Dương Hướng was born in 1948 in the northern province of Thái Bình and currently lives in Quảng Ninh. The author of six books, he is best known for his novel *No Man River* (*Bến không chồng*), which won Vietnam's most prestigious prize for fiction in 1991. Considered one of the three best novels about the American War in Vietnam written in the reform era, it has been widely read, studied, critiqued, translated into French and Italian, reprinted several times, and twice adapted into film. For his outstanding achievements, Dương Hướng received the National Hồ Chí Minh Prize for Literature and Arts in 2017.

Quan Manh Ha is professor of American literature and ethnic studies at the University of Montana, USA. He is the co-translator of *Other Moons: Vietnamese Short Stories of the American War and Its Aftermath*; *Hà Nội at Midnight: Stories* by Bảo Ninh; *Luminous Nights: Pioneering Vietnamese Short Stories*; *The Termite Queen*, a novel by Tạ Duy Anh; and *Longings: Contemporary Fiction by Vietnamese Women Writers*.

Charles Waugh is the co-editor and co-translator of Tạ Duy Anh's novel *The Termite Queen* with Quan Manh Ha in addition to the story collections *Wild Mustard*, with Văn Giá and Nguyễn Liên, and *Family of Fallen Leaves*, with Nguyễn Liên. A professor of English at Utah State University, USA, he is also the associate editor for fiction at *ISLE*, the journal of the Association for the Study of Literature and Environment.

ADVANCE PRAISE FOR *NO MAN RIVER*

'*No Man River* is an honest portrayal of life in the rural north of Vietnam during and after the American War. It recounts a tragic story of how the war has taken away all the strong, young men and left behind their beloved women who desperately long for their returns. A heart-rending novel about loneliness, unfulfilled happiness, and outdated cultural practices that stifle human joy and aspirations.'

—Bảo Ninh, author of *The Sorrow of War* and *Hà Nội at Midnight: Stories*

'A captivating read that grabs the reader's attention from the beginning! *No Man River* is a significant contribution to the understanding of the psychological toll of the American War in Vietnam, long after the war has ended. There is no glory in wars, we learn, and the sorrow and trauma continue, despite all the government propaganda and exaltation. The translators demonstrate virtuosity and cultural awareness of both languages, especially in their capturing of linguistic and literary subtleties.'

—Andrew Lam, author of *Stories from the Edge of the Sea*

'What is the Vietnam War to Americans is the American War to the Vietnamese. The tragic power of *No Man River* brings new dimension to the cost and permanent consequences of that conflict. Wars never happen to just one side. This novel will move you past the smoke and mirrors of a single perception. A novel of great authority and humanity—a necessary read!'

—Donald Anderson, author of *Fragments of a Mortal Mind*; editor of *Aftermath: An Anthology of Post-Vietnam Fiction*

'*No Man River* is a vital addition to the canon of Vietnam War literature, offering English-speaking audiences access to a Vietnamese classic. The translators capture the novel's panoramic scope as well as its tender love for the land of Vietnam and its people. The insightful introduction and carefully placed footnotes, which illuminate the cultural references and historical nuances that shape the novel's world, are a welcome addition. Readers worldwide will welcome the sensitive treatment of this powerful book, which is sure to find a wide readership and enhanced appreciation for its author.'

—Naomi Mandel, author of *Disappear Here: Violence after Generation X*

'*No Man River* is one of those rare books that combines the highest level of critical acclaim with widespread popular appeal. A rich and multilayered depiction of village life through the war-torn decades of mid–late twentieth century Vietnam, this powerful novel shows how, long after the fighting is over, war continues to cause further tragedies, even in rural communities far from the frontline. Professors Ha and Waugh have produced a bright and lively translation that, for the first time, makes this modern classic available to English-speaking readers.'

—Timothy Allen, translator of Nguyễn Du's *The Song of Kiều*

'Adding to the small but growing body of Vietnamese literature translated into English, *No Man River* presents a vivid portrayal of childhood, family life, courtship, love, and loss in a small northern village set against over four decades and three wars in Vietnam. Dương Hướng deftly illuminates the lives of women often overshadowed and neglected by the war heroes celebrated by the state. This is at once a perverse love story and a reversed war story, translated by Quan Manh Ha and Charles Waugh in a nuanced style that allows the machinations of the plot to slowly reveal themselves.'

—Sylvia Shin Huey Chong, author of *The Oriental Obscene: Violence and Racial Fantasies in the Vietnam Era*

No Man River

Dương Hướng

Translated by
Quan Manh Ha and Charles Waugh

PENGUIN BOOKS
An imprint of Penguin Random House

PENGUIN CLASSICS

Penguin Classics is an imprint of the Penguin Random House group of companies whose addresses can be found at global.penguinrandomhouse.com

Published by Penguin Random House SEA Pte Ltd
40 Penjuru Lane, #03-12, Block 2
Singapore 609216

Penguin Random House SEA

First Vietnamese edition published by the Vietnam Writers' Association Press 1990

First English translation published in Penguin Classics by Penguin Random House SEA 2025

10 9 8 7 6 5 4 3 2 1

ISBN 9789815233834

Typeset in Minion Pro by MAP Systems, Bengaluru, India

www.penguin.sg

Foreword

Dương Hướng's *No Man River* (*Bến không chồng*), along with Bảo Ninh's *The Sorrow of War* (*Nỗi buồn chiến tranh*) and Nguyễn Khắc Trường's *A Land of Many Humans and Ghosts* (*Mảnh đất lắm người nhiều ma*), shared the highest prize for prose awarded by the Vietnam Writers' Association in 1991. Since then, they have gained substantial attention from Vietnamese critics, scholars, and readers, and the novels have been reprinted multiple times and translated into many languages, primarily because they best represent the literary renaissance that took place in Vietnam during the last decade of the twentieth century.

The year 1986 marks the onset of the reform period in Vietnam, and although its initiatives primarily dealt with economic reform and political liberalization, it had a tremendous impact on literary and artistic production, as well as on various other aspects of life. From 1945 to 1975, Vietnamese literature was political, ideological, and propagandistic, in that it had to serve the country's nationalist and socialist cause. Therefore, the communist government in the north encouraged writers to extol heroism and revolutionary romanticism and to invigorate people to fight for the country's independence and unified patriotic endeavour. In other words, authors were assigned the role of propagandists in promoting the Party's policies and ideals by glorifying stereotyped characters and celebrating prescribed themes that best represented the 'goals of the collective struggle'.* Thus, 'the human facets of the war and

* John C. Schafer, 'The Collective and the Individual in Two Post-war Vietnamese Novels,' *Crossroads*, vol. 14, no. 2, 2000, p. 13.

the full scale of the trauma of combat were meticulously censored to present a sanitized vision of the war construed primarily as a eulogy of patriotism, revolutionary zeal, national unity, and the competence of communist rule'.[*] To the contrary, war martyr cemeteries were constructed in towns, cities, and provinces throughout Vietnam, honouring and commemorating the deaths of more than one million soldiers who fought on the communist side. During the ten years after the country's reunification in 1975, Vietnamese literature remained a political tool as writers were more concerned with ideological correctness than critical realism, as the country recovered from the long war and built a socialist republic, and more importantly, as the Party remained in control of the monolithic national memory of the war. Critic Viet Thanh Nguyen insightfully observes that '[f]lat, heroic characters' and 'revolutionary heroes and heroines, virtuous and smiling, chiselled and fierce' remain dominant motifs in art, propaganda posters, museums, and monuments.[†]

The transition from epic heroism to individualistic realism in the late 1980s and 1990s granted Vietnamese writers more creative freedom and a 'space for revisiting the past'.[‡] They started to scrutinize realism more honestly and depict the human experience more truthfully. Characters were portrayed with more psychological complexity, and their agency and individuality were celebrated. According to scholar Quan Manh Ha, authors during this time period became more interested in exploring and exposing 'various frustrating, anguishing social issues, as a response to the new mission of Vietnamese literature'—to offer candid critiques of reality and to examine human aspirations in depth.[§]

[*] Dana Healy, 'From Triumph to Tragedy: Visualizing War in Vietnamese Film and Fiction,' *South East Asia Research*, vol. 18, no. 2, 2010, p. 327.

[†] Viet Thanh Nguyen, *Nothing Ever Dies: Vietnam and the Memory of War* (Harvard UP, 2016), p. 29.

[‡] Hue-Tam Ho Tai, Introduction: Situating Memory, *The Country of Memory*, edited by Hue-Tam Ho Tai (U of California P, 2001), p. 3

[§] Quan Manh Ha, 'When Memory Speaks: Transnational Remembrances in Vietnam War Literature,' *Southeast Asian Studies*, vol. 5, no. 3, 2016, p. 473.

The academic discussion on *No Man River* has often focused on its portrayal of a post-war northern village and women's fates during and after the war. For instance, critic Nguyễn Phan Hách states that *No Man River* can be read as a 'chronicle of a village',* and Nguyễn Văn Long observes that the novel's main characters are 'both the victims and the agents of their own tragedies and that they must be accountable for their destinies'.† While *The Sorrow of War* received controversial and paradoxical reviews and criticism upon its initial release, *No Man River* was an instant success, and it quietly and effortlessly gained a stable status as a magnum opus in the body of post-reform literature. Recently, some dissertations and theses have attempted to examine the use of symbolism and discourse analysis in the novel in order to highlight its literary and aesthetic values. However, critical interpretation of *No Man River* has not been as copious as that of *The Sorrow of War*, because critics and scholars tend to be more interested in the more experimental novel that employs innovative plot development and characterization, whereas *No Man River* conforms to a conventionally linear plotline, employs common and clear language, and does not evoke contradicting interpretations as one sees in the literary works of Bảo Ninh and Nguyễn Huy Thiệp. However, *No Man River* is placed on the same pedestal with Bảo Ninh's *The Sorrow of War* and Lê Lựu's *A Time Far Past* (*Thời xa vắng*)—both of which have been translated into English. These three novels accentuate post-war tragedy, the rediscovery of individuality, and self-realization. They give 'representation to individual suffering in a broader context of pervasive social trauma' by exploring the 'bleakness and hardships of war rather than its glories'.‡ The male protagonists Kiên in *The Sorrow of War* and Giang Minh Sài in *A Time Far Past*

---

* Nguyễn Phan Hách, 'Hai bức tranh hiện thực nông thôn (Nhân đọc *Bến không chồng* và *Mảnh đất lắm người nhiều ma*),' *Tạp chí Tác phẩm mới*, vol. 5, 1991, pp. 24–25.

† Nguyễn Văn Long, 'Bức tranh làng quê và số phận người nông dân qua những biến thiên lịch sử,' *Báo Văn nghệ*, no.12, March 23, 1991, p. 3.

‡ Christina Schwenkel, *The American War in Contemporary Vietnam* (Indiana UP, 2009), p. 63.

embody the idea that living truthfully with one's passion and self must be honoured over living according to someone else's or the collective's ideals. In *No Man River*, the characters Vạn and Nghĩa represent the anti-heroes and social misfits, and they differ from the fictional, stereotyped soldiers and veterans commonly found in the Vietnamese fiction of the previous era.

No Man River delineates the daily life of a village in the north during the most important historical moments of twentieth-century Vietnamese history: the August Revolution against the French in 1945, the Land Reform from 1953 to 1956, the American War and its aftermath, and the Sino-Vietnamese War in 1979. The novel's characters suffer due to war, prejudice, and outdated beliefs. Vạn loves Nhân and wishes to devote the rest of his life to her, a widow with three children, but he must suppress his affection because he is afraid of rumours and gossip, and of his dead ancestors' curse. Nhân also has feelings for Vạn, but she must conform to the exemplary image of the faithful wife, caring mother, and chaste widow.* Their suppression of emotions illustrates how socialist realism trivialized personal lives, viewed sexuality as 'invisible', and treated male–female amorous relationships as 'asexual camaraderie'.† One commonality between *The Sorrow of War* and *No Man River* lies in their exploration of how the traumas of war continue to reside inside people's bodies, psyches, and souls long after the fighting ends. In *No Man River*, the male characters Vạn and Nghĩa can never return to their pre-war normal lives and have to shoulder the onerous responsibilities assigned to men. The female characters cannot find happiness after the American War ends because its ghostly hands have snatched away their loved ones and deprived them of either motherhood or marriage. Dương Hướng says that he wrote *No Man River* primarily to show how the war continues to have detrimental effects on the countryside, with some impacts even worse than those from fighting on the

* Dana Healy, 'Laments of Warriors' Wives: Re-gendering the War in Vietnamese Cinema,' *South East Asia Research*, vol. 14, no. 2, 2006, p. 237.

† Ibid., p. 238.

battlefield, because for every soldier who died at the front, a host of loved ones, including parents, wives, or fiancées, siblings, friends, and relatives were also impacted.[*] By decentring the ideological framework of heroic collectivism, the author shifts the centre to individual sorrow and interpersonal conflicts, thus challenging the generalized, monolithic view of the war endorsed by the mainstream history. Compared to the other war novels mentioned above, *No Man River* is distinctive in its portrayal of women and their melancholia because it elevates 'women and female identity to the centre' of attention.[†] The title of the novel accentuates the absence of young, able-bodied men because they have enlisted to fight the war, and the village is populated only by the elderly, the disabled, and women and children. The author's humanistic perspective on Vietnamese women demonstrates his empathy with them as they suffered not only the consequences of war but also the shortcomings of an intensely patriarchal culture. He exposes the ugliness of some villagers, including their superstitions, parochial worldview, avarice, and fear of gossip, but he always manages to do so without treating them sarcastically or disdainfully.

Another salient trait of *No Man River* lies in its vivid depiction of a typical pastoral village, with images of green rice paddies, a meandering river and riverfront, a stone bridge, and a pier, among other features. The novel offers the readers a better understanding of the northern countryside, its customs and culture, and its people. The riverside and the pier are where villagers meet and gather, where young couples spend their romantic time together, and where they bid farewell to one another. In Vietnamese folklore and proverbs, the pier often symbolizes the faithfulness and longing of the person who stays behind, while the boat represents the mobility of the person who departs. In *No Man River*, the riverside and the pier are associated with the desperation and misery of those who long in vain for their loved ones' return. The women in

---

[*] Đỗ Mai Hà, 'Gặp ba tân khoa Giải thưởng Hội nhà văn Việt Nam 1991,' *Tạp chí Văn nghệ quân đội*, no. 11, 1991, pp. 115–116.

[†] Dana Healy, 'Laments,' p. 243.

the novel suffer but show resilience rather than simply accepting their poor fate. After the August Revolution in 1945, a new image of Vietnamese women emerged as heroic, indomitable, talented, sincere, and faithful. The female characters in *No Man River* refuse to be bound within outdated social and traditional norms. Unlike her stoic mother, Nhân, Hạnh defies prejudice and marries Nghĩa, despite the two families' disapproval. She becomes a woman of action, and her female friends also make choices for their own happiness. However, scholar Dana Healy offers a counterargument about this reading of gender resistance in the novel: 'The gender bias towards infertility is implied in the fact that it is the woman who is automatically blamed for not fulfilling her fundamental role in life.'[*] Because the war denies many women motherhood, several characters risk pregnancies out of wedlock in order to conform to the social expectations of motherhood.

No Man River, a classic of contemporary Vietnamese literature, enriches the corpus of Vietnam War literature from the perspectives of the Vietnamese. It deglorifies the war by unmasking the real war that the Vietnamese fought against the Americans and by encapsulating the magnitude of the damages, trauma, losses, casualties, and sorrow that Vietnamese people experienced. Each character in the novel represents a personal loss and agony, juxtaposing their individualized tragedy against the collective triumph embellished by the Party's official accounts of memory and remembrance. The novel articulates the humanistic themes of human suffering, empathy, forgiveness, memory, and sociocultural ramifications of military conflict, and it empowers the victims' voices and vocalizes their perceptions of the war.

—Đỗ Hải Ninh, PhD, Literature Institute, Vietnam Academy of Social Sciences

[*] Ibid., p. 252.

Note on the Translation

There were two substantial challenges to the translation of this novel, in addition to the many, small difficult choices we had to make along the way. The first was the title itself. The title of the novel in Vietnamese, *Bến không chồng*, literally means 'riverside without husband', and refers to the river, the riverside and banks, the pier alongside the river, and the area in general where villagers would gather to swim, bathe, wash their clothes and buffalo, catch fish, and relax. The name comes from a story about a widow who drowns herself in the river out of grief and gets at the complicated relationship the villagers have with a river that both sustains them and at other times terrifies them. But the title in Vietnamese also has a kind of wonderful sound to it, and an economy of language that is hard to reproduce in English. We chose *No Man River* to try to replicate that simplicity of language and good sound, while still conjuring the original sense of the whole riverside area and the sense of loss the villagers associate with it.

The second challenge was how to manage the many overlapping familial titles and pronouns in this story of a tightly knit village community. Vietnamese pronouns draw on familial relationships and change according to the relation the speaker has with the person being spoken to, whether they are related by blood or marriage or not. In a village where a third of the people are members of the same vastly extended family, and everyone else is still referred to as 'uncle' or 'aunt' or 'sister', depending on their age in relation to the speaker, who is actually related to whom and how they are related becomes tricky to convey. The novel further complicates the situation by having multiple point of view characters, so what a character is called will change, depending on which character is the main one in a given passage. So you might see Mother Khiên in relation to Hạnh, or Aunt Khiên in relation to Vạn, or Mrs Khiên in relation to Dr Thủy or her husband, Khiên. Another quirk of Vietnamese is that a married woman's name is often presented as her husbands' with a different gendered title, as in the example above. Did we mention it's complicated?

We've used a mix of strategies to try to represent both family and civil relations, while relying on relation-less pronouns like he, she, you, and I for simplicity's sake and to prevent tedious repetition. It will be good for the reader to remember that even though the text might read 'Grandfather Nghiên' or 'Uncle Xung', those characters might not be the actual grandfather or uncle of everyone in the scene. In those cases, those familial titles should be read as honorifics that show respect to someone about the age of an uncle or grandfather. We maintained them where we could also to help show how a sense of family is replicated within the larger social context, with many of the same senses of obligation and respect, and also to show how strong the sense of community is in this village, and in Vietnam in general.

PART I

Chapter 1

Nguyễn Vạn adjusted his rucksack and opened his shirt after climbing the dike to look out over his home village. The lush canopy of the big mango tree at the front of the commune house occupied a wide swath of the horizon, backlit by the setting sun. The villagers wouldn't recognize him now, grizzled as he was and with such red-rimmed eyes. He had been just a poor, orphaned teenager when he left years ago to fight the French, but no villager would dare look down on him now after seeing all the shiny, sparkling medals pinned to his shirt.

The river rippled gently against the dike. The sky looked ominous, like a roiling purple sea. But, damn! That breeze felt so good! Vạn pulled down his zipper to relieve himself and then straightened his clothes afterward. He wanted to see his neighbours again. He limped along the dirt road pocked with countless dried buffalo prints. In the distance, two small shadows turned onto the road toward him, and when they got close enough, he could see that they were two little kids, each shouldering a bamboo pole with two hanging baskets. The boy had a dark, broad face and high brow above a crooked nose that made his nostrils flare. The little girl was quite a bit shorter, about the height of the boy's ears, and looked rather stern.

'What are you two doing?' asked Vạn.

The boy gave Vạn a strange look. 'I'm collecting buffalo dung,' he said.

'I'm cutting grass,' whispered the girl. She stood shyly behind the boy.

'Who are your parents?'

'My father is Dĩ, and my name is Sinh,' said the boy, 'but people call me Ngốc.'

Vạn continued down the road with the confused children still staring after him. Of course, the kid with a face like that has a beautiful name. Only an idiot would name a kid like that Ngốc.[*] What bad luck! Why did he have to run into that kid just before reaching the village? In the nearby rice paddies, villagers who had been busy working now lifted up their heads to look at him. That's right, look carefully, thought Vạn. I'm Nguyễn Vạn, a victorious Điện Biên Phủ soldier now returned![†] His shoulder had been injured, and one of his legs badly broken and poorly set, so he limped as he lurched forward again. As a child, Vạn had been known in the village for being fearless. When wounded on the battlefield, he had bled profusely and was in excruciating pain, but he forced himself to laugh heartily so he wouldn't cry. He laughed until he fainted.

Vạn kept going. A flock of parrots flashed a green arc across the sky. The ancient *duối*[‡] tree at the entrance to the cemetery had just a few leaves left on its curved branches. The cemetery was densely populated with graves, but he could still recognize his father's, located right between the edge of the rice paddy and a small shrine made of brick. The thigh-sized log that had been planted to mark the front of his father's grave had begun to rot and now looked like a piece of broken bone. As an orphaned child, Vạn had loved to play in the cemetery. He had worked as a buffalo herder for a wealthy landowner named Mr Hào whose psychological abuse he would never forgive nor forget. Vạn had worn the same pair of filthy shorts year-round, with no shirt to cover his dark, skinny back, and it seemed other than working with the buffalo, he'd spent

---

[*] Ngốc means stupid; the child has a developmental disability. An old superstition held that the first person you see at the beginning of Tết or when exiting your home or in this case arriving somewhere determined your luck.

[†] The epic battle at Điện Biên Phủ was where the Vietnamese defeated the French in 1954 and forced them to relinquish control over Indochina.

[‡] Sometimes called a toothbrush tree, *Streblus asper* has long been cultivated for its twigs, which, when chewed, have antibacterial properties.

almost his entire childhood in this graveyard. Vạn knelt before the rotting log marking his father's grave and clutched at the grassy earth. His eyes stung. Two warm tears trailed down his cheeks. The tears unsettled Vạn and he stood abruptly. Crushed grass and dirt fell from his hands to the ground. This may have been the first time in his life that Vạn cried.

At the village gate, a group of children gathered around him, some with their younger siblings dangling on their hips, some racing around or jumping up and down joyfully. The children looked at Vạn with curiosity. A few elderly women peeked out from behind their doors as if unsure what was causing all the commotion.

'Where are you going?' one of the kids asked, tugging Vạn's shirt.

'To visit the People's Committee. Do you know where it meets?' He knew the answer but wanted them to say it.

He smiled when several voices sang out, 'In the communal house!'

The children led Vạn to the wide, single-storey house in the centre of the village. He set his rucksack down beneath the mango tree and dug inside to find some candy. Shyly, they held out their little hands to receive it. Vạn studied the children's faces but he couldn't tell who their parents were. Excited by the candy and the visitor, the children raced around the courtyard. Vạn's heart beat faster as he climbed the three shiny, green steps. The men sitting at the table inside peered at him intently.

'I would like to meet with the commune chairman,' Vạn said to the young man with a pallid face standing closest to the entryway. The young man pointed at the fellow sitting behind the gleaming ironwood desk in the middle of the room. Vạn immediately recognized the chairman's crinkled eyes—it was Đột, Mr Hách's son. Vạn remembered him as a kid running around the village naked from the waist down, wearing only one of his father's old, patched shirts. In the afternoons, he had liked to stroll along the dike catching frogs to make bait for catching crab.

'Damn! Is that you, Đột? Don't you recognize me?' Vạn blinked back the tears that had suddenly welled up again, dropped his rucksack to the floor, and clasped Đột's hand. 'It's Vạn.'

'Vạn? Is it really you?'

'Of course!'

'You look so heroic! Who would've guessed you'd end up a soldier? What a surprise!'

Vạn smiled and pinched Đột's thigh. 'And you, chairman of the commune!'

Their laughter echoed through the chamber.

An elderly man with silver hair tottered in, leaning heavily on a cane. The old man came before the desk, pulled a folded paper from his shirt pocket, and offered it respectfully to the chairman. Đột's face turned serious. Not knowing better, he held the paper upside down.

'Please help me with this document,' said the old man.

'Are you selling your house?' Đột asked, scratching his neck.

'No. My water buffalo calf has grown up and is big enough now to pull a plow. I'm asking for permission to sell its mother.'

'Oh, of course, I see.'

Vạn found their conversation tedious. He raised his eyebrows and smiled at Tý Hin, the young woman sitting at the smaller desk right next to Đột's. She blushed but returned Vạn's gaze for a moment before demurely looking away. She had been a skinny little girl when he left and now she was a beautiful woman. Despite her shy expression, her cheeks remained rosy.

'Is that Tý Hin?' Vạn asked Đột.

'Who else? She's now my chief of staff. Her life will never be the same!'

Chapter 2

It had long been said that Đông Village had many passionate people, both talented men and beautiful women. The village had the largest communal house in the district, the biggest mango tree, the most beautiful stone bridge, and the purest, coolest river water. No wonder the mothers there sang so many lullabies that honoured their village's many virtues. The elders often said the village had been founded on the back of a dancing dragon—the Đình River—whose waters flowed from the Linh Tributary before twisting and turning through the district. They said its water was the mother's milk that fertilized the land and nurtured the villagers throughout their lives.

The bucolic village was typical, with several large banyan trees, a pier alongside the river, a communal house, young women who wore pink blouses and shawls and sang *cô đầu*,* and carefully selected beautiful young people who were costumed as generals, mandarins, elephants, and other chess pieces on festival days also celebrated with loud, beating drums.

Over time, the talented and beautiful young ones became elderly men and effervescent, betel chewing women. On special occasions, they told their children and grandchildren once-upon-a-time fairytale stories, reminding them that all the villagers had to know their history.

---

* Also known as *ca trù*, *cô đầu* is a type of Northern Vietnamese musical storytelling that features a female vocalist and that since 2009 has been on UNESCO's list of Vietnam's Intangible Cultural Heritage.

Grandfather Nghiên, the head of the Nguyễn clan—the largest clan in Đông Village—often sat cross-legged in the centre of the floor of the communal house's middle room, which was also the ancestor worship room, telling stories like these to his grandson, Nghĩa, and to the other children of the village. Nghĩa often sat alongside a girl named Hạnh, who was a member of the Vũ family and who also loved to listen to the stories. Her mouth would gape, and her eyes would go wide as she listened. By the time she was five or six, she could retell all the stories without missing a single detail. Grandfather Nghiên would stroke his beard and smile as he gazed out over his rapt, young audience.

One of his stories began like this:

'In the middle of the largest rice paddy, there is a pond whose water remains clear all year round. Some villagers call the pond the fairy's belly button, and some call it the fairy's vagina, but I call it the fairy's eye, because only a fairy's eye can be so clear as to see through a woman's heart to her innermost feelings. But once upon a time, the pond was just a stinking, muddy bog where buffalo wallowed. Ringed with reeds, the bog was full of ugly bottom fish, a home to swamp hens, leeches, frogs, and toads. Back in those days, a woman named Ngần was the most beautiful of all who lived in Đông Village. Her round, twinkling eyes were like two shiny lychee seeds. Her smooth skin was ivory, her hair like long silk. At sixteen, her parents married her off to a man she did not love. So on her consummation night, she ran to the pond and drowned herself. After the suicide, the reeds, leeches, carp, and swamp hens all disappeared, and the water of the pond turned clear. And ever since her death, all the women of Đông Village have considered the pond a refuge, and to this day will bathe there when they hope to wash away misfortune. This is also why the women of our village have smooth, ivory skin and look like fairies, and why they call the pond the Fairy's Eye.'

Hạnh liked this story the most, while Nghĩa preferred the story about Hero Hill, which was located near the pond and also had a second name, the Son of Heaven's Grave. Surprisingly, despite the fact that people farmed all around the hill, and that rats dug holes all through it, the hill never eroded away. Instead, it just grew bigger and perpetually nourished the trees that grew there. Old Nghiên told the story like this:

'Once upon a time, one of our village men returned home after a decade away fighting a war. Now a war hero, his eyes were sharp, and his eyebrows thick. Sword against sword, no one could defeat him. As he came to the mound in the rice paddy just outside the village, the farmers working there told him immediately that his wife had not remained faithful while he was away. Heartbroken, he stood atop the mound and cried out to lament the betrayal. Suddenly, blood spurted from his mouth, and then, as he stood there in shock, he keeled over dead. Ever since that moment, any time one of our villagers passes that spot, they toss a handful of soil onto the mound to honour the hero who survived a war only to die of love. Over the many years, the mound has grown bigger and bigger. Now it's commonly said that Đông Village men are extraordinarily brave because they share the same blood as that hero.'

There were many other stories the village elders liked to tell. One was about a ghost that lived under the duối tree in the graveyard. The ghost had eyes as red as a *gấc* fruit* and a tongue as long as a hand. His enormous penis was the size of a plough beam. The ghost wandered among the graves and chased after widows. If he managed to catch one, she'd have no choice but to become his wife. On rainy, windy nights, the ghost's bride would feel compelled to wander out to the cemetery and sleep with the ghost beneath the duối tree until dawn.

Another scary story claimed a water monster lived below the wide, wooden pier in front of the Nguyễn lineage temple. Every year or two, it would abduct a child. It had a long, black body, and its spindly red legs looked like the roots of a chinaberry tree. As big

* A fruit in the melon family native to Southeast Asia remarkable for its high levels of beta-carotene and lycopene, hence its bright red aril and seeds and orange rind

as a basket-boat, the water monster could drag even a grown man down below the surface and drown him.

Despite these legends, embellished and made more terrifying by various storytellers over the years, no one was really scared. The villagers still loved to bathe and swim in the beautiful river. In the winter, the clear, slow-moving water would become so shallow that the riverbed's perfectly white sand could be seen glittering under the sunlight. During the monsoons, the water would rise and turn all the trees green. The village ancestors called the whole riverside area No Man River,* but over time some people also came to call it the River of Love. Bends in the river divided it into three sections and also kept each stretch secluded from the others. Boys and men used the upstream part to bathe and swim, and women and girls used the middle, which left the part downstream for water buffalos and their herders.

In the afternoons, pimply teenaged buffalo boys would jump into the water from the backs of their buffalos. The bulls liked to take this time to flirt with the cows and sometimes tried to mate with their partners in the water. The boys would jump and dive into the water until their eyes turned red and only ever went home once it got dark. Bare-chested elderly men liked to take their grandchildren to the pier, fathers carried their kids on their shoulders, and young men and women farmers often ended their workdays by walking from the rice paddies directly to the river to bathe for a while, take off their mud-stained clothes and rinse them clean. The gentle breeze and slowly flowing water caressed their bodies like invisible hands, helping them forget their sorrows and hardships. Simply put, the cool water made people feel good. That's why so many young married couples often bathed in the river together and never thought twice about the legends of the water monster or the red-eyed ghost.

---

* The title of the novel in Vietnamese, *Bến không chồng*, literally means 'riverside no husband', and refers to the river, the riverside and banks, the pier alongside the river, and the area in general. The name comes from a story about a widow who drowns herself in the river out of grief.

But the seductive beauty of the river did actually cause some tragedies. Maybe the most tragic of all was the irreconcilable feud that arose between the Nguyễn and Vũ families. Late in the evening of the day the whole extended Nguyễn clan had celebrated the inauguration of their lineage temple—the largest one in Đông Village—the only daughter and most beloved child of the Nguyễn patriarch went to the river to bathe. In the dark, she did not see the young Vũ man swimming downstream, nor he her. Suddenly their naked bodies met. Both were terrified, each thinking the water monster had come to drown them. He swam straight for the shore. But she fainted and drowned.

The next morning, some fishermen found the Nguyễn woman's naked, floating body caught against the Silver Stone Bridge. When it was revealed that the young Vũ man had also been swimming in the same place at the same time, the two families erupted into a bloody fight. That's when the Nguyễn patriarch uttered a curse that would be repeated endlessly over the years. *The Đình River will always flow. The Silver Stone Bridge will stand forever. The River of Love will always be beautiful and romantic. And the Nguyễn–Vũ feud will never end.*

Chapter 3

To Hạnh's dark, adolescent eyes, Đông Village was an entire mysterious world, stunningly beautiful with its green bamboo groves, tall areca trees, and lovely reflections of the mango tree and the Silver Stone Bridge on the gentle Đình River.

A timid and sensitive girl, Hạnh felt afraid each time she had to pass the two stone dogs snarling at the entrance to the communal house. And she was particularly fearful of the red-eyed ghost living beneath the duối tree in the cemetery. At the same time, she was resolute. Despite her fear, she kept following her older twin brothers, Hà and Hiệp, past the graveyard to the rice paddies outside the village. She wore her mother's torn conical hat and liked to run along the dike as her brothers cut grass or caught crab and fish. They gave her the chore of catching grasshoppers to feed to their family's pet birds. She loved to talk to the birds and would often say to them, 'You should come to the paddy with me, or the cat might eat you alive!'

Hạnh felt mesmerized by the countryside's simple beauty. She would dance with joy just watching rice stalks, sweet potatoes, and corn baking in a bonfire in the middle of a field. Her eyes brightened any time she heard the crackling of white rice grains and corn popping among the burning coals.

In spring, the farmers planted peanuts. To scare away the birds, they also erected scarecrows and hung colourful strings wherever they could. But without a strong wind, the scarecrows stood still as ghosts in their torn clothes and hats. And the birds were not stupid. They'd swoop down anyway and eat the buds just starting to emerge from the ground. One rainy day, Hạnh stood protectively among the straight rows of buds beneath the drizzling sky.

'You can sit in the shelter,' her brother Hà told her, gesturing toward the little hut that they, like the other farmers, had put up for the season. 'You don't have to stand out in the rain. Hiệp and I are going to set some traps to catch birds.'

Hạnh did as she was told. Her brothers had roofed the low shelter with freshly cut banana leaves. She proudly thought that their shelter was the biggest and nicest one of all in the colourful field. Sitting there, gazing out at the drizzling rain, she thought about so many things. She lay down on her stomach with her chin resting on her arms to get a closer look at a big, red dragonfly with shiny yellow wings that was being eaten by a swarm of ants. After a while, old man Nghiên's grandson, Nghĩa, walked by. She sat up, stuck her head outside the shelter, and called to him.

He came over and stood in front of the shelter, holding a trowel in one hand and a string of dead rats in the other.

Hạnh stared apprehensively at the string of rats.

'Want some baby rats?' Nghĩa asked. He dropped the trowel and pulled a handful of tiny, nearly naked rats from the pouch he had slung from his shoulder. He gestured as if to hand them to her.

'No! They're scary!'

'Why? You could take them home and feed them to your cat.'

'That sounds terrible! Put them away—I don't even want to look at them.' After a minute she changed the subject, pointing at a steeple visible in the far distance. It was the tallest building in the district. 'I would like to see that church over there sometime. Will you take me?'

Nghĩa put the baby rats back into the pouch. 'Your brothers won't let you.'

'They don't have to know,' she said. 'You could take me, right? Here, let me give you something.'

Hạnh took Nghĩa's hand and pulled him into the shelter. It was still drizzling outside. The two adolescents sat on a pile of leftover banana leaves.

'Here,' said Hạnh, handing him a sweet potato. 'You can have the big one, but you have to take me to the Thượng Church tonight, okay?'

Nghĩa didn't answer but was clearly pleased as he ate the sweet potato. For his willingness to take her to the church, she had given him a dry place to sit and a nice snack. He told her what he knew about the church and the French and Vietnamese Catholics who built it, and she listened attentively while gazing toward the tall steeple. She had never gone so far from the village before, but three times a day, the church bell rang and its echoing tone made her very curious. When the rain let up, a line of people wearing colourful clothes came out of the church, headed their way.

'That looks like a procession.'

Nghĩa sat up and peered over her shoulder at the small group. Suddenly he snatched the trowel and jumped to his feet.

'What are you doing?' asked Hạnh.

'I'm going to teach those parishioners a lesson,' he said. 'Last time I went near their church with some friends, they bullied us.'

Hạnh followed Nghĩa across the paddy to the main road and watched as he hurriedly dragged the trowel through the dirt in the shape of a cross. Gleefully, he told her, 'If they want to walk along the road here, they'll have to step on their own symbol!' When finished, Nghĩa took Hạnh's hand and they ran back to the shelter to wait for the brightly dressed parishioners to pass. It looked like several of the men were carrying the priest in a red hammock strung between them, followed by a few elderly men and women.

'Uncle Xình told me these parishioners are reactionaries,' said Nghĩa. 'They're spies who use the excuse of escorting the priest from one church to another to travel wherever they want and organize against the government.'

Hạnh trembled with fear as the parishioners approached. The ones at the front saw the cross Nghĩa had scraped into the dirt and seemed agitated. First one, then another, and then all of them touched their heads, stomachs, and both shoulders. Hạnh heard the first man say quite loudly, 'God will punish those who dare blaspheme Him.'

The priest in the hammock frowned and directed the parishioners to turn onto the singletrack path skirting the peanut field. Hạnh quivered, feeling as if she had just done something terribly wrong.

'Maybe God will punish us, Nghĩa,' she said.

'There's no God,' said Nghĩa. 'Uncle Xình told me so. All I see is a lazy old priest lounging in a hammock while his lackeys carry him around. We should treat these reactionaries the same way I deal with rats.'

Nghĩa gathered up dry straw and twigs from the shelter and made a pile in the dirt outside. He pushed the thickest stick into the ground in the centre and looped the string of rats around it before sprinkling kerosene from a small jar he'd had in his pouch. He struck a match to set them ablaze. 'Burn, disgusting rats!' he shouted as their skin sizzled and their eyes popped. He was about to drop the baby rats onto the fire when Hạnh swatted his hand and sent them flying. Starting to cry, she turned her back on Nghĩa's surprised face and marched back into the shelter and sat down.

'Burning rats, huh?'

Hạnh's brothers, Hà and Hiệp, had returned carrying a water snake and a couple of toads. Horrified, she shrieked and quickly looked away as she saw that the boys meant to behead them with Nghĩa's trowel.

'Stop!' she shouted. 'The toad is Heaven's uncle.'

Hà scoffed at her. 'You're so stupid. If it were Heaven's uncle, why would it be here?'

'I'm serious. It was Grandfather Nghiên who told us that and also that if you hurt one, Heaven will make you pay.' Without waiting to see what they'd do next, she ran out to the main road and nearly all the way back to the village before running into Nguyễn Vạn.

'Are you Nhân's daughter?' asked Vạn. 'You look just like her.'

'Yes, sir—that's right.'

'Where are your brothers?'

Hạnh pointed, and then led Vạn back to the peanut field. He gazed coolly at what the boys were doing to the animals they'd caught but said nothing.

'Did you just come back from the war?' Hà asked. 'Were you in my father's unit?'

'Yes.'

'When will my father come home?'

'I don't know,' said Vạn. 'I can't say right now.'

The children accompanied Vạn back to the village and waited in the courtyard while he spoke with their mother inside the house. After a while, they heard their mother crying and Hà and Hiệp rushed inside. Vạn came out to the courtyard and held Hạnh by the shoulders and said, 'I told your mother already but shouldn't keep it from you any longer. Your father died in battle. He's a hero.'

Hạnh wailed at the news. Vạn caught her as she crumpled and carried her inside, where her mother and brothers were also weeping. Several neighbours heard the commotion and came to see what was wrong. Nhân hugged Hạnh and cried, 'Oh child, your father is dead!'

*

Nhân felt as if she'd come to live in another world where every single thing seemed menacing, even deadly. After lying a long time in bed, unable to force herself to get up, she finally dragged herself out of the house. In the sty, their pig lay very still with its nose buried in a heap of compost. She thought it looked dead so she poked it with a stick. The pig screeched and stood up. She realized it had been many days since she'd last fed it and felt a bit of relief that it was still alive. Hạnh had gone to the village's communal house to stay there and help Uncle Vạn. Her twin sons rarely made an effort to care for the pigs and chickens.

For the next several days, she slept a lot, dreaming frequently that her husband had come home. He'd stand by her bed but say nothing.

'Are you back?' she'd say to the shadow of her husband. 'Oh, no! How did you stain your face like that? Our dear friend Vạn has come home with lots of medals. Please don't scare me like this! Come lie down next to me.'

Then the shadow of her husband would descend to the bed, down onto her body. She'd feel like she was falling from a cliff. Numb all over, she'd kick her legs, trying to sit up, screaming, 'Stop or I'll die!'

The previous night, her cries woke Hà. 'Ma, you're talking in your sleep again,' he groaned. 'Quit scaring us.'

She stirred when she heard him, then woke fully as a couple of cats wailed outside like babies. They made a racket as they chased each other over the roof. Before going back to sleep, Nhân staggered out the door and beat a stick across the thatch, sending the scared cats scrambling into the front garden. In the breeze, yellow moonbeams danced on the banana leaves laden with dew.

Now, after feeding the pigs, Nhân took a basket out to the pond to pick some duckweed. A few carp roiled the surface, gulping, making her think they looked desperate for oxygen. A pain swelled in her chest. Her vision blurred.

Just as Nhân was about to step down into the water, her son Hà called, 'Hey, Ma, go get some rest. Let me and Hiệp do it.'

Then Hà stripped off his clothes and plunged into the muddy water. Hiệp came to her holding up a string of sparrows he had caught. 'We caught about twenty,' he said. 'But I gave half to Uncle Vạn and Hạnh.'

She stared at the struggling birds. Some of them were already dying. Since Vạn's return and the news of her husband's death, she had been easily moved to tears. Following Hiệp home in the yellow afternoon sunlight, she tried not to look at her or Hiệp's long, distorted shadows on the water. She had never imagined her immature, sometimes cruel, twin boys would be a comfort to her, until now. Recently she had noticed they had started to take care of things around the house.

'Ma,' said Hiệp in a quiet voice, 'are we war martyrs now?'*

'Who told you that?'

* The Vietnamese government routinely called those who died fighting for independence martyrs.

'Uncle Vạn. He said Pa was very brave and died heroically. He also said a man must fight during war.'

Hiệp dropped the string of birds to the ground and rubbed his hands together, telling them, 'I'll cook you soon, little birdies.'

Later, after Nhân and the boys had eaten, Vạn and Hạnh came to visit. Hạnh hugged her mother tightly, as if she'd been gone a long time.

'I told her she had to come back here every now and then, or she'd get homesick,' Vạn said. 'She says some strange things sometimes, like our eating those birds was sinful. But the birds tasted really good.'

Nhân caressed her daughter's head. It felt good to have her home, but she also pitied Vạn for having to live alone in the back room of the communal house. So, she hadn't said no when Hạnh asked to stay at the communal house to help take care of him.

Nhân felt she herself had to become stronger. Peace had been restored. Her sons could take care of the house. The bad old days of the wealthy colonial landowners were over.* The working class would rise and govern the country, building a socialist paradise. The world would live in harmony. No one could have imagined Đột would become chairman of the commune.

---

* The French concentrated land holdings with just a few Vietnamese families who would cooperate with them. Seventy-five per cent of Vietnamese during this time became landless labourers.

Chapter 4

The village leader and Nguyễn family patriarch, Grandfather Nghiên, had a son named Khiên and a grandson called Nghĩa. Known for his talent and upright morality, Nghiên had earned the villagers' respect. All the children in the village loved him because of his wonderful stories. He managed his allotted acre of land without ever pilfering even a single kilo of rice for himself. Every year on the death anniversary of his great great grandfather, he always took perfect care of every detail. On his own deathbed, Nghiên looked meaningfully at his son and grandson and said to them, 'For each generation, we have had only one son to carry on the family line, and that man must be our family's anchor. Khiên, you'll soon be head of this family and this village, and you must protect this land. Our ancestors gave their blood, sweat, and tears to it—you must keep it intact.'

His voice echoed through the family's lineage temple, which was devoted to the worship of their ancestors. It had three sections and two rows of main pillars and smaller pillars, sixteen in all. Each of the massive ironwood columns shone a glossy black atop a heavy blue stone with veins of white marbling that contrasted against the main rooms' red brick floors. The back room's floor had been laid with bricks made of sand, mortar, and limestone powder, and was really hard. On the altar, colourful gilded dragons flanked a central wooden throne. Just in front of the throne, an incense bowl held several smouldering joss sticks that emitted a pleasant fragrance. Four parallel verses graced the four main, solemn-looking pillars.

After Nghiên gave his son and grandson his final instructions, he looked into his only son's eyes. 'Khiên,' he said, 'please bring me the family ledger.'

Khiên removed the handwritten book from the altar and placed it in front of his father. The crimson cover had its title painted in bright yellow.

'This is our family's most valuable asset,' said Nghiên. His hands trembled as he opened it. He took out two loose sheets of paper and gave them to his son. Nghiên's great grandfather had written four things on the first sheet: *morality, talent, loyalty, courage*. 'Every Nguyễn must possess these four qualities,' he said. On the second sheet had been drawn the family tree, and beneath that had been written a description of the eternal feud with the Vũ family, as well as the patriarch's curse.

'Let me tell you my last words.' Nghiên pulled his son's hand to his chest. 'A person must have morality. It is the most important quality. Even a thief or a murderer respects this.'

Just a few moments later, old man Nghiên died. Khiên recorded the death in the family ledger this way: *Nguyễn Văn Nghiên, eleventh village head and leader of the Nguyễn family, passed away on 12 January 1957.*

Khiên took over his father's duty to lead the commemoration of the anniversary of the great great grandfather's death. Only in his early forties and already head of the clan, he was nervous. The clan elders didn't help, telling him, 'Peace has come at last, so this year's memorial has to be really special.'

After dinner one evening, Khiên's wife swept the entire lineage temple, spread out mats for everyone to sit on, and prepared tea. Khiên carefully washed the tobacco water pipe, sat down on the mat, and then waited for the elderly members of the clan to arrive to discuss the preparations for the anniversary.

The first person to come was great Uncle Xung.

'Is anyone here?' called Uncle Xung from outside the gate.

'Please come in and have some tea,' said Mrs Khiên cheerfully. 'You're the first to arrive.'

'Damn it! Nobody's here but me because there's nothing to eat or drink.' He kicked at a cat to shoo it away. 'Pour me a cup of rice wine so next year people will know to come early. People who show up first should get wine, those who come after, tea, and after that just plain water.'

Uncle Xung rubbed his feet against each other, sat down on the mat, and glared at Khiên. Then he tapped the water pipe.

'I'm serious. Bring some wine. Then write down the expense in the book. Tomorrow nobody will dare say a word. You're head of the family now, so be flexible. Don't be stingy like your father.'

Uncle Xung grinned and called for Nghĩa. The boy ran from the back of the lineage temple and respectfully crossed his arms in front of Uncle Xung. He told the boy, 'Go tell Uncle Kình and Uncle Phỏng I'm here. And tell them there's wine.'

In a moment like this, Uncle Xung liked to act imperiously, but normally he wore shorts everywhere and his business involved going to the Quài Market to buy piglets that he'd then resell for a tiny profit at the Đình Market. The other villagers usually called him Pig-dealer Xung. He had three sons: Xeng, Xèng, and Xình. Any time he called all three of his sons' names at once, his voice sounded like a set of musical gongs. Fortunately, his youngest daughter, Thao, was a strong woman who knew how to run a business, so his family prospered.

After the others arrived, the discussion of the death anniversary of the Nguyễn family patriarch quickly reached a consensus: there would be ninety tables and each would have seven dishes. They'd employ seven cooks, six kitchen maids, two strong young men to chop wood for the stoves, four women to carry buckets of water from the well, and several other people to help with miscellaneous chores.

The others all left after the meeting, but Uncle Xung stayed a bit longer to finish a last cup of wine. He whispered to Khiên, 'Are you going to let Vạn move into the lineage temple?'

'Yes,' said Khiên. 'I can't let him keep living in the communal house. The other families will laugh at us for not taking care of him. He's our village's greatest hero.'

'Listen to you! Everybody knows Vạn is a hero and has made a huge contribution to the country and our people, so let the government take care of him! His family hasn't done anything for the Nguyễn clan. Their whole lives, his parents and grandparents barely had enough food to eat. The whole lot of them had to work for landowner Hào. But things have changed. Don't be so ignorant. Let Vạn keep living in the communal house. Sooner or later, one way or another, Hào's line will die off. Don't you get it? When he dies, the property will go to Vạn for sure—a nobody. Just watch and you'll see! Everything has changed now. Nobody knows what's coming.'

'I couldn't care less about all that,' said Khiên. 'A moral person is afraid of nothing.'

'Don't be such an idiot! Sometimes a moral person starves to death.' Uncle Xung drained his cup. 'Talking to you is like spilling wine.'

*

Very early the next morning, Nghĩa woke to having his cheek pinched very hard.

'Wake up,' said great Uncle Xung.

Still only half awake, Nghĩa just barely understood that Uncle Xung had asked him to keep an eye on the cooks and kitchen maids all day to make sure no one stole any meat, sticky rice, or fruit for their own families at home. Nghĩa had been told that when he grew up, he would be head of the Nguyễn clan. The boy had no real understanding of the significance of that position but he did know that every member of the clan feared Uncle Xung, who was his grandfather's younger brother. His grandfather and Uncle Xung also had three more younger brothers—Kình, Phỏng, and Rinh—who all now had grey hair and long wispy beards. Some of their children were actually younger than Nghĩa, but he still had to call them aunt or uncle, and he hated them because even though he was older, they always behaved toward him in a superior, condescending way.

All day, Nghĩa watched the adults prepare for the big event. The lineage temple was packed with people. Outside in the courtyard and in the kitchen, adults hurried back and forth, carrying platters full of meat, baskets stacked with yellow rice cakes, and bamboo trays heaped with red sticky rice. Nghĩa noticed that all the members of the Nguyễn clan, regardless of age, seemed cheerful and had put on their best clothes. Each individual household in the clan was different from the next. But they all worked hard all year round and on this date each year maintained the tradition of gathering to honour the extended family.

'Have you seen Uncle Vạn?' Nghĩa's father, Khiên, had come up from behind and tapped him on the shoulder. 'Run to the communal house and tell him to come here right away.'

'Dad,' said Nghĩa, 'I'm busy.'

His father raised his voice. 'Go now!'

Nghĩa ran to Uncle Xung and whispered in his ear, 'I have to go get Uncle Vạn.'

'Have you caught anyone stealing?' asked Uncle Xung.

'Kind . . . of . . .' Nghĩa stammered.

'Don't be afraid. Tell me.'

'But . . .'

'Go ahead and tell me. I'll teach them a lesson.'

'Your son, Uncle Xeng,' lied Nghĩa. 'He stole some meat and a bottle of wine and hid them in a bamboo basket. Then he covered them with cabbage leaves and gave them to his wife to take home.'

Uncle Xung's face blanched. He was speechless for a moment, but then he grinned and patted Nghĩa on the shoulder. 'You're too honest! My son probably gave the meat to our dog. Don't you remember I have a huge dog? When she has puppies, I'll give you one. Here, have a few *hào** to buy some marbles. Don't tell anyone about this.'

Nghĩa took the coins and ran to the back room of the lineage temple. He put two bananas in his pocket, and then ran to the communal house. In the courtyard, he found Hạnh sitting on one of the stone dogs, reading.

'Aren't you afraid of the stone dogs?' Nghĩa pinched her cheek. 'Where's Uncle Vạn?'

---

* An old subunit of Vietnamese currency equivalent to a tenth of a *đồng*

'Ow! You're terrible—you pinched me too hard! Uncle Vạn is inside.'

'Here are some bananas. Put them away inside and then come join the party with me.'

'What party?'

'At the Nguyễn lineage temple. Today's our ancestor's death anniversary.'

'I'm not a Nguyễn.'

'You live in the same house as Uncle Vạn, so we can consider you an honorary member of the family.'

'Uncle Vạn won't let me go for sure. Plus, I'm afraid of old man Xung. He's made it very clear that no Nguyễn boy can be friends with a Vũ girl.'

Nghĩa went inside to look for Uncle Vạn. He didn't know why, but Hạnh was right. Uncle Vạn wouldn't let her go to the party. Nghĩa sulked angrily behind his uncle. Normally he'd be so proud to follow behind the village hero. Even so, he had to admit, Uncle Vạn looked really great in his new shoes and military uniform with all the medals pinned to his chest.

At the Silver Stone Bridge, Vạn slowed to gaze down at his shadow rippling on the water. As a boy he used to swim here in the river with landowner Hào's buffalo, and now the burbling of the river made him imagine it was delighted to see him again. Vạn felt many contradictory things all at once. Since his return, this would be the first time he was reacquainted with the whole Nguyễn clan. He didn't know what to say if people asked him about his relationship with Nhân's family. Did he love her children, or did he love their mother, Nhân? That he was very close to her family was a natural thing. But the villagers' gossip evoked in him unsettling thoughts about her.

The Nguyễn patriarch's curse had caused so many small tragedies. Over the decades, several couples had been in love but could not be together. Others had eloped, resettled elsewhere, and never come back. Vạn had mixed feelings about the clan too. On the one hand, he was very proud of his extended family. On the other, he felt quite detached from them. He loved them but he also frequently disliked them. The tall row of areca trees and mossy roof of the lineage temple came into view. By the time they reached the courtyard, Nghĩa was walking proudly by his side. Everyone stared in amazement at Vạn in his uniform with all his medals. He stood there in silence taking in the moment before smiling wide and greeting everyone. Uncle Khiên hurried out and shook his hand and led Vạn by the arm inside.

Only Uncle Xung crabbed at him. 'You're late, Mr Hero!'

Vạn said nothing, feeling overwhelmed by the event's bustling, festive atmosphere. When he was a kid, he had worked as a buffalo boy and as a servant for landowner Hào, and all he really understood was that people gathered on this date annually to eat and drink. Back then, he had dared only to linger around the edges of the party, hoping to get a handful of sticky rice or a banana, which he'd take somewhere else to eat.

'Please forgive me for being late,' said Vạn. 'My work at the commune office keeps me very busy.'

'I'm sure,' said Uncle Xung sarcastically while tapping the water pipe. 'The commune office is of course much bigger than this lineage temple.' Xung's brother Kinh gently poked Xung in the ribs and whispered, 'Do you want us to go to jail? Never insult a commune official.'

'I didn't!' said Uncle Xung, raising his voice. 'I'm just saying he's shown no respect for his ancestors.'

'Calm down,' said Khiên. 'Because of his situation, he's had to live far away from the village ever since he was a child, so there are some things that he's not aware of. Now that he's returned, it's a blessing for our clan. No one else from our village has gone to war and returned a hero safe and sound like Vạn.'

'We all know already about his heroic deeds.' Uncle Xung gulped down the rest of his wine and leered at everyone with red-rimmed eyes. He glared at Vạn and said, 'And now, what about your relationship with Nhân? Maybe you were too busy fighting on the battlefield and forgot about Great Great Grandfather Nguyễn's curse. Let me remind you what he wrote.' Uncle Xung tapped his chopsticks on the tray of food as he recited the lines of the curse like poetry, his voice echoing through the lineage temple. *'The Đình River will always flow. The Silver Stone Bridge will stand forever. The River of Love will always be beautiful and romantic. And the Nguyễn–Vũ feud will never end.'*

While everyone else was busy eating, Nghĩa stole bananas, sticky rice, and rice cakes and took them to the communal house. Nghĩa placed the food on a table, and he and Hạnh played a game of hide-and-seek in the back rooms where she and Vạn were living. Afterward, they laughed and joked as they ate. Then the conversation turned a bit more serious.

'Who's bigger,' Hạnh asked, 'the saint of this communal house or the god in the Christian church?'

'Uncle Vạn says there is no saint and no god. We have only the Party. The Party is the biggest and the strongest. They're the ones who put food on our tables and warm clothes on our backs.'

'Then why do people clasp hands and bow to saints and gods?'

'Superstition.'

After eating, Hạnh and Nghĩa went to the river to swim. Usually, Hạnh stayed in the shallows because she was afraid of the water monster. But with Nghĩa, she felt brave enough to swim to the middle of the river.

'Nghĩa, do you know where the river comes from?'

'Why do you ask such silly questions?'

'I want to know everything!' She laughed and splashed Nghĩa's face. 'The main canal in the paddies comes from this river. It runs by Hero Hill and the Fairy's Eye, and it runs through my family's rice paddy.'

Even the rice paddies of Đông Village evoked Hạnh's curiosity. She wanted to know where everything came from. Hạnh and Nghĩa walked downstream along the riverbank. The sun was setting into a bamboo grove in the distance, its simple pastoral beauty mesmerizing. They chased each other and caught grasshoppers from the long grass and put them in their pockets. They passed an old brick kiln. The river curved to the left and then a new vista opened before them. The river widened into a long, straight stretch. Hạnh suddenly gasped with joy when she saw a concrete structure towering in the distance on the horizon.

'The Linh Canal return,' Nghĩa said.

'Have you been there?'

'No.'

'Let's go!'

'I'm afraid it'll be dark by the time we get there.'

'Don't be a scaredy-cat!'

'Okay, fine. Let's go.'

They held each other's hand and ran on and on, never feeling tired. The structure grew closer, rising before them. They climbed to the top of the dike. From up there they could see all the way to the vast ocean for the first time in their lives. Hạnh imagined this must be the kind of world that existed only in the fairy tales that Nghĩa's grandfather had told them. Was she dreaming?

The moon had risen and now cast their shadows onto the grass. Linh Canal glowed faintly with the light from some fishermen's lanterns, which looked like stars twinkling on the water. Every now and then, the fishermen hoisted the bamboo poles holding the big nets, making the ropes shriek over the bamboo structure. Hundreds of shining silver sardines flickered as they jumped in the nets. Water pouring from the canal return into the river sounded like a waterfall beneath the bright moon.

They held hands on the long walk home too. As they neared their village, they jumped into each other's arms when an explosion on the river startled them. A column of water rose up and spattered noisily down. Then everything became quiet until two shadows splashed into the river.

Nghĩa breathed a sigh of relief. 'It's Uncles Xèng and Xình,' he whispered. 'They're using explosives to catch fish. You go back to the village that way. I'll wait, then keep going this way.' No Nguyễn would understand the new world they had just discovered.

Chapter 5

Not a soul begrudged Vạn when the land reform reassigned Hào's house to him. Old man Khi got a share too—a huge stone mortar—which he couldn't carry home himself and had to pay deaf brother Nhương two đồng to cart to his home. Aunt Nhị got a rice mill, Mr Đang several bags of dried sweet potatoes, and Miss Vòng four clay barrels used for pickling cabbage—two of them still full. The poor villagers saw for the first time just how much food and how many valuables Hào had accumulated by collaborating with the French. All his property was confiscated and piled up in the yard, including hoes, shovels, rice, pots and pans, bronze trays, bowls, and plates. One of Hào's former servants, Miss Sen, claimed that her master had hidden two more bronze trays somewhere, but Hào refused to say where. The militia beat the hell of out him but still he would only say, 'Công hid them.' His son, Công, had committed suicide when the French lost at Điện Biên Phủ and he saw the writing on the wall. Chairman Đột ordered the militia to search the property thoroughly, so they even raked through the pigsty and dug up the ground inside the cowshed. They searched under the banana and jackfruit trees in the garden too but found nothing.

Uncle Xung whispered to Chairman Đột, 'Ask the grandkid.' Chairman Đột glanced around and saw Công's son, Tốn, sitting glumly beneath a lychee tree. He still wore the mourning headband for his father's death. Chairman Đột asked Tốn in a sweet voice, 'Young man, where did your father hide the bronze trays and other things? Tell me and I'll give you some candy.'

Tốn just glared back at him, so Chairman Đột raised his voice, demanding, 'Where did he hide those things?' When Tốn remained silent again, he pinched the boy's ear, making him squeal with pain until he blurted, 'The pond!'

Four militiamen stripped to their underwear and splashed into the muddy pond. In just a short while, they found all the missing things.

The reappropriation of Hào's property was a big, boisterous affair that attracted all sorts of people who had been exploited by the former landowner. The most unfortunate person, the buffalo dung collector Dĩ, was given the central roller of a rice husking machine. He couldn't waste a day of work to retrieve it, so he sent his middle son to get it instead. The husking machine roller was very heavy. It took several men to load it onto the cart, and then a bunch of kids from the village excitedly helped push the cart to get it moving. But halfway home, the roller fell off the cart and hit Dĩ's son in the head as he was pushing from behind and killed him.

During the first night in his new home, Vạn could not sleep because he could not get over the shock of living in the house of his former master, a rich landowner. It was the first time in his life he could call a place his own.

Quietly, he called to Hạnh in the other room. 'Are you asleep?'

'Not yet.'

'Tomorrow you should go tell your mother to come and get her share of Hào's redistributed stuff. I already accepted them for her.'

'She said she won't take them because there are poorer families who need them more than us.'

'Your mother is exaggerating. These things aren't so valuable. What your father sacrificed is worth a lot more.'

Despite what Vạn said, deep in his heart he had always longed for a place to call his own home. But he also always thought it would be a place he built himself, on his own piece of land. No one begrudged Vạn, but he saw the bitterness and anger in Hào's grandson, Tốn's, eyes. He couldn't care less what that little spoiled brat thought.

Later that night, Hạnh was deep in her sleep, but Vạn felt wide awake. He tossed and turned for a long time, but then finally got up and went outside. The heavy wooden door made a terrifying screech, so he left it open. The kitchen building was quiet, its door shut. It was the only part of the property Hào had left for Công. Something fragrant wafted through the air. Công's wife, Hơn, must have been burning incense for her husband after his recent suicide.

Vạn picked his way silently to the pond, and then stood on the little bridge beneath the bright moon gazing down at the muddy water. Earlier some kids had dived there repeatedly, hoping to find anything else Hào might have hidden in the water. Hào had bricked the pond all around as if it were a swimming pool, but in the frenzy to find everything, the villagers had dug up all the bricks and left the place an ugly mess. Hào's own incredible greed and arrogance had made him their target. The power of the people had triumphed! Hào had also built a stable, a cowshed, and a pigsty, but within just a few hours, the villagers had turned everything into a disaster zone—not a single brick, lath, or rafter was left untouched.

In the moonlight, Vạn saw someone sneak into the banana garden. He thought for a moment to get his rifle but decided not to, worried he might lose sight of the intruder. Maybe it was one of Hào's loyal servants, returning for some still hidden treasure. Vạn had had a very difficult childhood and had fought for his life on the battlefield, so now he held no fear of anyone or anything. Within seconds, he snuck up behind the shadow searching the banana garden, and then, fast as a squirrel, seized the intruder's hands and held them powerfully behind the man's back. Of course it turned out to be Uncle Xung, who didn't fight back at all because he was old and weak.

'Vạn?' said the old man.

'What are you doing here?'

'Well . . . I just . . .' mumbled Uncle Xung. 'I have to go to the Quài Market early tomorrow, so I came here to get some banana leaves. I'm a pig dealer. You know that!'

'But I saw you digging.'

'You've been watching me, eh? Okay, fine—so what?' Then he whispered, 'Haven't you wondered whether Hào hid some gold here in the garden?'

'You need to report yourself to the commune office,' Vạn said gravely. 'You've been caught not telling the officials everything you know. Yesterday, you should have told them about the gold.'

'Huh? How could I report it if I don't know where Hào hid anything? It was just a guess.'

'You still have to report it even if it's just a guess.'

Uncle Xung shook with anger or fear or both.

'Plus, you've violated the curfew. After nine o'clock, no one except the commune officials can have a light on or leave their residence. I'm head of our local militia now. I insist you report to the commune office.'

'Are you trying to intimidate me?'

'Of course not!'

'You are *Nguyễn* Vạn,' said Uncle Xung, emphasizing the family name to remind his interrogator that they were both part of the same clan. 'Don't you know the Nguyễns have the biggest lineage temple in the whole village? Have you forgotten our ancestors' teaching? All members of the clan must love and protect one another!'

'I've forgotten nothing!' said Vạn, raising his voice. 'I also remember the oath a revolutionary soldier takes—to be loyal to the Party. Just remember, even if my own father were still alive, I would not protect him if he had betrayed the revolution. Now go, please.'

'You're the betrayer,' hissed Uncle Xung as he shuffled away. 'Traitor.'

*

When Vạn entered the gate of Nhân's courtyard, she had just finished washing her long, black hair and stood combing it in the yard. It's said a long-haired woman will have a hard life, and Nhân's hair reached all the way to her knees. Her son Hiệp sat on the step peeling a cassava root with a knife. His twin brother, Hà, stood in the corner chopping bamboo poles to be used to hang banners. The two boys cried cheerful greetings when they saw Vạn come into the yard. Nhân hurriedly tied her hair into a big bun and blushed when she noticed Vạn watching her. Awkwardly, she rushed inside without saying a word to him. He, too, felt awkward, realizing suddenly he had no real purpose for visiting. Since the death anniversary commemoration, Vạn had not seen Nhân except in passing, and they both knew why. If it weren't for the rumours about them, they could stand in the yard and talk to one another like regular people. Vạn followed her inside the house.

'Oh my!' gasped Nhân. 'Who could've guessed old man Xung and his family are reactionaries?' Nhân peered at Vạn as if trying to read his mind.

'Uncle Xung is still being investigated,' said Vạn. 'His sons Xèng and Xình were caught damaging the Linh Canal return with explosives. The investigation also uncovered members of the Nationalist Party operating out of Thượng Thủy Church. They've been secretly contacting their allies in the region. At a meeting in Hamlet Three last night, they caught Hinh blowing a leaf-bugle to signal the Nationalists.'

'Really?' Nhân exclaimed. 'Everybody says Hinh is a nice, quiet man, but I guess no one really knows what he's been up to.'

'Hinh is a sly fox! He said he was afraid of being late for the meeting and didn't have time to smoke his water pipe before leaving home, so on the way, he cut a banana leaf and made a pipe. When he reached the hamlet leader's house, he said he accidentally blew into the pipe, which made a sound like a bugle, and that he wasn't actually sending a signal to the Nationalists. That's when the militia jumped out and arrested him. Can you believe such a crazy story?'

'It's all such a mess.' Nhân sighed. 'I thought since peace had been restored, everybody could live peacefully, but now the Nationalists have become another big problem. Be careful, Vạn, and remember to lock your door before you go to bed. Reactionaries could sneak in and kill you at any time. Tell Hạnh to be careful too. And watch out for Công's wife and son—they might try to take revenge.'

'No need to be fearful.' Vạn smiled. 'Công's wife and son would never dare do such a thing. Hạnh is doing fine, by the way. She can cook rice now and has been a big help. We all need to be resolute if we're to do what's necessary to be rid of those bastard collaborators. Whatever share of Hào's stuff has been allotted to you, you need to claim and take home. Otherwise, you might be accused of not following the Party's policy, or worse, showing sympathy for the collaborators. That's why I signed you up for your share.'

'You don't understand. There are so many poor people in our village. Look at Mr Dĩ. One of his sons died in the war. Now another one has been killed too. All he has left is the boy with the developmental problems, and he's hardly any help at all.'

'No, you don't understand!' said Vạn. 'No one will see your refusal as the kindness you mean it to be. Look at how suspicious everyone is about you and me.' Vạn blushed and looked away. 'I feel so sorry for your sons when I think about their father. When he died, I searched through his rucksack and found all kinds of empty bullet shells and pieces of aluminium. I remember him telling me that once peace was restored, he would make toys out of them for his children. He also told everyone in the unit that you were the most beautiful woman in the whole village. At that moment, I remembered the time when we were kids and you also tended buffalo, and the bull I was riding saw your cow and ran towards it and dumped me to the ground. Your buffalo got spooked and charged into the river. I remembered thinking you must be a pretty skilled rider not to fall off.' Vạn meant for his story to cheer Nhân up, but her expression remained sombre. Vạn said, 'I love your children, and I want to help them now that their father is gone. I often want to stop by for a visit but I'm afraid of starting more rumours.'

'Then don't come,' Nhân said flatly. 'I hated seeing you living all alone at the communal house so I gave Hạnh permission to stay with you to keep you company. And you know what people said? They said I was using my daughter to seduce you. That infuriated me but I didn't tell you. Let the fools gossip, even if words cut deeper than swords. And if my kindness makes you uncomfortable, don't visit again. And send Hạnh back here to live with me.'

Vạn had not expected their conversation to turn so sour.

'You're overthinking it,' he said. 'I don't want Hạnh to leave unless she wants to and I won't let a bunch of idle gossips take her or our friendship away.' He stood abruptly and walked out to the courtyard.

'Uncle Vạn,' called Hà. 'Tell me if I wrote this slogan correctly.' He pointed to the banner he'd just painted, which read, *Down with cruel landowners!*

Chapter 6

Nghĩa had become convinced the world was nothing but chaos. He had only just seen the people of his village celebrate the return of peace and now the Nguyễn lineage temple had become a prison for colonial collaborators and reactionaries. What astonished him most was that great Uncle Xung turned out to be a reactionary too, and his sons, Xèng and Xình, were actually spies who had tried to destroy the Linh Canal return on purpose. Nghĩa stared at the two militiamen who had been transferred from Hạ Village to patrol Đông Village. Their severe, unfriendly faces and the way they held their guns told him the situation was serious. Maybe even more serious than the day earlier that week when the North Vietnamese Army had launched an attack on the Nationalists' staging area. Nghĩa had stayed up that whole night.

Just after sunset, armed NVA soldiers had come into town and packed into the communal house to prepare for the attack. His mother, Hạnh's mother, Uncle Xung, and Aunt Xeng kept busy cooking for the soldiers, rolling grapefruit-sized rice balls and cooling them on bamboo trays. Nghĩa's mother put salt, sesame, and four grilled shrimp on each rice ball. Before his uncles Xèng and Xình were discovered to be reactionaries, they joined their brother Xeng and the soldiers and prepared with them to attack the Nationalists, apparently to maintain their cover. At nine o'clock, the soldiers crept into the dark night, and the communal house fell silent. Nghĩa and Hạnh's mothers, and a few other village women sat together to wait for the attack to begin. At midnight, the sound of gunfire filled the air. Nghĩa climbed to the lineage temple roof and saw the Nationalist outpost sending flames high into the sky. An hour later, the communal house had filled again, this time with wounded men. Its wooden doors were taken down and used as surgery tables or beds, and Nghĩa held an oil lamp so the medics could treat the injuries. Strips of cloth to be used as bandages lay everywhere. That was the first time Nghĩa had seen so much human blood.

Later that morning, once all the wounded had been treated, Nghĩa's mother called to him from the next room. His parents were sitting with Chairman Đột.

'Sit down, son,' said his mother, 'and tell the truth, no fibbing. Up to now, what have great Uncle Xung, and Uncles Xeng, Xèng, and Xình given you?'

Seeing his parents' and Chairman Đột's stern faces, Nghĩa knew he couldn't refuse to speak. He tried to remember every detail.

'Great Uncle Xung gave me a few hào to buy marbles, and Uncle Xình gave me four ears of corn. I kept one and gave the others to Hạnh and her brothers.'

'A ha! What the boy just said is exactly what the villagers told me,' Chairman Đột said to Nghĩa's parents. His eyes brightened.

'Nghĩa,' said his father, 'did Uncle Xình give you a trowel?'

'Yes, Sir.'

'A ha!' Chairman Đột thumped Nghĩa's shoulder.

'Uncle Xung said I could take the trowel to his cornfield to dig up rats,' Nghĩa said, looking at Chairman Đột. 'That day I caught several big rats and a bunch of baby rats.'

'Did you draw that big cross on the road?' His father looked worried.

'Yes, Sir.'

'That's enough evidence!' Chairman Đột exclaimed. 'They know how to take advantage of children. Many people saw you draw that big cross on the road leading to Uncle Xung's house.' Chairman Đột bolted from his chair and hurried outside. Nghĩa's father followed just behind.

'For heaven's sake, Nghĩa, you're such a fool!' cried his mother. Her eyes filled with tears. 'Don't you know the cross you drew is the Nationalist Party's symbol? That's what told their members—

the parishioners—to go to great Uncle Xung's house. Uncles Xèng and Xình took advantage of your innocence and gave you that corn to get you to do this bit of dirty work for them. In fact, it means you inadvertently showed the reactionaries how to get to Uncle Xung's house!'

'What are you talking about? I just drew a cross in the road—no one told me to do that. And it was my idea to borrow Uncle Xình's trowel to dig up rats. That day I just drew the cross on my way to return it to his house.'

'Don't say another word!' Nghĩa's mother bawled. 'And stop doing such stupid things! You'll wind up in jail.'

Nghĩa felt miserable that he had caused his parents so much trouble. It was like everything had turned upside down. He had just been playing a trick on the parishioners, hadn't he? Could he have inadvertently helped the reactionaries?

That evening, when Nghĩa went out to the back garden to pee, a shadow emerged from behind the banana tree and grabbed his hand, scaring him so bad he peed his pants. He recognized the voice immediately as Aunt Xeng, great Uncle Xung's daughter-in-law.

'I hid some rice balls in the haystack,' she said with a shaky voice. 'Find a way to give them to your uncles Xung and Xèng and Xình, or they'll die of hunger. They're locked up in the lineage temple.'

Stunned by her frightening, sudden appearance, Nghĩa said nothing, but she quickly and quietly vanished into the banana garden as if being chased. After learning that morning how his actions might be misinterpreted, Nghĩa didn't want to get involved in any more adult business, but he also didn't want his uncles to starve.

Nghĩa found the rice balls Aunt Xeng had hidden. And later that evening, when his mother told him it was time for the family to study revolutionary doctrine, he complained of a stomach ache, and said he was going to go out to the field to dig up some ginger root. As he passed through the village, Nghĩa realized how difficult it would be to fulfil Aunt Xeng's request. Two militiamen stood guard outside the entrance to the lineage temple. But then Nghĩa remembered the broken latch on the window in the lineage temple's back room. He thought he could climb through. When the guards took a break to smoke their water pipe, Nghĩa hung the bags of rice balls around his neck and quickly scurried into the garden, snatched a chair that had been left there, placed it below the window with the broken latch, and climbed inside. The back room of the lineage temple was cold and musty because no one had burnt incense there for more than a week. Nghĩa tiptoed to where his uncles were being held. Several people sat leaning against the pillars, their ankles in chains. Nghĩa gagged at the stench of human waste and urine. An oil lamp at the door cast enough light to recognize Uncles Xung, Xèng, and Xình, Mr Ninh, and a few people he knew from Hồi Village. Nghĩa split the rice balls into portions, passed them out, and then fled. As Nghĩa returned the chair to the garden, voices came from the temple entrance. The land reform committee chairman was speaking with Tý Hin—Chairman Đột's younger sister. Nghĩa worried they'd heard him. But in the moonlight, he saw them slink to the rear of the lineage temple. Nghĩa lay flat beside a canna bush, held his breath, and strained to follow the shadows in the dark. They stopped beneath the jackfruit tree, embraced, and fell upon one another.

*

Drumbeats punched through the village. Hạnh, and everyone, regardless of age, rushed to the communal house courtyard. Youngsters carried flags and banners, and traipsed among the crowd, chanting, 'Down with cruel landowners!'

'Down with them! Down with them!'

'Down with reactionaries Xèng and Xình. They tried to destroy Linh Canal.'

'Down with them!'

The jeering crowd pumped their fists.

Hạnh searched the crowd for Nhân, ducking through until she saw her mother and brothers. She gave Nhân the two rice balls Vạn had asked her to keep. All around them people filled the communal house courtyard, many standing on the walls, some sitting on the roof. Hạnh worked her way through the throng to the high platform at the front decorated with slogans and red banners. She had to stand on one of the stone dogs to see Nghĩa, who sat with his parents in the front row, which had been reserved for people who had denounced landowners publicly. An open space yawned between the platform and the crowd, thanks to the deep pit that had been dug there. Hào, the cruel collaborator, stood in the hole with his head lowered, his grey hair a mess. Hạnh elbowed her way through the crowd and sat next to Nghĩa. Vạn stood at the rear holding his rifle from the army. On the left side of the platform, a few people with tied hands stood waiting for the prosecution—among them old man Xung as well as his sons Xèng and Xình. Scanning the crowd, Hạnh's eye caught on Chairman Đột's sister, Tý Hin, who looked quite beautiful with her rosy cheeks.

'Tý Hin looks majestic today,' said Hạnh.

'Majestic my ass,' blurted Nghĩa.

'Why would you curse at her?' Hạnh gaped at Nghĩa.

'I saw her fooling around with the head of the land reform committee behind the lineage temple.'

'Bite your tongue! She could throw you in jail!'

'Go ahead and tell her!'

Hạnh said nothing. Surreptitiously, she kept staring at Nghĩa to consider his sad and grumpy face, her mind whirling with many strange feelings. The crowd seemed anxious under the hot sun. The banging of a gavel and a sudden shouting from the platform startled her to attention. Based on what was said in the court, she got a simple sense of why old man Xung, his sons, and the others were found guilty. Xung had searched Hào's garden and harvested banana leaves illegally, Hinh had blown the leaf trumpet to warn the reactionaries, and Xèng and Xình had used explosives to destroy part of the Linh Canal.

At noon, everyone scattered into the shade to eat lunch. Hạnh's mother gave her back the two rice balls and she circled the courtyard and grounds looking for Uncle Vạn. She finally found him inside the communal house, sitting at the desk with Chairman Đột.

'You didn't denounce Xung publicly this morning,' Chairman Đột was saying. 'You're no coward, so why didn't you speak up?'

'I left when I was just a kid,' Uncle Vạn explained, 'so I know nothing about his reputation or standing with the village. And when I caught him in the banana garden, I told him then he had to report to the commune.'

'I know you still have some reluctance to speak against anyone in the Nguyễn clan,' said Chairman Đột. 'If it turns out we can't punish Xung, the father of the reactionaries Xèng and Xình, you'll be held partly responsible. You have to criticize yourself for this.' Then Chairman Đột lowered his voice, saying, 'But it's okay. On the execution day, you just have to show everybody you're a brave rifleman, a real Điện Biên Phủ hero. I'm still your friend, so I'm just telling you like it is. I think your hesitation to speak up today has raised some suspicions with the head of the land reform committee about your perspective on the revolution and social class.'

Uncle Vạn smiled and said, 'I'll volunteer to shoot landowner Hào.'

'No. You can't do that. We'll have Thước shoot him.' Chairman Đột grinned back at Vạn, blinked, and then whispered, 'This is a chance for Thước to show his loyalty to the Party because he was Hào's favourite servant. Get it? The duty of shooting Xèng and Xình in the head has to fall to you.'

Uncle Vạn nodded. 'Okay,' he said. 'Fine.'

Uncle Vạn stood slowly beneath the weight of this decision and staggered to where Hạnh was standing behind a pillar.

'Are you hungry?' he asked. 'We can sit right here and eat.'

'Did you just volunteer to shoot Xèng and Xình?' asked Hạnh, her eyes wide.

'No, it's just my duty. A revolutionary soldier must do what's necessary to rid ourselves of colonial collaborators and reactionaries so that everyone can live fairly and happily.'

Hạnh nodded and asked, 'Are you and my mother mad at each other?'

'Who told you that?'

'No one. I just guessed because I saw her earlier and she didn't ask about you, which seemed strange.'

*

Vạn spent a long time cleaning his rifle with a rag and oil, just as he had done so many times before. But even with his gun now shiny clean, he still felt uneasy. He would probably have to use this rifle to shoot great Uncle Xung's sons, whom he had not so long ago sat with at the same table eating and drinking in the Nguyễn lineage temple. Vạn hung the gun from its strap on a nail in a pillar and stood in the open doorway. Công's wife, Hơn, quietly passed by carrying a bamboo basket. God only knew what was on her mind. Her husband had killed himself, and very soon her father-in-law would be executed. She might be looking for food—only now did she begin to understand the plight of being a poor farmer.

Hơn was quite attractive. Công had deliberated very carefully when choosing his wife. Her eyes were black, her waist small, and her skin rosy. If there had been no land reform and Công hadn't committed suicide, Hơn would surely have given birth to several children. Suddenly Vạn heard some kids shouting in the garden, so he stepped out beyond the wall and saw that they had set up a pretend court to 'prosecute' Hơn's son, Tốn. The kids had made a platform from bricks and tied Tốn's hands behind his back. Tốn sat on the ground behind bars the kids had made from bamboo. The judges included a few older children, Tý, Tường, and Hương, and the audience was mostly younger children with runny noses and wide eyes. Two boys on one side were using slingshots to pelt Tốn with chinaberries, and with each hit, Tốn screamed. Vạn rushed into the garden and shouted at them to stop. Green papayas and jackfruit lay scattered all over the ground. A few lemon trees had been dug up too.

'Who said you could destroy the garden?' Vạn yelled, glaring at the kids.

They looked at each other and said nothing. After a while, Tý said innocently, 'We only dug up the trees because we wanted to uproot the cruel landowners.'

Vạn snorted. 'Well, this garden no longer belongs to a cruel landowner. I forbid you to come back here. Now replant those trees and clean up this mess.'

That evening, Hạnh went home to spend the night with her mother, and Vạn felt very lonely. It was already dark when he finished his dinner. He lit an oil lamp, and as he sat on the mat drinking tea, Công's widow, Hơn, came in and knelt beside him. She placed her hand on his and said, 'You left the village when you were really young, so you probably don't know much about me. I'm Father Hào's daughter-in-law, Hơn, and I've never done anything to hurt other people. I've never abused anyone or exploited them. In fact, I've been secretly helping many poor people in the village. I was born into a poor family myself, in Hồi Village, but because people think I'm beautiful, Công married me. But beauty can also be a curse. I have only one son, Tốn. My husband is dead. Even though Tốn is the grandson of a collaborating landowner, I promise to teach him how to live a simple peasant life. Please don't hate him. I beg you. Please don't let the village kids beat and bully him. His eyes and face are so swollen now. I saw the kids beating him but I didn't dare say anything because I was afraid their parents would accuse me of oppressing the poor. I have no one now to share my sorrow—that's why I came to you to ask for help.'

Her pleas embarrassed Vạn. He had told the kids not to torture Tốn, but he couldn't promise to help her any further. Vạn sat very still, not daring to look into her blazing eyes. He didn't know what was on her mind. But his silence seemed to puzzle her even more.

'Please, sir, promise me you'll help. I beg you.' Tears trailed down her cheeks. 'I've spoken with you honestly. I have no family other than my son. What if . . .?' In desperation, she clasped Vạn's arms. Her eyes were like flames. 'Help me, and you can do whatever you want with me.'

She fell into his arms. Her body heaved against his chest. Vạn gathered his fortitude and gently pushed her away. He stood and said, 'You should go. I promise to help. I promise.'

'Thank you, sir. Thank you very much for your kindness!' She sat up onto her knees, bowed deeply, and then rose and dashed outside.

*

The people sent the criminals to be shot. Nghĩa and Hạnh followed the crowd escorting them, and at the stone bridge, could see that the whole district had come out and people were all rushing excitedly toward the graveyard.

'Will they shoot them in the head?' asked Hạnh.

'For sure,' Nghĩa replied, 'in the head.'

'Will they give them funerals?'

Nghĩa wondered the same thing. He liked that Hạnh often came up with questions he wouldn't think of. But he didn't know the answer. He guessed Vạn would be in charge today. Nghĩa and Hạnh followed Vạn into the graveyard, which had already started to fill with people. Each village and commune had its own assigned seats, separated by ropes and banners. Hạnh held Nghĩa's hand tightly as the criminals were led to the front and tied to poles.

The crowd shouted:

'Down with cruel landowners!'

'Down with them!'

'Down with the Nationalist Party!'

'Down with reactionaries!'

The crowd whooped and yelled and raised their fists—the same things Hạnh had seen at the courtyard of the communal house.

'I'm scared,' said Hạnh.

'There's nothing to be afraid of,' Nghĩa said. 'Look at Uncles Xèng and Xình. They're tied to poles and about to be shot, and they don't look scared at all. Don't be a scaredy-cat.'

Hạnh looked around, hoping to see Uncle Vạn again. Chairman Đột and the head of the land reform committee sat at a table off to one side signing some papers. Then she saw Uncle Vạn step away from the crowd and stand with Mr Thước across from the criminals to prepare himself to shoot. The atmosphere grew quiet. Everyone seemed to take a deep breath.

'Blindfold them,' someone ordered.

Hạnh couldn't understand it, but Uncle Xình was tied up and blindfolded and still he shouted, 'Long live the Vietnam Workers' Party!' And then, 'Long live President Hồ!'

All the people around Hạnh seemed astonished to hear the words 'Long live President Hồ!' coming from the mouth of a criminal.

Three gunshots rang through the air. Hạnh felt so terrified that her eyesight blurred, and her ears felt clogged and muffled. She held Nghĩa tightly without looking at the crumpled bodies of the dead.

The execution was over.

Hạnh jostled through the crowd following Nghĩa toward the riverbank.

'Fire!' someone screamed. 'The village is on fire!'

Chaos erupted as the crowd alongside the river started to run every which way.

Hạnh's arms and legs went limp as she looked toward the village and saw a vast column of smoke billowing from behind the bamboo grove, and then, a bright sheet of flame. Nghĩa took Hạnh's arm and ran, pulling her to the Silver Stone Bridge. Then they heard someone shout, 'The Nguyễn lineage temple is on fire!'

Nghĩa dropped Hạnh's hand and raced off toward the temple. People were crying out, yelling, and screaming over the popping and crackling of the fire that sounded to Hạnh like exploding firecrackers. Ashes filled the air. Trembling, Hạnh searched the crowd for Nghĩa. People started a bucket brigade from the pond, dumping pots and buckets full of water over and over to try to kill the blaze. Some men removed the thatched roof of Nghĩa's house next door so the fire wouldn't spread. Finally, the fire was out, and the exhausted firefighters all sat in the yard looking like they were still in shock. Nearly the whole lineage temple had been destroyed, except for the back room, and the walls that had been made from brick. The pillars were still smoking.

'Who torched the lineage temple?' someone asked.

'The whole village had gone to watch the execution, so it must have been Nationalists from Thượng Church.'

'We should interrogate the two militia guards.'

'They were guarding the criminals, not the lineage temple.'

'Manure collector Dĩ wasn't at the execution. When I ran here, the first things I saw were his baskets of buffalo dung over there.'

'Bring Dĩ here immediately.'

Soon Dĩ stood in front of the crowd gathered in the yard, saying, 'I didn't start the fire. I was carrying a load of manure and saw flames coming from the corner of the temple, so I dropped the baskets and ran to see what was going on. The two militia guards were both asleep at the entrance. I shouted, 'Fire!' and they woke up and immediately ran inside. They dragged Xung, Ninh, and the other criminals out to the yard.'

Hạnh found Nghĩa lying propped against a banana tree in the garden. Soot blackened his face. She sat next to him, sniffling and crying a little as she took in the sight of the burnt banana and areca leaves.

'You should sleep at my house tonight,' she said. 'It's good your house didn't burn, but it'll take a while to put back together. Where else would you sleep?'

*

The following day, Nghĩa and Hạnh chopped down the burnt banana trees and tied the trunks together to make a raft to transport bales of sedge from the other side of the river. Though Hạnh was living in the house with Uncle Vạn, she sometimes helped her mother by cutting the sedge she would use to make mats and other things. Nghĩa's parents chopped down the burnt bamboo from the yard and tossed it in the pond so termites wouldn't eat it. They had nearly finished the work when they heard people shouting from the road.

'That trial was bullshit!'

'They should be beaten to death!'

Mrs Hinh, Miss Ngọ, Miss Tý Hin, and Chairman Đột all ran into the lineage temple, their clothes dishevelled and torn. Terrified, they sprinted to the still intact back room and locked the door shut. A group of fierce-looking men brandishing sticks rushed up to Nghĩa's parents in the courtyard and shouted angrily, 'Where are you hiding those bastards?'

Nghĩa's parents just stood there, too stunned to speak.

A voice that sounded like Uncle Xung's said, 'I bet they're in the back room.'

The angry men rushed into the temple and banged on the locked door and yelled, 'Open up!'

'Kill them all!'

'Cut off their tongues and fill their mouths with shit!'

'Stop!' Uncle Vạn shouted as he ran into the yard. 'Everyone, just wait a minute!' He stood there with his gun in his hand. The angry mob came back out to the courtyard and glared at him in silence.

'Here! Take my gun.' Uncle Vạn dropped the rifle onto a heap of straw. 'If you want revenge, go ahead and shoot me, Nguyễn Vạn.' And then he opened his shirt wide to show the many scars on his chest, and starting with Uncle Xung, stared at each person, one by one.

Shaking with fear, Hạnh rushed to Uncle Vạn and wrapped her arms around him. He pushed her behind him and then stood there defiantly, his scarred chest thrust forward.

Suddenly, Uncle Xung threw down his stick and charged inside the lineage temple. He stretched out his arms and wrapped them around one of the burnt pillars. He shook as he glared up at the vast blue sky and howled, and then suddenly he burst out laughing like a lunatic. Several vessels had burst in the corners of his eyes turning them a terrible, bloody red.

PART II

Chapter 7

Seven years later, the charred pillars of the ruined Nguyễn lineage temple still stood, and Nghĩa had become a strong young man. Hidden behind his bright eyes was his ambition to rebuild the family temple, and only Hạnh could read his mind. The things they'd witnessed during their childhood were etched deeply into their memories. Any time Nghĩa saw the burned ruins of the temple—the symbol of the Nguyễns' collapse—his heart ached. He hoped one day he'd be able to rebuild it. When he told his father his intentions, Mr Khiên's eyes lit up. He patted his son's shoulder and said, 'You're a good son. You deserve to be head of the Nguyễn clan. Your mother and I want to rebuild the temple too, but it will have to wait. We just spent everything on your sister's wedding.'

Nghĩa knew his parents were kind-hearted people to allow Duyên to marry Minh. His mother and father had died when he was a child, so he'd been forced to move in with his older sister's poor husband's family. Nghĩa's parents had paid for the wedding and thrown a huge party. Mr Khiên had said paying for everything was the only thing to do. As head of the clan, he had to set a good example for everyone.

Seven years had passed, but still no one knew who had set fire to the lineage temple. When Nghĩa and his father prepared to rebuild the front rooms of the temple, a few wicked villagers started the rumour that Mr Khiên himself started the fire so he could build a new house for his only son on the land.

But that was ridiculous. Before starting the renovation, Khiên asked every household in the clan for permission. No one objected because the half-burnt ruins were such an eyesore. And the new house looked so impressive! Khiên had two couplets carved into wooden planks that he hung from the pillars to remind everyone that the arsonist would eventually be punished—*Eliminate criminals and the ancestral hall burns. Injustice and hatred will not be forgotten*. He also built a bedroom for Nghĩa in the new house and hoped his son would one day restore the family's honour and heritage.

Khiên's strict parenting had turned Nghĩa into a mature person. When he was young, he had studied the old Confucian verses with Teacher Thảo, and Khiên never forgot his teacher. Although their family could barely make ends meet, each year on the first day of Tết,* Mr Khiên brought Nghĩa with him to visit Teacher Thảo and give him rice wine and *bánh chưng*.† Mr Khiên often said to Nghĩa, 'First study manners, then study literature—if a man wants to be literate, he must first study the way.' Raising Nghĩa, Khiên was both loving and indulgent, as well as extremely strict. He bought several musical instruments for Nghĩa to learn to play. At first, Nghĩa felt tormented every evening when forced to practice. But gradually, Nghĩa developed a passion for them. Any time he took a buffalo out to the field, he'd bring a flute tucked into his pants. Along the river, he'd sit on the back of his buffalo and play songs on the flute. He found life so beautiful then.

In those days, Hạnh always followed Nghĩa, probably because she loved the sound of his music. Now a young woman, Hạnh had become as beautiful as a chrysanthemum. Her black hair was long and silky like her mother's. Her breasts were round and full. Whenever Hạnh looked at Nghĩa, her eyes were like two flames that made his heart melt. Since Hạnh had moved back into her mother's house, Nghĩa had not seen her much, but each day he tried to find some reason to visit.

Sometimes Nghĩa thought Hạnh was Miss Ngần, the woman from the story about the fairy's eye his grandfather used to tell. In fact, Hạnh did resemble a seductive fairy, but no one knew whether

* The Lunar New Year

† A traditional Tết dish made from sticky rice, mung beans, and pork

she would have to suffer injustice like the fairy had. Because of the Nguyễn–Vũ feud, no couple from both those families had been able to live happily together.

At the end of a music lesson at Uncle Vạn's house, Hạnh surreptitiously poked Nghĩa in the ribs, signalling him to stay afterward. Nghĩa went out with the other students, but then stopped at the pond to wash his feet. When the others and the teacher had gone, he came back inside. Hạnh hugged him tightly, and they wrestled and tickled each other, laughing on Uncle Vạn's bed.

Her eyes flashing, Hạnh asked sadly, 'Will we always have to keep our secret?'

'Maybe we should tell Uncle Vạn,' said Nghĩa. 'He's probably the only one who might understand.'

Together with Hạnh, the evening felt very peaceful. Widow Hơn's black cat suddenly jumped down from the roof and ran into the house. It sat and stared strangely at Hạnh and Nghĩa.

*

After the lineage temple burned, Vạn had encouraged Hạnh to go back to her mother's house. In general, the Nguyễn clan was not pleased with his murky relationship with Nhân, and many people said that the Nguyễn ancestors were punishing them because of his violation of the family curse. Vạn was by no means a superstitious person. A revolutionary never believed in angels or evil spirits. No ghost could punish him. Not afraid of dying or the dead, Vạn worried only about violating the Party's teachings. Vạn had dared to convert the village communal temple into the commune office, and he was still alive. He'd even pissed on the shrine at the village gate when it was taken down. All the other villagers had considered it sacred and wouldn't even curse when passing it by. In everything Vạn did, even the small things, he considered whether it was in the people or the Party's best interest. He knew in his heart he was in love with Nhân, but in his mind he considered those feelings a weakness. To have a relationship with a fallen comrade's wife seemed unfitting for a revolutionary, and perhaps a betrayal of some kind, or at the very least, not the example he wanted to set for the village. His youth may have passed, but he still had his pride.

Now people turned their suspicion toward Nghĩa and Hạnh, who had been playing together in Vạn's home since adolescence. Vạn loved them both as he would his own children, but he'd never considered that they might fall in love. A few years ago, when he mentioned the curse and the feud between the two families, they had looked at each other with surprise. And now, recently, when it came up again, they had covered their mouths and giggled in front of him.

This morning, before going to the commune office for a day full of meetings, he had given Hạnh a key so she could use the house for music practice. He'd asked her to drop off the key at his office when she finished. But it was now nine o'clock in the evening and Hạnh had not yet come by. Maybe they were still practising, or would practise all night? Vạn walked home. Next door, Widow Hơn had already turned off her light and gone to bed. Outside his door, he could hear Hạnh and Nghĩa's voices and laughter. He pushed open the door and found them lying on the bed together. Hạnh sat up when she saw Vạn. If she gets pregnant, Vạn thought, it will be his fault. The young couple didn't seem embarrassed. In fact, they were cheerful.

He looked at them sternly and asked, 'What's going on here?'

'We're just playing,' said Hạnh between giggles.

'From now on, you two are forbidden to play such deadly games.'

'Deadly?' she scoffed, her hand half hiding a mocking smile. 'Who's going to die?'

'If you keep playing this particular *game*, you'll wind up getting pregnant, and then everyone will blame me. The whole village will come after me for encouraging your bad behaviour. Then one of us might die, probably me.'

'But we didn't do anything bad.'

'Let's not hide anything from him, Hạnh,' said Nghĩa. The young man clasped Vạn's hand and said, 'Hạnh and I love each other, Uncle. We can't live without each other. We . . . we know only you can understand us . . . and explain the situation to our parents.'

Vạn stood very still, looking at them. He felt a bit shocked by their openness. The younger generation was very different from his, talking about love so freely, as if it were nothing. When he was their age, he hadn't known a thing about girls, or about love. But he knew for sure now that the entire village would say that because he could not marry Hạnh's mother, Nhân, he was setting the two of them up, and that would kill him.

Hạnh could see the battle raging silently behind Vạn's brow. She placed her hands atop Vạn and Nghĩa's, and said, 'You're the only person we trust. Please help us, Uncle.'

'Stop!' Vạn hissed, taking back his hand and glaring at the young couple. 'Stop it and get out of here right now!'

Hạnh and Nghĩa looked shocked, then heartbroken, and then hurried out of the house.

Vạn realized suddenly that he'd never yelled at them before. He staggered to the door and called out, 'Hạnh and Nghĩa, come back.'

They turned around and shuffled to the front steps and stood sheepishly before him.

'I'm sorry I yelled,' Vạn said, ushering them back inside. 'But I have let you two go too far. Eventually this fling will fall apart anyway. Please come to your senses. You don't realize how much suffering there's already been and how much more trouble this will cause. Nghĩa, you have to think this through. You're trying to restore the family's name. You can't let everything burn again.' Then he lay a shaking hand on top of Hạnh's and said, 'You probably don't know I was once in love with your mother. If I hadn't controlled my feelings, I would've lost everything.'

'You're a big coward,' she said. 'You have no heart.'

Once again Nguyễn Vạn stood dumbfounded as Hạnh yanked her hand free from his, took Nghĩa by the arm and pulled him out of the house. Vạn felt his chest swell with excitement and confusion. Maybe they *could* free themselves from the past.

It was still quite hot outside, so Vạn decided to cool off in the pond before going to tell Nghĩa's parents everything. But at the pond, he found Widow Hơn already there, half submerged in the water, her naked back glowing with moonlight. Not saying a word, he turned and began to creep away, but then Hơn said sweetly, 'Vạn, have you come to swim? Don't go back—I'm finished. The water feels so nice and cool.' She pulled up her wet blouse to cover her breasts and then emerged from the water. As she passed him, she said, 'When you're done, stop by my house. I need to ask you something.'

Vạn splashed into the pond, wondering what the young widow wanted to say to him. It all seemed so strange, and he found himself embarrassed that she may have thought he was spying on her. After cooling off, he came back to the yard and found the door to Hơn's house wide open. He passed by on his way to speak with Khiên and his wife, but Hơn called out again, 'Oh, Vạn! Please wait just a moment. I need to ask you something.'

Hơn had put on a white, sleeveless blouse. She poured tea into a cup and held it out to him.

'Please, have some tea,' she said. 'You're my next-door neighbour, but we rarely have a chance to speak.'

'I'm very busy.'

'I know. You are always very busy. But I often remind my son about how you helped us. You're very kind. If you hadn't intervened that day, my son might . . .'

Vạn waved a hand. 'It was nothing. No need to dwell on that.'

'I'm not an ungrateful person.' Hơn smiled and glanced up at him coquettishly while holding her teacup. 'I've been wondering why you don't get married.'

Vạn snorted. 'I'm old and disabled. Who would want to marry me?'

Hơn covered her mouth with her hand and giggled. 'You're joking! You're not old!'

Vạn thought maybe she was teasing him because she thought he'd been spying on her at the pond. 'Whether I get married or not has nothing to do with you. Why don't *you* remarry? Then you'll have someone else to tease.'

'Oh, Vạn! I'm not teasing. And actually, getting married is what I want to talk to you about.' Hơn lowered her voice. 'I thought you had something going on with Hạnh's mother, but I guess that's not true. But what about me? Do you think I'm pretty? And how about this? If you agree, I'll move in with you. We can turn my place into a little restaurant. Tốn can also help out. Every night I already feel very close to you, knowing that you're sleeping in the bed that used to be mine and my husband's. I also . . .'

'What . . . an . . . interesting proposal,' Vạn said as he got up hastily and hurried out the door. 'I've got to go now!'

Along the main road, he chased his own shadow beneath the bright moon. The village was so peaceful at night. That Hơn is very naughty, he thought. And he wasn't exactly comfortable with naughty. Her eyes were like fires. And he still couldn't tell whether she was teasing or serious. He couldn't believe she had the nerve to mention the bed she had shared with her husband. If he hadn't helped her son, would she have dared to make such a suggestion? The moon was now high in the sky. The shadow of the mango tree looked huge, and beneath it, the commune office glowed white. On the Silver Stone Bridge, Vạn's shadow split in half, part on the bridge, part on the water.

He heard someone splashing below and then saw a shadow rise up onto the riverbank like a ghost. It was Uncle Xung. He wore only a short shirt and was naked from the waist down. He whirled his arms around as if practicing martial arts, and then picked up a walking stick and started to sing. 'Praise the skilful lamp maker, horse, dog, horse, dog, in the blink of an eye, it turns around . . . When . . . When will you tie the knot?'

The whole village had already heard plenty of Uncle Xung's 'Tickle Song'. He sang it all the time now, wherever he was, whatever he was doing. When meeting someone for the first time, he sang even louder. At the end, he leaned on his cane, looked up at the moon and laughed. His mind had snapped the day Xèng and Xình were executed and the lineage temple burned. At first, people had thought he was faking so they wouldn't keep him in chains. But then people had realized it wasn't pretend. The death of his sons had driven him insane. Xung clattered onto the bridge and froze when he saw Vạn watching him.

'Uncle Xung,' Vạn shouted. 'Go home right now. Or I'll have the militia arrest you.'

'Arrest me? Who are you? Oh, I see—it's Nguyễn Vạn. Have you forgotten our ancestors' teaching? Let me recite it . . . *The Đình*

River will always flow. The Silver Stone Bridge will stand forever. The River of Love will always be beautiful and romantic. And the Nguyễn–Vũ feud will never end.'

Vạn shook his head as he walked away. 'Crazy!'

He felt confused and a bit disoriented after meeting Uncle Xung. Maybe the Nguyễn family really was cursed.

*

The young couple walked hand in hand along the river. It had been a long time since Hạnh had asked Nghĩa to take her to Linh Canal, and now they were walking along the same stretch of riverbank again. A full moon in the sky and a full moon on the water had followed their footsteps that night, and did this night too. Only human life was subject to change. Back then, everything had been mysterious to Hạnh. Now, she understood the way of the world. And she knew her love for Nghĩa was true.

'I guess now we know for sure Uncle Vạn really did love your mom.'

Hạnh sighed. 'Another cursed love.'

'I don't care about that stupid curse. We'll be the ones to break it.'

'Can we?' asked Hạnh. 'Are we strong enough?'

'When they're in love, people say nothing else matters. I just want to have a happy life, living with you in the house my father built for us. Eventually, I'll be head of my clan and I'll lift that stupid curse from our families so Nguyễn and Vũ boys and girls will be free to love whomever they choose. After our wedding, I'll cut down a patch of bamboo to make a boat we can take down to Linh Canal any time we want.'

'The moon is so beautiful tonight,' Hạnh said. 'Look how pretty it is on those tall areca trees in the front of the lineage temple.'

'My ancestors said that land is really fertile. Any tree can grow there.'

As Hạnh and Nghĩa returned to the village entrance, they saw Uncle Xung wandering in the communal house courtyard and heard him reciting the ancestors' curse.

'Let's run,' Hạnh said. 'I'm afraid of him.'

'You don't have to be afraid. He's crazy, but harmless.'

They passed through the gate to Nghĩa's courtyard. Hạnh's heart thumped in her chest. Her face felt hot.

Nghĩa squeezed her hand. 'Let me take care of everything.'

The evening was still hot, so Nghĩa's parents had spread a large mat and were sitting together in the middle of the front yard to catch the breeze. They seemed surprised to see Hạnh with their son.

'Where've you been to come back so late?' asked Mrs Khiên. She glanced at her husband, who was preparing tobacco for his pipe and said nothing.

'We have something we want to talk to you about.'

'The music performance?' asked Mr Khiên. 'When you're ready, just let us know and we'll be there.'

'Not about that.'

'Then what?'

'Something important.' He took Hạnh's hand and held it up. 'Hạnh and I have been dating.'

Mrs Khiên gaped at Nghĩa and then at Hạnh. Mr Khiên had begun to inhale the smoke from the water pipe and now spluttered and coughed. He set down the pipe and stared at his son as if unable to believe what Nghĩa had just said.

'You're not joking?'

'No! We're serious. We've been in love a long, long time.'

'Stop! Stop this nonsense right now.' Mr Khiên lifted his face to the heavens as if in prayer.

'Don't be foolish, Nghĩa,' said Mrs Khiên. Then she turned to Hạnh and said, 'Hạnh, you can ask your mother about this. We don't hate you but you can't marry our son. We are Nguyễn. You are Vũ. So many terrible things have happened.'

'Mom, you can't say that. Our families, not Heaven or fate or the ancestors, have caused all the bad things to happen. How can it be wrong that Hạnh and I are in love?'

His parents looked stricken.

'I believe that you don't hate me,' Hạnh said hesitantly, unable to meet Nghĩa's parents' gaze. 'But you can't really think the non-existent relationship between my mother and Uncle Vạn caused the lineage temple to burn or Uncle Xung to go insane or his sons to be executed. You need to know I've been thinking about this for a very long time. I love Nghĩa. It's up to you to decide whether to love me or hate me. I should go now. Please, with your permission.'

Hạnh got up and turned toward the gate.

'Hạnh, don't go yet!' said Mr Khiên. 'I suspected already you two were in love, but you have to understand our families have been enemies for generations. We live on the lineage temple land. Our whole clan will say I allowed our mortal enemy to desecrate the land of our ancestors, that I let an elephant trample the ancestors' graves.* We can't take this lightly.'

Nghĩa said, 'We'll build a house somewhere else.'

'You'll be head of the clan, son,' said Mrs Khiên. 'Don't forget that! How can you even think of not living on our family land?' Then she turned to Hạnh. 'I beg you to leave him. Please don't destroy our family.' Mrs Khiên broke into sobs and wrapped her arms around Nghĩa.

Hạnh felt terrible—frightened and angry and powerless. She rushed from the yard all the way home, where she fell onto the bed and burst into tears.

'What's wrong, sweetheart?' Nhân whispered, stroking her hair.

Hạnh buried her face in her mother's arms and wailed, 'Why am I so unlucky?'

* Vietnamese folk saying

Chapter 8

As if to mock the two families' prejudice, the local Youth Association threw a huge wedding party for Nghĩa and Hạnh in the co-op storehouse. They decorated the place magnificently, with curtains and lights like the stage setting for a play. They hung the blue canvas backdrop for the musical performance and brought out drums to beat noisily before the ceremony. They had also done some fundraising to buy sweets and cigarettes for the party, so the wedding became a hot topic of conversation throughout the village. Some criticized the younger generation for being spoiled. Some criticized Mr Khiên for not doing his duty and punishing the upstarts. Some blamed Nhân for setting a bad example with Điện Biên Vạn.* They said her daughter was now just following her footsteps.

A big round of applause kicked off the celebration at seven that evening. The whole area of the village around the storehouse shone brightly with lights. All the young people in the village showed up, and many children too. Of course, the older generation—the parents, aunts, and uncles—refused to participate because they worried doing so would taint their reputations. It was the first time Đông Village witnessed such an unusual wedding. The Youth Association performance group got to show off their singing voices amid their friends' laughter, providing joyful cover for the bride and the groom to bury the sorrow of their elders' disapproval

* The villagers' nickname for Vạn, because he had fought at the victory at Điện Biên Phủ

deep in their hearts. Right in the middle of all the fun, Uncle Xung appeared, tapping his cane.

'Are you having a meeting?'

'Yes, Uncle,' replied Dâu, the most cheerful young woman at the party, before inviting him to take a seat.

'What kind of meeting is this?' asked Uncle Xung. 'Why aren't you chanting slogans?'

His questions made the youngsters laugh and laugh.

Nghĩa hurried over to Uncle Xung and said, 'Please have a piece of cake, Uncle. This isn't really a meeting. It's my wedding.'

'Your wedding? If this is a wedding, where's the sticky rice, meat, wine, and tea?'

'It's the new way, Uncle,' said Nghĩa. 'We have only sweets and cigarettes.'

'Oh, really? If my sons Xình and Xèng were still alive, I'd throw them the biggest wedding party this village has ever seen.'

The young people who had gathered around Uncle Xung smiled and laughed, the whole room bright and boisterous and cheerful. It was so loud, some neighbour women thought a fight had broken out and called for their children to come home.

After the party, the village became quiet again. Hand in hand, the newly-weds strolled down to the river. Nghĩa carried the blue canvas backdrop too. The sounds of the drums and firecrackers and laughter still rang in their ears. When they reached the riverside, they finally managed to forget their sorrow completely. They had nowhere to go, except here. In the whole world, there had never been any newly-weds who spent their wedding night like Hạnh and Nghĩa. The sky was full of stars, the air cool.

'We could walk like this all night,' Nghĩa said, squeezing Hạnh's hand.

'We're lucky it didn't rain.'

'And it's cool but not cold.'

'It's funny—I can't believe we're husband and wife.'

'And we just had the best wedding the village has ever seen.'

Nghĩa spread the blue canvas on the grass near a turn in the river where an irrigation canal diverted water out to the fields. He sat and gently drew Hạnh down next to him.

'This is such a beautiful spot, isn't it?' said Nghĩa. 'This is the centre. From here we can see the Linh Canal and the whole village. And the river here is like two arms wrapping us in a big embrace.' They lay down on the blue canvas. He held Hạnh tightly. The night sky blazed with stars.

'We're husband and wife now,' Nghĩa said, unbuttoning her blouse with trembling hands. She placed his hands on her warm chest, thinking this was the best moment of her life so far.

When the eastern sky turned pink, the two lovers reluctantly said goodbye. Hạnh skirted the edge of the pond coming home, worried someone might see her and give her a hard time. At home, she gently pushed open the door to her mother's room. Tears trailed down her cheeks. Hạnh hugged Nhân tightly. After such a happy night, Hạnh loved her mother even more.

As a mother and a woman, Nhân could tell that Hạnh was feeling quite emotional, but even so, she wasn't completely sure her daughter was happy or not. Despite the advice she had offered Hạnh about marrying Nghĩa, she knew Hạnh would do what her heart told her to do. She imagined Hạnh's love for Nghĩa was probably much stronger than her own love for Vạn. Last evening, like so many others, she had cooked a meal and placed it on her dead husband's altar. It was so complicated—she still loved him too. Nhân had hoped Hạnh and Nghĩa would come back to the house together after the wedding. When she heard the pop of the firecrackers coming from the storehouse, she ached to run to the wedding but didn't dare. Instead, she went back to bed to wait for them. She had waited all night.

'Did you spend the night at the storehouse?' asked Nhân.

'Of course not! We walked along the river and slept up on the bank where we could see all the way out to the canal. It was so pretty—our sweet honeymoon!'

Nhân felt a chill rise up her spine. Her heart ached.

'Maybe you two will end up wandering like that forever?'

'Oh, Ma, you don't understand,' said Hạnh. 'We've planned everything. Now that we're married, we can apply for some land. Then the Youth Association will help us build a small house. It doesn't have to be fancy. Even a little hut with clay walls and a thatch roof will be fine. When we earn enough money, we'll build a bigger house.'

'I feel so sorry for Nghĩa,' said Nhân. 'His parents have such a big house, but he can't live there with you. Where did you eat dinner yesterday, by the way?'

'We were too excited to eat.'

'Let me cook something for you. It won't take long.'

'Let's just wait 'til everyone's awake. This way you can rest here with me a little while longer.' Hạnh sighed contentedly, and then after a moment said, 'Oh, Ma, you and Uncle Vạn should be together too!'

'Oh, stop!'

'It's true. And now he'll never marry because he's still in love with you.'

'Don't blame me. I never stopped him from marrying someone else.'

'I know, Ma.' Hạnh hugged Nhân and stroked her hair. 'You're still so beautiful. I think I just realized that love can turn into marriage very quickly. It's like jumping over a fence. You just do it and then you're on the other side and never have to worry about it again. I wish you and Uncle Vạn could jump over the fence like that.'

Nhân rolled her eyes. 'Clearly this girl of mine has lost her mind! Now let me go so I can make some breakfast!'

Alone in the bed, Hạnh felt very peaceful. She reminisced happily about the night before, the moment of ecstasy still electric on her skin. That was the first time each of them had seen the other's naked body. She smiled, thinking it was all very funny. She thought even the trees, the grass, and the stars in the sky had all probably thought it was very funny seeing them make love on the blue canvas. All of nature empathized with their love! Hạnh closed her eyes so she could feel deeply the darkness of her mother's room. Focusing intently, she could hear the wind and the rushing of the river. From out in the yard came the sound of her mother's footsteps walking out to the water tank and back. Light from the kitchen fire danced on the window. Hạnh had already dozed off, imagining that Nghĩa lay right beside her, his fingers caressing her neck.

When Hạnh woke, it was already bright outside. She went out to the yard. The sun had come up bright red in the eastern sky. She unlatched the gate of the chicken coop, and all the chickens scurried out and scattered around the yard. The rooster hopped up to the top of a bush and crowed loudly. Her brother Hiệp stood by the jackfruit tree fixing a harrow. He blinked at Hạnh.

'After the wedding, Ma told me to go look for you, but I couldn't find you anywhere!'

'Really? Did you really go look for us?'

'Ask Ma. She waited for you all night.'

Hạnh went into the kitchen, hugged Nhân and laughed. 'Ma, you're so wonderful,' she said. 'You really aren't mad at me and Nghĩa, are you?'

Her mother teased her, saying, 'You've already taken a husband and yet you're still such a child!'

The fire in the stove glowed warmly on the faces of mother and daughter alike. Nhân said Hạnh was childish, but she knew it was more complicated than that. Hạnh was just like Nhân when she was that age. All girls are the same—they want to look confident and mature when they're out and about, but at home, they still want their mothers to take care of them.

'Did you really wait up for me and Nghĩa last night?'

When Nhân remained silent, Hạnh wondered if her mother was sad. After all, on her only daughter's wedding day, not only could she not attend the ceremony but the groom's family had also not given any wedding gifts. There were no betel leaves and areca nuts for Nhân to share with her neighbours. Of course, Nghĩa's parents didn't want to treat the bride's family improperly, but they were in a difficult situation and couldn't have done otherwise. It all just felt wrong. Hạnh sat on the mat by the tray that held the bowls of rice and chicken. Two tears rolled down her cheeks.

'I thought you two might come back here last night, so I cooked this meal to offer to your dead father and get his blessing.' Nhân sighed. 'You should go ask Nghĩa to have breakfast with us.'

'Ma, you're so thoughtful!'

Hạnh wiped the tears from her eyes. It would be so nice if Nghĩa could join them, but Hạnh did not dare to go to his house to invite him.

'We'll have to wait until we have our own home. Then Nghĩa and I will have you over to celebrate.'

Nhân put the biggest piece of chicken into Hạnh's bowl and said, 'If Nghĩa isn't coming, you'll have to eat his share.' Nhân smiled at Hạnh. 'I have a surprise too. I got a letter from your brother yesterday.'

'Really?' Hạnh cried out happily. 'Can I read it, please?'

'Finish eating first,' said Hiệp. 'The letter's on the table.'

Ignoring her brother, Hạnh stood, snatched the letter and read it out loud.

Hoà Bình, 4 September

Dear Ma, Hạnh, and Hiệp,

The big news first! I've been chosen to take a training course to become an officer. Out of forty people in my platoon, only two get to do the training: me and a guy from Nam Định named Mạnh. He finished high school already and his father was killed fighting the French. I heard that after I finish the training course, I'll be stationed somewhere far way . . .

Since I left, not a day has gone by without my thinking of you all. Please send my best to Uncle Vạn and Hồng. And please tell Hồng I'm sorry I can't write to her personally . . .

All my love,

Hà

Hạnh laughed. 'Hà revealed his secret love! Ma, he's introducing his future wife to you. No wonder Hồng kept asking me about him last night.'

'He's a boy but he writes letters like a girl,' said Hiệp.

'Just wait and see when you live far from home,' Hạnh said to him. 'You'll cry for sure.'

'Go to hell!'

'Enough bickering!' said Nhân. 'Finish your breakfast.'

Hạnh asked her mother, 'Do you want me to help you bail water today?'*

'You can stay home today,' said Hiệp. 'I'll help Ma. Go tell Nghĩa to submit a land allocation form to the commune office. When you have your land, I'll ask my friends to help you build a house.'

'Dâu told me the same thing.' Hạnh smiled and gave her brother a sly look. 'By the way, what do you think about her?'

Hiệp made a strange face. 'She's kind of awkward. She always grins like a goof before she says anything.'

'You're too picky! She's just very friendly, and what's wrong with smiling at people? If you could win her over, she would be . . .'

'Hey! Are you trying to make me help you take over the Nguyễns?'

'Enough, please, you two!' said Nhân. 'Hạnh, please don't mention this again. Don't you see how much gossip your marriage has already stirred up? And, Hiệp, I don't think falling in love with any Nguyễn girl is a good idea.'

Nhân put down her chopsticks and went to the kitchen. Hạnh regretted upsetting her mother. Staring at the tray of food that would not be shared with her new husband, Hạnh felt a lump in her throat. She knew she would trade her own happiness to heal the division between the two families. But she didn't fully understand why. Was it her love for Nghĩa? The more the Nguyễn clan resisted her, the fiercer the fire in her heart grew to burn down the hatred between the two families. Only then could she love Nghĩa freely. She had been born a timid girl but falling in love with him had made her bolder, stronger, and more strategic.

'You're talking crazy,' Hiệp whispered.

'And you're so lame!' said Hạnh. 'All the boys in the village are lame too. They know the village elders are old-fashioned but no one dares say a word. For years, our young men have had to go to other villages to get married. And all our young, well-mannered women have been forced to be daughters-in-law somewhere else.

---

* Rice paddies often need water to be moved from one level to another, which is sometimes done with a large, mounted scoop.

Why won't people own up to what Miss Toan and Miss Sang went through after they were forced to marry in Hạ Village? Toan was beaten by her husband and went crazy. Sang's mother-in-law kicked her out of the house and she had to come back here to live in disgrace. How can people be so cruel?'

Hiệp looked stunned. Maybe he'd never considered these things before.

'I'm serious,' said Hạnh. 'You should give Dâu a chance—she's really sweet.'

'Shh,' said Hiệp. 'If Mom hears, she'll give me hell.'

'Just give her a chance,' Hạnh whispered.

Hiệp remained silent. But silence meant yes. A satisfied smile spread on Hạnh's lips. She had an ally.

A gong sounded from the co-op storehouse. Time to start the day. Hiệp got up quickly and readied himself to go help his mother bail water.

Hạnh watched them leave for the paddies, their long shadows rippling on the pond.

Chapter 9

One day, word spread that a district official named Mr Hòa would come that evening to share important news with the village. Bright lights lit the co-op storehouse's seven long, empty rooms. Nghĩa and the whole village came to listen. Elderly men with white hair and beards walked in with their canes, looking quite solemn. Middle-aged people came in their work clothes and seemed strong and contemplative. Excited adolescents joked and laughed among themselves, while younger children ran in and out and from room to room playing games as if the meeting were a festival. Many of the adults were talking about a comet that had been visible early that morning, saying that a sword in the eastern sky meant some kind of terrible violence lay ahead. To avoid collective tragedy, they advised the owner of four newly built houses to stain the pristine walls with mud. Young women should dye any bright, new clothes black or brown. The children got excited when several jets roared overhead, flying in from the sea.

The whole affair reminded Nghĩa of the time in the early 1960s when he and other villagers had beat drums loudly around the village chanting, 'Down with Diệm!' On festive occasions over the years, village kids loved to make effigies of President Diệm* out of banana tree trunks, with faces painted from soot so that he looked like a monster. Whoever could hit his head with a thrown rock or stab him in the chest with a wooden sword while blindfolded won the game.

---

* President Ngô Đình Diệm led the Republic of Vietnam (South Vietnam) from 1955 until his assassination in 1963.

The storehouse went quiet when Mr Hòa stepped up to the head table covered with a blue, flower-patterned tablecloth. Uncle Vạn had put a vase of yellow mums on the table as well. Along with some members of the Women's Association, he, Mother Nhân, and the other families of soldiers who had died fighting the French were seated in the first row.

'Ladies and gentlemen of Đông Village,' said Mr Hòa, 'your village has a great patriotic tradition. Before we go any further, let's give our Điện Biên Phủ hero, Nguyễn Vạn, a big round of applause.'

Mr Hòa then praised the heroic mothers and wives whose sons or husbands had died as martyrs fighting the French and cast their great patriotism in the same light for allowing the next generation to join the fight against the Americans. Nghĩa looked around to see Uncle Vạn and Mother Nhân's faces glowing during the speech. Hạnh, on the other hand, was whispering something to Dâu. Mr Hòa continued, his voice rising:

'Let's take a look at the world. Our socialist cause is getting stronger, especially in the Soviet Union and China. The American imperialists are losing terribly in South Vietnam, and in their desperation, they act like wild dogs. On 5 August, they bombed the North. And our people and soldiers have already shot down American planes in Quảng Ninh, Bến Thuỷ, and Hàm Rồng.'

Murmurs arose from the audience.

'My son is in Quảng Ninh.'

'Your son's not the only one there.'

'Women work in the kitchen and don't understand anything,' said old man Thịnh as he stroked his beard. 'They hear about bombs and get scared to death.'

'Right!' snapped Mrs Nhị, sitting next to him. 'Everyone knows you're such a big hero. When we attacked the Nationalist outpost, you were last in line, back behind the women you say were so scared.'

The people sitting nearby covered their mouths and snickered. They all knew Mr Thịnh had claimed to have diarrhoea that day, because he'd told everyone the same thing countless times. His wife had made clam soup for him the night before and it made him sick. No one believed it and Mr Thịnh very quickly fell out of favour with the village women.

'Everyone, quiet!' Uncle Vạn barked. 'Each person in this village needs to demonstrate their love for our country right here and now. We have to encourage our young ones to join the fight against the Americans if we're going to save our country.'

After the meeting, Nghĩa left to meet Hạnh as usual at the Silver Stone Bridge. Since their wedding day, they had been forced to continue to get together in various places outdoors because their dream house had not yet materialized. Nghĩa had submitted a land application on the first day, and it was initially approved by Chairman Đột, but the commune committee had yet to agree. With their great enthusiasm for the newly-weds, the Youth Association had been so excited to build a house by the riverbank that they didn't wait for the final approval. They finished building the house in two days, and the newly-weds were just about to move in, but then the commune official told them it had not been approved. In the meantime, the commune let the co-op use the new house for raising ducks.

Nghĩa ambled along the riverbank, waiting for Hạnh. The river sparkled with starlight. Just upstream from the bridge footing, two boats carrying bananas had moored to wait for the water to go down so they could pass beneath the bridge. It had been raining the last few days, raising the water level, and the surface of the river looked vast. One of the boatmen was humming a song, and from the other side of the river, a woman hummed back in reply. Her voice sounded sincere and seemed to fly in the star-lit sky. Nghĩa recognized Hạnh's silhouette hurrying down from the bridge. She rolled up her pants and waded into the water, kicking her feet and stirring up tiny sparkling waves.

'It might be a good thing we don't have our own house,' Hạnh said, holding Nghĩa's arm. 'We can still meet here like this, like when we were dating. It's very romantic!'

Hạnh's words touched Nghĩa's heart. He knew she had said that just to comfort him. While the Youth Association was building their house, Hạnh had been so excited. Her eyes shone bright the whole time. He knew she desperately wanted a place to call their own.

The couple wandered past the duck house, the one that should have been their happy home. The ducks startled as they passed and raised a quacking ruckus. The duck tender, Mr Nhương, called out, 'Who's there?' and then stuck his head out and saw Nghĩa and Hạnh. 'Oh, it's you again. You know, you're married now, so when you want to do it, you should just do it in the commune office. After the militia catches you a few times, the commune will have to give you a piece of land!'

Hand in hand, they walked away quickly to escape Mr Nhương's laughter and any more embarrassing suggestions. Nghĩa took a cigarette from his pocket, struck a match, and smoked. He'd been smoking a lot recently. Before the wedding, he had only smoked every once in a while, when he was in a good mood, but now it seemed he lit a cigarette any time he had something important to think about. Nghĩa was like his father. When Mr Khiên worried about something, he used the water pipe frequently. As Nghĩa shook out the match, a lone duck lost from the flock flew by.

'We have something important to discuss,' Nghĩa said, pulling Hạnh into his arms. 'I've got to enlist.'

Hạnh shuddered. Was the lost duck a sign of their separation? All young men had to serve—that's just the way it was. But Hạnh hadn't thought Nghĩa's turn would be so soon. He was the only son in his family.

Strong winds gusted over the countryside, unsettling the evening's tranquillity. Hạnh watched a star fall from the sky in the distance and vanish into the horizon. They reached the honeymoon spot where they had spent their first night together and lay down on the grass, overwhelmed by new emotions. Unlike before, their passion now gave way to anxiety and apprehension, their feelings about the world around them crowding out their feelings for each other. Before, Hạnh couldn't care less about where they met. She cared only that Nghĩa lay next to her, and that they could gaze at one another affectionately and listen to each other's heartbeat and breath. Perhaps, the mysterious paradise they sought was already right here—in the press of her young breasts against his chest, her smooth, silky skin against his. But this night, they did not press themselves together. Instead, they lay side by side, gazing deeply into the starry sky, their hands entwined.

'I know you'll let me go,' Nghĩa said. 'But my father? He'll never let me leave. He thinks my only future is on our ancestral land.'

Hạnh squeezed his hand and sighed.

He said, 'If we had a baby already, when I come back home, he'd know how to call me Papa.'

Chapter 10

Nguyễn Vạn frowned at the couplets hung at the entrance to the lineage temple and then limped to each of the bonsai that his cousin Khiên tended every day. Vạn smiled as he inspected the ancient trees' gnarled roots and trunks. They reminded him of an old man's long hair and beard. The courtyard's patch of shiny yellow bamboo did not impress him though. They had no scent, no beauty, no value. He limped to the fish pond where the koi swam around and around the little mountainous landscape Khiên had made with cement. On the little mountain stood two miniature deer with curvy horns looking rather regal. Villagers often said Mr Khiên was just like his father, Nghiên. Both of them would rather wear torn clothes or starve than give up their bonsai garden. People said Mr Khiên even watered the plants with washed rice water. Vạn didn't really understand how Khiên could be so interested in such a hobby—it seemed rather bourgeois to him. He entered the house and found Khiên lying in bed, looking back at him wearily.

'How can you still be in bed?' asked Vạn. 'Listen, it's been a whole year since Nghĩa and Hạnh got married. You need to let them move in with you here. They have to meet each other every night at the river or in somebody's cabbage garden. It's embarrassing!'

'This is our ancestors' land,' said Khiên in a feeble voice. 'My wife and I have no right to offend them.' He blinked at the ceiling.

'Don't be so old-fashioned!' Vạn said angrily. 'Haven't you noticed you live in a socialist country now? In socialism, there's no such thing as "ancestors' land". The land belongs to the people. And there's no hatred or superstition in a socialist society. You need to take down those couplets over there that use the words "injustice" and "hatred". Who do you hate? Do you hate the government?'

Seeing the blank look on Khiên's face, Vạn realized not a word he said had sunk in. Khiên remained silent.

'I'll say it very clearly for you. If you don't take down those couplets, I'll have to report you, and they'll lock you up. These days, while everyone else is fighting the enemy, growing vegetables and raising livestock, you're indulging yourself in pointless superstition and a bourgeois hobby.'

Khiên just lay there, still and silent as a block of wood.

Vạn let himself down into a chair in the middle of the room and glared at Khiên.

'I actually came here today to tell you something else,' he said. 'Nghĩa has to enlist.'

At this, Khiên jerked upright. 'What are you trying to do?' he said. 'Kill me? I beg you. Nghĩa's my only son. Our whole Nguyễn clan has only him . . .'

Vạn burst out laughing, startling the black cat that had been asleep near the broom in the corner. It ran to the door before turning back to stare daggers at Vạn.

'Oh, you still have ambitions for Nghĩa?' he asked sarcastically. 'I thought you'd given up on him. If you still love your son and care about his future, let him do his duty and fight the Americans. Look at me! I'm who I am today because I fought the French. You're just being selfish and old-fashioned. A man has to fight for his country. It's shameful to cling to the wife or mother's dress at home.'

With that, Vạn hauled himself out of the chair and hobbled home.

Khiên sat up, his expression gloomy. Nghĩa's marriage to Hạnh had made him lose face with the whole clan. The marriage was done—there was nothing he could do about that—but he couldn't let Hạnh move in without the entire Nguyễn clan complaining that they'd destroyed the family's reputation. Since the wedding, he'd been careful to tend his bonsai garden and koi pond in secret because he didn't want more scrutiny. But he really did have high hopes for Nghĩa. He'd taught him very well ever since he was a baby, certain that Nghĩa would become a talented and virtuous leader.

Khiên was the most educated man in the district. Illiterate women would come to him to write letters to their husbands or sons. When Nghĩa finished high school, Khiên had written a poem for the occasion and proudly recited it in front of all the parents and teachers. He didn't want Nghĩa to pursue any career other than living and working on the ancestors' land, and nothing gave him greater satisfaction than simply to hear Nghĩa play the flute in the evening. But now, everything had turned upside down. The couplets were just supposed to remind everyone that the person who had set fire to the lineage temple had never been caught or punished. He was as steadfastly loyal to the country as he was to the Nguyễn family. But now, Vạn had accused him of not following the Party's rules.

Khiên blew out a deep sigh and lay back down. The world around him seemed to spin, making him dizzy.

This morning was like no other morning in Mrs Khiên's life. She had not slept the whole night previous. Since the day she'd married, this was the first time she'd ever kept the truth from her husband. She felt guilty and kept glancing at him furtively. But she knew she had to lie to him. Nghĩa had enlisted that very morning. She would bear any retribution willingly as long as Nghĩa could do his duty and fight the Americans. At breakfast, she tried to stay calm and quiet so she wouldn't give anything away. Nghĩa seemed more confident. She watched anxiously as her son scooped rice and broth into a bowl and served it to his father and hoped only she would notice his unusual demeanour. Had Nghĩa considered she would be the one who'd have to answer to his father about his decision to enlist, after he'd already left? Just as they were finishing breakfast, their daughter, Duyên, and her husband came to the house.

'Are you feeling better, Daddy?' asked Duyên. 'We brought you a hand of ripe bananas.' She set the bananas on the table and surreptitiously slipped Nghĩa some money. She asked him whether he would attend the farewell ceremony for the new recruits later that day.

'Yes,' said Nghĩa with a smile before casting a cautious glance at his father.

I see, Mrs Khiên thought to herself with a sigh of relief. They've come to say goodbye. Now she had to confront the reality. Her head felt about to explode. If Khiên suddenly caught on and asked what was going on, she would faint. She pitied Nghĩa, whose marriage had made his life so hard, and who now faced another hardship because of having to keep his enlistment secret.

After Duyên left, Mrs Khiên sat at the well to wash dishes. Nghĩa was pacing in and out of the house, maybe feeling a bit conflicted now that the time to leave had actually come. I hope you don't cry, thought Mrs Khiên. Nghĩa stood at the door to take one last look at his father in his bed and then bent down to pet the cat, who meowed and ran inside. Nghĩa came to the well and gave Mrs Khiên a big hug. The touch of his fingers made her shoulders ache. She felt like she might faint when he whispered into her ear, 'I've got to go.'

Her whole body felt cold as she watched him pass out of sight down the lane. She stood and went inside to the kitchen. Tears trailed down her cheeks. She tried to restrain herself from sobbing.

*

When Nghĩa entered the gate to Hạnh's courtyard, Uncle Vạn was already there. He gave Nghĩa a satisfied grin. 'I was worried you'd spill the beans and get stuck.' Uncle Vạn squeezed Nghĩa's shoulder. 'Okay, time to go. Nhân and Hiệp, you should stay here and let Hạnh see Nghĩa off.'

Hạnh came out and stood next to Nghĩa, hugging the bag of clothes he had brought over the night before. Nhân clasped Nghĩa's hands, deeply moved.

'Remember to write your parents,' she said. 'They'll need to know you're okay.'

'I'll keep an eye on them for you too,' said Uncle Vạn.

'Bye, Nghĩa,' said Hiệp, shaking hands. 'You're going first, but my turn's next. Maybe we'll see each other on the battlefield.'

Hạnh, Nghĩa, and Uncle Vạn arrived at the district office where the new recruits had been told to assemble. The vast, boisterous crowd of people filling the area around the office made it seem like a festival. Hạnh saw countless women in her same situation, saying goodbye to their husbands. Many were sobbing. Standing with Nghĩa, though, Hạnh could not cry. She didn't know why. Nghĩa went inside to change clothes and came back out. He looked so mature and handsome in his new uniform. He handed her the bag of civilian clothes and hugged her. Neither could utter a word.

'Time to get on the bus,' Uncle Vạn told Nghĩa. 'Follow the example of the brave men from Đông Village and fight well. Do what I did and live!'

'I have to go now,' Nghĩa whispered to Hạnh. He gave her one last squeeze and then joined the line of new recruits.

Hạnh's eyes blurred as she tried to keep sight of Nghĩa among the sea of hands waving farewell from the bus windows. The bus grumbled to life and left with a roar, and then everything went silent. Hạnh stood there in quiet shock until a group of young women took her hand and pulled her to a coffee shop.

'Your brother Hiệp didn't come to see Nghĩa off?' Dâu held Hạnh's hand and drew her to an empty corner of the shop. 'Wait here and I'll get us some bowls of *phở*.* You haven't eaten anything this morning, have you?'

Dâu gently pressed Hạnh's shoulder, prompting her to sit, and then hurried out. Of all her friends, Dâu probably understood Hạnh the best. Energetic, strong, and passionate about so many things, Dâu had been her close friend since grade school. She had just been an average student, but she loved to read fiction and watch movies, so no one could hide anything from her. It was like she could read people's hearts and minds. She spoke her mind too—maybe too directly for some people—but Hạnh loved Dâu's forthright nature.

Hạnh also knew quite well that loneliness often lurked behind Dâu's laughter. Sometimes Dâu would joke or fight with guys with real bravado, but then later she'd crumple in Hạnh's arms and weep. When Dâu learned Hạnh and Nghĩa didn't get the commune's

---

* Noodle soup

permission to build their house, she was the first to hug Hạnh and cry. Dâu returned with two steaming bowls of phở. Hạnh knew already that Dâu would become her main source of comfort while Nghĩa was far away.

'You're so skinny!' Dâu chided light-heartedly. 'Eat so you have more strength. "Men must fight on the battlefield, women must fight in the rice fields."' Dâu giggled, and Hạnh giggled too—she'd been imitating Uncle Vạn.

'Hey, what did you tell Hiệp?' Dâu stirred a few slices of red chili pepper into her phở and looked inquisitively at Hạnh. 'I love hot, spicy food, so don't tell your brother anything sweet about me.'

'I didn't tell him anything.'

'Don't lie!' Dâu laughed. 'I know how men are. A few days ago, I ran into him, and he looked at me in this very strange way, so I knew you must've said something. Anyway, let's not talk about him. Love should come naturally. It's more fun that way!' Dâu took a sip of her phở broth and added a few more chillies. 'Are you okay? With Nghĩa gone, you should move in with his parents. Fear no one! You're a soldier's wife now. Nghĩa and his parents built that house, and you are his wife and their daughter-in-law. You have every right to live there. If anyone complains, you'll win for sure!'

'I've thought about it, but I can't just move in. I need his parents' blessing.'

As they finished their phở, the other young Đông Villagers they'd come with left the coffee shop to return home. Dâu suggested they go back along the Diêm dike shortcut. From on top of the dike, surrounded by rice paddies, they could see Đông Village on the horizon, looking vibrant and green. It was noon, so no one was out working the fields. A flock of black, long-legged swamphens wandered over the dike, and when they saw Hạnh and Dâu, some splashed into the rice paddy and some flew off. Birds and animals know humans are dangerous, thought Hạnh. Even water snakes swim away when they see us coming. It was roasting hot. Little crabs had climbed up many of the rice stalks to hang there and catch the breeze.

'So many crabs!' Hạnh cried out. 'Let's catch some before we go home.'

'It's too hot today. You don't want to get sick.'

Hạnh cast a regretful look at the crabs but kept going. A little farther on, they saw three shirtless young men wriggle out from inside a mound. The men stood there wiping mud from their faces and bellies.

'Those guys catching snakes are from Diêm Village,' Dâu said. 'Don't look scared or they'll think we're weak and mess with us.'

The men grinned and spread their legs wide, waiting for Hạnh and Dâu to come closer. Then they lay down across the top of the dike so Hạnh and Dâu couldn't pass without stepping over them.

'Hey, let us pass,' said Dâu. 'My baby's waiting at home, thirsty for my milk.'

'You'll have to step over us,' said the first guy.

Dâu began to step over, but the guy reached up and grabbed her hand. Quickly, she spun around and turned his wrist and nearly threw him into the canal, but he caught her hair and then they both tumbled into the canal together. The second guy slid down the embankment to tackle her, and she fought against both of them in the water. The third guy pounced on Hạnh like a madman and held her tightly in his muddy arms. They rolled away from the canal, down the dike, and to the edge of the rice paddy. When he laid his dirty hands on her breasts, Hạnh gasped, and in a fury, she scooped up a big handful of mud and smacked it right into the bastard's eyes. Then she grabbed the bag of clothes and ran back up to the top of the dike. After a minute, she saw Dâu climb up the dike on the other side of the canal.

'Hạnh!' Dâu cried out. 'Wait up!'

Dâu slid down into the canal, swam across towards Hạnh and laughed. Her shirt was torn, showing her ivory breasts.

'How did you escape?' Hạnh asked.

'I was just worried about you. Those guys were nothing.' Dâu chuckled. 'When they unzipped their pants to show me their things, I used my ju-jitsu to wring their little birdies' necks. They screamed in pain, and I ran. Oh no! You lost your hat!'

Only then did Hạnh realize her hat was missing, but she didn't know when it had come off. Probably when she had splashed into the paddy. When they reached the Đình River, they eagerly waded into the water and rinsed off.

It had been a while since Hạnh and Dâu bathed in the river together. They took off their clothes and washed them. Noticing Dâu staring at her chest, Hạnh flushed and turned away, unable to meet Dâu's gaze. Hạnh knew her breasts had gotten fuller. Dâu threw her clothes to the riverbank, spun Hạnh around, and jumped into her arms.

'Wow!' she said. 'This is the first time I've seen your gorgeous breasts! No wonder Nghĩa loves you so much! How did your boobs get so big so fast?'

Hạnh flushed again. 'You'll know once you get married.'

Dâu laughed and tickled Hạnh's ribs.

'Quit messing around!' she said, laughing. 'We should hurry. It's almost time for people to get back to work in the paddies. If they see us like this, they'll say we've lost it. We're lucky I still have Nghĩa's clothes. Our shirts are so torn!'

They each put on one of Nghĩa's shirts, which were quite big on them. When they reached the village gate, a group of young boys stopped playing and looked at them with surprise.

'Um, Dâu and Hạnh, are you wearing men's clothes?' asked one of the boys, making them all laugh.

Hạnh and Dâu ducked their heads and ran, laughing and poking each other all the way home. The sun shined gloriously bright through the green trees.

Chapter 11

At breakfast, Hạnh had just sat down when her mother said, 'Nghĩa's gone now, so you have to be careful when you're out. You're a married woman. You don't want to run into trouble.'

The previous evening, Hạnh had repaired the torn shirt and sewed the buttons back on. Her mother must have seen her and guessed something happened.

'Have I done something wrong, Ma?'

'I'm just warning you. Everyone knows a woman has to be chaste.'

'Hiệp, when do you plan to enlist?' Hạnh asked, changing the subject.

'Soon. "A man must fight on the battlefield,"' Hiệp said, making Hạnh giggle by imitating Uncle Vạn. All the villagers now quoted Uncle Vạn.

While Nhân, Hạnh, and Hiệp ate, Mother Khiên walked in, trembling, and Hạnh startled at her unexpected presence, thinking something bad must have happened. Hạnh set down her chopsticks, invited her mother-in-law to sit, and offered her a cup of tea.

'Tell me truthfully,' she said to Hạnh, 'has Nghĩa gone already?'

'Yes, Mother, he left yesterday just before noon.'

'I'm sorry to ask, but the problem is Nghĩa's father . . . Well, actually it was Mr Dĩ's fault. Last night he came over unexpectedly and asked us why we didn't throw a big going away party for Nghĩa. His question shocked my husband, who sat up in his sick bed, stunned. Then I had to deal with all his questions and curses, so I told him everything. His face turned pale, and he asked whether Nghĩa was still in the district. I told him he'd be all the way to the province capital by now, but Khiên didn't believe me. He was about to leave the house and go to the district headquarters, until I yelled, "Are you crazy? It's midnight. You can't go now!" Then he threw off his jacket and collapsed onto the bed. He tossed and turned all night but didn't say a word. This morning, though, after he ate breakfast, he announced he was going fishing. I thought he'd gone crazy. He'd been lying in bed sick for days and suddenly he wanted to go fishing? He headed off toward the river. I knew he was only pretending to fish so he could go to the district and catch Nghĩa, so I snuck after him and saw that he was going to the Linh Canal return. I think he must have gone there hoping he'd see Nghĩa marching on the way to the province headquarters.'

Mother Khiên took a big breath and sighed and then gazed pitifully at Hạnh.

'Don't worry, Mother,' Hạnh said. 'Let me go to Linh Canal and find Father.'

Hạnh hurried into the kitchen, snatched her mother's conical hat, and headed for the river. Once again, she found herself walking the familiar riverside to the Linh Canal, but this time there was no Nghĩa, no moon, and no stars, so she felt as hollow as an empty gourd. But at least the river flowed quiet and peaceful as usual. And the morning breeze felt wonderfully cool. The dew on the grass sparkled like gold in the early morning sun.

Mother Khiên had guessed correctly. At Linh Canal, Hạnh found the fishing net on the canal works, and then, a minute later, saw Father Khiên sitting up on the dike, watching the district road just below. Hạnh's heart ached. Since the wedding, Father Khiên had changed drastically. He'd become quiet and got sick a lot. Hạnh remembered he used to sing, play music, and recite poetry at village weddings. Now he looked like a starving beggar.

A column of dust curled up from the district road as a line of vehicles made their way toward the canal. Nghĩa's father jumped up as three trucks carrying tobacco slowed down, switched gears, and belched black smoke right into his face. Stupefied, he just stood there watching as the trucks climbed the hill. The last vehicle was a bus making a stop to pick up some passengers. Father Khiên's hand trembled as he grasped the step handrail and climbed up to look inside the bus. Hạnh thought he might even take the bus to the district.

'Has anyone seen my son, Nghĩa?' he asked.

'Nghĩa who?' replied one of the passengers.

'Nguyễn Nghĩa—a newly enlisted soldier,' said Khiên.

'This is not a military vehicle, sir.'

'Are you looking for Nghĩa or begging for money?'

'You're crazy,' said the driver's assistant. 'Please get off.'

Father Khiên stepped down and watched gloomily as the bus lurched away and climbed the hill. Hạnh sat nearby in the grass, observing him and trying to regain her composure. When Father Khiên turned around and stared at the river in a daze, Hạnh approached and stood in front of him.

'Father, why are you here?' she asked.

Khiên shifted his blank gaze to her, seeming utterly baffled, and then said, 'Ah . . . I . . . I'm . . . fishing. I got bored of lying in bed all day.' He rummaged through his pocket for a small bag of tobacco and a pipe.

'You should come home and rest,' she said. 'You don't look well.'

'What are you doing here?' asked Khiên, peering at Hạnh. 'Did you come here to meet Nghĩa? I know he'll pass by soon.'

'Father, he left at noon yesterday.'

Khiên sat dumbfounded, his face dark. 'Cruel!' he muttered. 'So cruel!'

'Please, Father, come back with me.'

'Go away!' he shouted suddenly. 'Leave this rotten bastard alone. For Heaven's sake, why can't anyone understand me?'

Shakily, he got to his feet and slid down to the riverbank, picked up the fishing net, and lowered it into the water. Then he squatted down and remained still as a statue. The Đình River flowed by peacefully. The net's bamboo handles quivered in his hands.

Hạnh climbed to the top of the dike and looked down. The bottom of the canal looked very deep. The river water foamed as it flowed through the diversion. Looking down at the bottom of the canal made Hạnh feel dizzy.

'Hey, beautiful girl!' called out a man's voice. 'You look sad. Before you drown yourself, come here with me and I'll show you how beautiful life is.'

Surprised, Hạnh turned and saw an unkempt man grinning at her from a sampan just a little upriver. The previous day's incident with the snake catchers at the Diêm rice paddy flashed through her mind, and she hurried down the dike and back toward Đông Village.

*

Mrs Khiên counted—it had been five days since Nghĩa left, and Mr Khiên had fished for three of those without a catch. Mrs Khiên was not surprised by this, since sardines swam in schools, and there had been times before with no catch even after Mr Khiên spent an entire week fishing. But often when he was lucky, there'd be so many he'd have to let some of the fish escape or the net would be too heavy to pull up. He often told her his fishing stories, which, in the end, all came down to the necessity of patience. It was easy to give up if you didn't catch anything for a day or an entire week, but you never knew. You might be just about to give up, and then a large school of sardines would swim right into your net.

She got up that morning at the same time he was coming in with the two buckets of sardines he'd caught overnight. She didn't know why but he told her not to sell any of them. Then he took a shower and went straight to bed.

'What are you going to do with all these fish?' Mrs Khiên asked from the door. 'If you won't let me sell them, I guess you'll want me to give them to the entire village for free?'

He didn't answer, so she went to the bed and shook him. He lay on his back in the bed, wearing dark purple silk pyjamas, with his legs stretched out straight and his hands across his belly. She touched his hand and screamed. Soon after, many people filled her front yard. The news of his sudden death spread quickly through the village. Some said he'd caught pneumonia. Some that he had committed suicide. A few maintained he died a sacred death—having gone fishing and then come home to die. Many of the older generation said because he allowed Nghĩa to marry a Vũ, his ancestors had punished him. But many also said he was lucky to die so peacefully.

Vạn threatened to throw in jail anyone who said Mr Khiên committed suicide because of Nghĩa's enlistment. He also had the couplets removed from the pillars. The rest of the Nguyễn clan kept busy preparing for the funeral. Xeng, Uncle Xung's remaining son, cleaned the ancestral altar. Uncle Kình was put in charge of selecting a butcher to slaughter the hundred-kilogram pig Mrs Khiên had raised. She also had a flock of nearly twenty chickens butchered, both roosters and hens, which actually belonged to Nghĩa and Hạnh. When Uncle Xeng handed out mourning headbands, he said Hạnh was not allowed to wear one because she and Nghĩa may have registered their marriage with the local authorities, but it had not been approved by the Nguyễn clan, so she was not considered an official daughter-in-law. Amid the mournful sound of funeral trumpets and lamenting, Uncle Xung hobbled in with a cane in his hand.

'We have to select the next family head,' Uncle Xung stated loudly. 'And he must be someone who can drink.'

'Listen to you!' someone said. 'The head of the family is based on heredity. It's not voted on like a village head or a chairman of the commune.'

Uncle Xung snorted. 'You're so stupid. Heredity, my ass. Nowadays heredity is a mess. Let me ask everybody this: Nghĩa's not here now, so what happens if he dies on the battlefield? Then who will lead the family?'

Vạn grabbed Uncle Xung's wrist and led him outside. Khiên's funeral was the biggest funeral the village had ever had. Many people came because they believed he died a sacred death or because they loved him. Many felt sorry for Mrs Khiên, who was now a widow with no children left at home. After they buried Khiên in the family's section of the cemetery, the whole Nguyễn clan came to the reception, where the women busily prepared and served food, and the men ate and drank, maybe too much.

Mrs Khiên couldn't hold herself up so she retired to her bedroom. After a little while, Hạnh brought her a bowl of rice porridge.

'Mother, try to eat something. You haven't had anything since early this morning.'

Mrs Khiên pulled Hạnh by the hand to sit beside her on the bed. Still in shock from her husband's death, she looked dreadfully pale as she passed Hạnh a letter that she took from her pocket.

'This is the letter my husband wrote to Nghĩa. I found it in his pocket. Please read it to me. I want to know what he wrote.'

Hạnh held the letter with trembling hands and read aloud to her mother-in-law:

My dearest son, Nghĩa,

I wouldn't be able to rest in peace if I didn't write you this letter. I am heartbroken because neither you, nor your mother, nor anyone else understands me. I have always tried to teach you how to live a meaningful life. You and your mother have disappointed me because you don't take me seriously. I didn't want you to enlist because I want you to lead the Nguyễn clan. You are my only son.

Of course, I can't and won't try to stop you. But you and your mother should not have hidden it from me. I could have thrown a farewell party for you. I feel so embarrassed because you felt you had to leave the house so secretly, which made everyone think that I am just a selfish, old-fashioned coward. I have saved some money, which I keep under the lamp on the ancestors' altar. I intended to give you this money for your wedding, but I never had the chance and this saddens me greatly. Whenever I think about that money, my heart aches. You are gone now, and Hạnh is miserable and lonely. I plan to give her the money—it's yours now—and hope that you'll live up to the reputation of the Nguyễn family.

I wish you well.

Your father,
Nguyễn Khiên

Hạnh embraced Mother Khiên and both women sobbed. Each wanted to comfort the other but neither could speak. Just then, Nghĩa's sister came in. Duyên patted their shoulders and said, 'Get some rest, Ma,' and then she pulled Hạnh out to the reception and a mat with a tray laden with food where Dâu and a few other young women were already sitting.

'Sit down and eat,' Dâu said and put a piece of chicken into a bowl for Hạnh. 'Don't be shy.'

The clan elders at the upper table were drunk already and had started to grouse at one another. 'Hey, Uncle Khoái!' called Uncle Kình as he put a piece of chicken into his own bowl. 'Mr Lý and his son from Hồi Village played the trumpet better than your people did today.' Kình grinned impishly at Khoái.

'You're criticizing our co-op trumpeters but praising Lý and his son?' said Vạn.

'Exactly!' Kình put his rice wine cup on the table and glared at Vạn. 'I heard the co-op trumpeters playing badly. I have to say it even if it makes Uncle Khoái unhappy. I told my son not to invite the co-op trumpeters to play at the funeral when I die.'

'Uncle Kình may be old but that doesn't make him wise,' said Khoái. 'He knows nothing but loves to criticize everyone else. Lý and his son play trumpet and drums, and each get paid a hundred đồng per funeral, while each co-op player gets just ten đồng, so how can you compare us to them? Pay us a hundred đồng apiece, and we'll outplay Mr Lý.'

'Let's change the subject!' suggested Uncle Xeng, setting down his bowl and chopsticks and looking around at the other elders. 'You've all been talking nonsense anyway. Let's get to the important business. The head of our clan just passed away, and it's a big loss for all of us. We don't know where Nghĩa is now. And we don't know whether he'll avoid the bullets and bombs and make it back. We shouldn't leave the duty of burning incense and maintaining the temple to an old woman and young girl.'

Everyone gasped at Xeng's suggestion.

'He sounds just like his father!' whispered Aunt Nhị to Dâu.

'The egg is wiser than the duck,' Uncle Kình whispered to Uncle Phỏng. 'Xeng has a poisonous tongue. He wants Nghĩa to die so he can be in charge.'

'I have a suggestion.' Phỏng raised his hand, in which he held a ball of sticky rice. 'Maybe Vạn should give landowner Hào's old place back to Tốn's mother and move here? Tốn may be the grandson of a cruel landlord, but he's in the army now fighting to defend our country from foreign invaders, so we should return the house to his mother. Vạn is still single so he could easily be in charge of the lineage temple and also take care of poor Aunt Khiên. She could use the help. Am I right, everyone?'

'Excuse me!' Xeng stood again. 'Uncle Phỏng is an elder but also an idiot. The whole clan can't live on our ancestral land. We can't forget hierarchy. My father is still alive. Don't forget that!'

'Sure!' said Phỏng. 'Your father's still alive, we all know that, but he's also crazy as a loon! If he's head of the clan, we'll all be eating shit one day.'

'You're old but speak like a child!' Xeng's face turned dark as he glared at Uncle Phỏng. 'I'll speak in a way you can understand. Even if my father goes crazy, I am still here. And if I die, I still have three sons, and each of them will have three sons, which means I'll have nine grandsons to continue the family line.' Then he turned to Vạn, who looked deep in thought, and said, 'And I suggest Vạn should keep his current house for the rest of his life. Don't listen to Uncle Phỏng's stupid ideas or try to act noble, or you'll be out on the street when Nghĩa comes home.'

'That's enough!' Vạn shouted. 'It's not the right time to talk about inheritances and family hierarchy. I will never move into this house. You're all so old-fashioned! Khiên's family rebuilt this house with their sweat and their money, and he may now be dead, but Nghĩa and his mother and his wife are all still alive. The door to the lineage temple is always wide open, so anyone can come in any time they like and burn incense and make offerings to our ancestors. Our clan doesn't have a single spare hectare of land left. On the annual death anniversary of our great great grandfather, each of us should donate money. Anyone who doesn't contribute will have to withdraw their membership.'

'Uncle Vạn is right!' Dâu stood up and put her hands on her hips. 'May I say something, too?'

'Dâu!' her father yelled. 'This is none of your business. Don't be rude.'

'Don't be old-fashioned,' said Uncle Phỏng as he poked Dâu's father in the ribs with a chopstick. 'The younger generation should have a say too.'

'Dâu, I beg you to stay out of this,' Hạnh whispered, pulling the hem of her friend's shirt.

'Let me speak,' Dâu said to Hạnh. Then she turned toward the elders. 'With your permission, aunts and uncles: as a family, we gather here to show one another love and support. This is something right in front of you, but you fail to notice it every single time. Uncle Khiên is dead. Aunt Khiên lies in a faint in the bedroom. Their son is in the army, unable to be here to attend his dear father's funeral. They have been working hard all their lives, teaching and farming and fishing, to build this house on our ancestors' land, hoping that Nghĩa will live a happy life. Isn't it ridiculous that Nghĩa and his wife are not welcome to live here?'

Dâu looked at each of the elders defiantly. Some nodded their heads, some glared back. Uncle Xeng was not pleased. Hạnh kept pinching Dâu's thigh.

'So,' Dâu continued, 'I propose Hạnh be allowed to live with Aunt Khiên and take care of her husband's mother. Nghĩa has gone to defend our country. Uncle Khiên is dead, leaving Aunt Khiên all alone. Nghĩa and his wife have done nothing wrong. They should not be made to suffer any longer.'

'Nghĩa is guilty!' said Uncle Xeng. 'Guilty of breaking our ancestor's law. And that's enough from you, Dâu. Stop being so arrogant. I know you're in love with Hạnh's brother, Hiệp, so stop pretending you're acting out of kindness. Stop trying to be a rebel and disrespecting the wisdom of our ancestors.'

Dâu's father lumbered toward Dâu, grabbed her wrist, and pulled her outside.

'Oh, please, everyone,' cried Aunt Khiên as she emerged from her bedroom, weeping and wringing her hands. 'Please. I beg you to stop talking about this. My husband has just passed.'

Each of the elders took a handful of sticky rice, stood up one by one, and left.

'Damn!' said Uncle Khoái. 'Eating at the same time as talking about things that make you lose your appetite is such bad luck! This morning, when I left the house, the first person I saw was Mrs Mực. That was really bad luck!' He stood up unsteadily, rattling the bowls and plates on the table against one another. Uncle Kình's daughter, Thắm, and Uncle Phỏng's daughter, Thư, stayed to help Hạnh and Duyên clean up.

It was cold that night in Đông Village. The sound of the funeral trumpets and drums as well as the elders' words at the reception earlier kept echoing in Hạnh's mind. It had been over a year since she and Nghĩa married, but only just now was she able to sleep in her husband's bed. Next to a framed portrait of him on the wall hung his zither, monochord, and flute. Hạnh thought he was smiling at her affectionately. She extinguished the oil lamp and lay down on the bed. She heard Mother Khiên quietly pad into the lineage temple to burn incense for her husband. The image of Father Khiên sitting frail and alone on the canal return lingered in Hạnh's mind.

After lighting incense, Mother Khiên came to Hạnh's bed.

'Mother, can't you sleep?' she asked.

'You're awake too? Good, I have to tell you something. Keep that letter but don't tell anyone about the money that's supposed to be under the lamp on the altar. Someone stole it. With all those people here, it could've been anyone. When Nghĩa writes to you, and you have an address to write back, send him a telegram and ask if he can request a short leave. And don't let what the elders said upset you. Tomorrow I'll talk with your mother about letting you live here with me. We haven't treated you right, and I promise as long as I live, I'll take care of you. I'm so sorry.'

'Mother!' Hạnh held Mother Khiên's dry, bony hands. 'You've done nothing wrong. I know you love me and Nghĩa.'

Hạnh could not sleep that first night in her husband's house. Mother Khiên's footsteps in and out of the lineage temple pattered throughout the night.

Chapter 12

Nghĩa was a bit surprised. He couldn't understand why his comrade Biển looked so cheerful when he too had received a telegram informing him of a parent's death. On their way back home, Biển even cracked jokes and flirted with the girls on the train they took from Vinh to Thanh Hóa. Nghĩa sat by the window.

'You look so innocent,' said Biển. 'Nobody in the unit believes you have a wife. Do you think the girls in this region are pretty? I heard they really love soldiers in the South.' Biển pinched Nghĩa's thigh and winked. 'If you sit by a girl and don't give her a little pinch or whisper in her ear, she'll think you're dumb. Look at this girl! She's gorgeous!' Biển nodded at the girl in the purple shirt sitting across the aisle. 'Any time I flirt with a girl, she always falls in love with me.'

Nghĩa was only half listening. He kept thinking about Hạnh's telegram, hoping somehow it was a mistake and his father was not dead.

'Cheer up!' said Biển. 'You can't take a telegram sent during a war seriously. Your father's still alive. Trust me.'

'How do you know?'

'You're so naïve! The war's raging, and your parents are afraid you might die, or your wife is so horny she can't sit still. Newly married women are like that. Once they get a taste for sex, they can't just give it up. When you get back, she'll ride you 'til your bones break. So, cheer up, you've got a lot to look forward to when you get home! When we get to Thanh Hóa, you can rest at my dad's place, and then we'll go see a movie or something. I'll take you to the bus station tomorrow.'

'You're not going home?'

'Nah. My dad has an apartment in the district seat. You think my mom just died? No way! She's healthy as hell.'

The whole time Biền was talking to Nghĩa, he kept glancing at the girl in the purple shirt. Night came, and Nghĩa fell asleep to the rhythmic clacking of the train. At some point, he woke to find Biền had switched seats to sit next to the girl. He was smooth-talking her, and in a voice like a chirping bird's, she giggled every now and then in response. He was telling her about 'love during war', which Nghĩa had already heard explained so many times before.

When they arrived in Thanh Hóa, the last bus to the district had already left. Nghĩa shouldered his rucksack and followed Biền to a three-storey building on Lê Lợi Street not far from the bus station. Nghĩa had just started up the staircase when an air raid siren wailed from outside. The street erupted into chaos. Most people were scurrying to the bomb shelters, others just stood there looking up at the sky.

'Damn it!' said Biền. 'We just get here, and the air raid siren goes off.' They had to step aside for the third-floor tenants to run down the stairs. A few minutes later, the siren stopped. Nghĩa followed Biền as he climbed quickly to the second floor and entered a very nice-looking room. A young girl stood dancing to music that played from a cassette player. She looked at Biền and Nghĩa with great surprise.

'Why didn't you run downstairs when you heard the siren?' asked Biền as he dropped his rucksack onto the floor. 'You're so stubborn! Nghĩa, this stubborn girl is my younger sister, Thủy. This is Nghĩa from Đông Village. We're in the same unit.'

The girl's eyes brightened as she glanced at Nghĩa and then again at her older brother. 'I can't believe you're back already! I thought you wouldn't be home for years!'

'Where's Dad?'

'His company had to evacuate to Châu Cúc. He might not be home tonight.'

After dinner, Biền made tea, poured himself a cup, and whispered to Nghĩa, 'Want to go see a movie?'

'I'm too tired.'

'Okay. Stay here and tell Thủy to turn on the cassette player for you. I've got to go see my girlfriend. I've been missing her so much!'

Biển went into his room to change clothes. After washing the dishes, Thủy primped in front of the mirror and tapped her feet and sang. Her lips were rosy, her eyes black, her smile cute. Every now and then she peeked over at Nghĩa. After Biển traded his uniform for brown pants and an ironed blue shirt, he looked much younger than Nghĩa.

'You're going out again,' Thủy said with a pout. 'I'm going to tell Dad.'

'Just stay here and entertain my friend. I'll back soon.' Biển winked at Nghĩa and left the apartment. Thủy sat down by Nghĩa and asked, 'Are you married?'

'I just got married a year ago.'

'Is your wife beautiful?'

'She's a typical country girl.'

'Me too.'

'But you live in the city, and it sounds like you'll become a famous singer one day.'

'You think becoming a singer is easy? It's much harder than farming. Being so young and already married must be hard too.'

'It's fate. We've loved each other since before high school.'

'Oh, first loves are the best! Would you like to hear me sing? I'll sing you one by Hoàng Vân called "Quảng Bình, My Home".'

Thủy pressed record on the cassette player and started to sing, her voice warm and clear. As she sang, she danced and swung her arms gracefully like she was performing on stage. When she finished the song, she rewound the tape to listen to her voice again.

'What do you think?'

'You sing beautifully.'

'Then why do you look so sad?'

'I received a telegram. My father might be dead.'

'Oh! Don't let telegrams like that scare you. Biển told me his girlfriend sent a fake message like that, saying my mother died, so he could come back and have some fun. If I were his captain, I'd never approve one of his requests for a leave. Anyway, let's not talk about it. Just enjoy yourself while you're here with me. Don't think about it too much. Soldiers can never tell what the future holds.'

Thủy smiled and gave Nghĩa a mischievous look. 'Let's make a beautiful, platonic memory tonight, so even if you go to the ends of the earth, you'll always be able to remember this moment. What game will we never forget?'

'Painting soot moustaches?'

'You're funny. That game is for children.'

Nghĩa didn't know what sort of game she had in mind. He'd never met a naughty girl like Thủy before. She stared at him as if she'd known him for years. Just as he was starting to think maybe she could read his mind, she burst out laughing and held his hand tightly.

'Don't pretend to be innocent!' said Thủy. 'Can't you guess what we should do to remember each other forever?'

'Are you joking? I'm married.'

'I know you're married.' Thủy gave Nghĩa that mischievous smile again. 'Why don't you kiss me like a friend or a brother? Westerners often greet each other in public that way.'

'I see what you mean, but that's in the West. Nobody kisses like that in Việt Nam.'

'Let's pretend we're Russian or actors in a film. Then you can kiss me really naturally, like this, and like this.'

Thủy stroked the back of Nghĩa's head and neck. Her perfume smelled like fragrant flowers. Her lips went down his forehead and cheeks. Nghĩa felt like he was dreaming. He realized that somehow, strangely, Thủy was both light and dark.

'Are you feeling anything?' she whispered.

'I still don't know what game you're playing.'

'I guess now that you're married, you've lost your youthful passion. Let's try one more thing.' She kissed him on the lips, again and again, and wrapped her soft arms around him. She pressed her round breasts against his chest, and in that moment, he imagined holding Hạnh. Thủy placed his hand on her left breast and said, 'They say this is where the heart is.' Then she released his hand and gave him another look. 'You're cheating,' she said, and then burst out laughing.

Nghĩa's face felt hot and he gaped at her, bewildered.

'Okay!' she said. 'Game over! You're Nguyễn Minh Nghĩa, right?'

'Um, yes?'

'Don't give me that strange look! And you used to be the best literature student in the district school, right?'

'You know me?'

'I'm not the only one who knows how smart you are. All the girls in my class had a crush on you.'

'What grade were you in?'

'One class below you.'

'Oh. But I didn't know you?'

'Well, now you know me,' said Thủy. 'And now you've kissed me. When I saw you come in with Biển, I knew you right away. I don't know why but you remind me of Pavel.* That's why I came up with that game earlier. Do I look like his sweetheart co-star?'

'It's like you're always dreaming.'

'Can you call a girl who doesn't dream a girl? Now I'm sure you'll never forget me. I wanted to go to medical school but I failed the exam, so my father helped me join the, *văn công*† even though it's not my passion. If I'd been able to study medicine, I'd volunteer to join the war like you and my brother.'

Early the next morning, while Thủy was still asleep, Biển took Nghĩa to the bus station. The whole bus ride, he couldn't get her out of his mind. He'd been in a different world the night before. The bus stopped near Linh Canal for Nghĩa to get off. He'd only been away three months but it felt like three years. He picked his way down the dike to take the dirt road to the village. It was late morning now, but still a little chilly. A group of children chattered among themselves walking from school.

'Hello, soldier!' said one of the kids. 'Where are you going?'

'Đông Village. Do you know if there's been a funeral there recently?'

The children looked surprised at Nghĩa. He realized he'd asked a dumb question.

---

* Soviet actor Pavel Kadochnikov (1915–1988)

† The North Vietnamese Army unit composed of singers and performers who travelled all over the country during the war to provide uplifting, patriotic entertainment to both soldiers and civilians.

From the road by the cemetery, he saw a wilted wreath on a grave covered with green grass and wondered whether it was his father's. He was unsure. Nghĩa kept trying to believe his father was not dead but a strange feeling repeatedly sapped his efforts. At the co-op storage house, Nghĩa paused to watch people husking rice by pushing and pulling the big stone in a circle. Familiar faces from Đông Village started to appear before him, but everyone, including his own mother, saw him but did not say a word. Just by looking into their eyes he knew now for sure his father was dead. Nghĩa burst into tears and ran to his parents' home. He kicked open the door to find the house empty. He dropped his rucksack, fell onto his old bed, and sobbed like a child.

After a while, he heard Dâu outside, saying, 'Leave him alone. Let his crying express his sorrow so every Nguyễn knows he's grieving.'

His mother and many of the people he'd seen at the storehouse came inside. Nghĩa heard Hạnh's voice as she poured tea for everyone. She shuttled in and out of the house, ushering everyone back outside. His mother came into his room and stood by the bed.

'Get some rest, son,' she said. 'I'm going to go pick some morning glory for lunch.'

Nghĩa followed his mother out to the lane. A flock of sparrows chirped from the hedgerow and then flew to the top of the areca tree. The late autumn sun filled the field near the riverbank with warm golden light. Nghĩa meandered to the front yard. He saw where the couplets his father had hung had been clumsily removed. Several potted plants in the courtyard were now going yellow. A reeking patch of algae floated in the dirty water of the koi pond, which looked devoid of fish. Nghĩa inspected the miniature landscape but the only thing he saw was a rotten fish head. The two little deer his father had made with cement were broken, their armature wires now visible and haphazard. Back in his room, he noticed Hạnh's clothes hanging on the hooks. He realized suddenly that the peaceful existence he and Hạnh had longed for so desperately had finally arrived, but at the cost of losing his father. Light footsteps came from outside. Hạnh crossed the yard holding two eggs and slipped into the kitchen. Just as he was wondering whether she had just gone for eggs or actually lived there, Hạnh rushed into the room and hugged Nghĩa tightly.

His mother returned carrying a basket of greens. Hạnh took the letter his father had written from the bureau and gave it to Nghĩa to read before going into the kitchen to cook rice. Just then, Uncle Vạn appeared in the doorway.

'Nghĩa, my boy, you're back?' Uncle Vạn's voice was loud. 'Wow! You really look like a soldier now! You've been to Sông Lam and Bến Thủy, right? Wonderful! That's our beloved Uncle Hồ's hometown, in heroic Nghệ Tĩnh Province.' Uncle Vạn finally seemed to take in the sad look on Nghĩa's face. 'Okay, things happen,' he said. 'Don't be sad, though. Sad makes a person weak. You're in artillery, right? That's cool! I was infantry. Have you fought in a battle yet?'

'No, not yet.'

'Well, you probably still need some training. It's not like the old days! They just took us in and sent us out to fight right away. I've heard the Americans are pretty tough though, right? Don't be scared!'

Uncle Vạn accepted a glass of water from Nghĩa and downed it in one gulp.

'Let me see your papers for how many days you have on leave. Whoa! Only seven? You have to leave day after tomorrow.'

'Please let him get some rest,' his mother called from outside, where she was washing the greens and removing wilted leaves. 'He just got home and already has to think about leaving.'

'Military regulations are strict,' said Uncle Vạn. 'Soldiers aren't like farmers who can come and go as they please.'

When lunch was ready, Nghĩa's mother invited Uncle Vạn to join them. They ate sautéed morning glory, *canh chua*,* and eggs fried with tiny, dried shrimp.

'I was just at Hạnh's mother's house,' said Uncle Vạn. 'Nhân said she'll make lunch for you two tomorrow. Then, for dinner

---

* Also known as sour soup, it is a broth made sour with tamarind, and often includes pineapple, tomato, elephant ear stalks, bean sprouts, and sometimes fish.

tomorrow night, I also want to cook for you, but you have to come a little early to help me slaughter the chicken. My whole life, I've never cooked for anyone but myself.'

Hạnh spent the afternoon at home with Nghĩa. It was October, so it didn't take long for the sun to rise above the areca tree. While Hạnh made dinner, Nghĩa followed the hedgerow across the village to visit great Uncle Xung. After Uncles Xèng and Xình were executed, Uncle Xung suffered a mental breakdown and could no longer work as a pig dealer. As a result, his family's finances deteriorated. His house had been a nice-looking, well-furnished place, but now looked dilapidated. The three-sectioned pigsty that used to be full of pigs of various sizes was now empty and had started to fall apart. After a minute or two taking in the place's poor condition, Nghĩa finally noticed just one little black pig lying with its nose buried in a heap of garbage.

When Uncle Xeng's children saw Nghĩa, they jumped up and down happily, shouting, 'Uncle Nghĩa is back! Uncle Nghĩa is back!'

'Where's your grandpa?' Nghĩa asked the kids. The littlest ones looked at the oldest, who lowered his head and shuffled his dirty feet, reluctant to speak. 'Where's Grandpa?' repeated Nghĩa. 'Can you hear me?'

The boy said quietly, 'My father has him locked up in the kitchen.'

'Do you have the key?'

The boy nodded.

'Give it to me.'

'Dad said he'd beat me if I let anyone in.'

Nghĩa shouted, 'Give me the key, damn it!'

The boy removed the key tied round his neck and held it out. Nghĩa snatched the key and opened the door to the kitchen. It was pitch black inside and smelled horrible. Uncle Xung squatted, nearly catatonic, in one corner next to a heap of garbage. Nghĩa's expression darkened when he registered the gauntness of Uncle Xung's bony face. Uncle Xung blinked at Nghĩa, bewildered. The kitchen was a complete mess, the floor covered with ash and garbage and rat turds, the whole place looking like it had been ravaged by a flock of chickens. The rats had chewed holes everywhere. Suddenly

Uncle Xung jumped up and ran outside. Nghĩa chased after him into the yard and caught him by his filthy hand.

'Uncle? It's me, Nghĩa.'

Uncle Xung glared at Nghĩa, and then covered his face and sobbed.

'Nghĩa . . . Nghĩa . . .' he muttered several times before it seemed to click. 'Oh, Nghĩa, you're still alive? I planned to make Xeng head of the family.'

Before Nghĩa could answer, they heard Xeng and his wife talking outside the gate, and Uncle Xung ran to the other side of the house.

'Hello, Uncle and Aunty,' said Nghĩa. 'Are you just coming home from work?'

'Yes. And hello.' Uncle Xeng scowled. 'What are you doing here?'

'What a question! I'm on leave for my father's death, and I came by to say hello to you both, your children, and Aunt Thao.'

Without a word of reply, Uncle Xeng threw the baskets and yoke pole he'd been carrying to the ground and stormed inside. Aunt Thao dropped the hay she'd carried into the courtyard on her shoulders and scolded the children for being lazy. Then she threw her sickle into one of the baskets and followed Xeng inside. Nghĩa came to the doorway.

Uncle Xeng was already sitting at the table smoking his water pipe. He gave Nghĩa a tired look.

'How's the family?' asked Nghĩa.

'Everyone says the Nguyễn clan is paying for bad karma. Do you feel humiliated yet? Our bad luck started when Uncle Vạn messed around with Hạnh's mother, which caused the burning of the lineage temple. My brothers Xèng and Xình were convicted and killed unfairly, which drove my father crazy. I thought then maybe our bad luck would be over.' Uncle Xeng hesitated and then glared at Nghĩa. 'But then you married Hạnh. That's why your father died. Get it? Don't you see our clan has been ruined? Wake up, Nghĩa!' As tears filled Uncle Xeng's eyes, he said, 'As long as Hạnh lives on our ancestral land, bad things will keep happening to our family.'

Nghĩa returned home with a heavy heart. He sat on the mat near the tray, which held a steaming tureen of fish soup, a plate of dried beef, and a plate of sautéed greens. Seeing just three rice bowls and three pairs of chopsticks, Nghĩa thought about his father, who would have been so happy to join them for this dinner.

'Where have you been, son?' asked his mother.

'I visited Uncle Xeng. He had Uncle Xung locked up in the kitchen.'

'No wonder I haven't seen him recently. What a shame.' His mother let out a big sigh. 'He used to be so strong and provided for his whole family. When he raised and sold pigs, his family lived so well and so happy together. And now, they're just miserable . . .'

*

The next night, after a long day of visiting with Nhân and Uncle Vạn, Hạnh and Nghĩa fell asleep holding each other tightly in each other's arms. When Hạnh woke, Nghĩa had just a few hours before he had to catch the bus back to the district. Gazing at his face in the oil lamp's dim light, Hạnh wondered when she would see her husband again, or would it be *if*? She lowered her head and gently kissed his lips, and then dressed and tiptoed into the kitchen.

Mother Khiên came out of her bedroom. 'I can't sleep,' she said. 'Let me do the cooking. You can go back to bed for a little while. It's still so early.'

Hạnh returned to the bedroom and lay down next to Nghĩa. She knew their mothers wanted them to have a baby as soon as possible. They didn't have much time together, so they made the most of it when they could. The questions circled through her mind again. When would Nghĩa be home again? Would he come home? Unable to put their imminent separation out of her mind, Hạnh suddenly felt a little panicked and hugged Nghĩa tightly, forgetting that he probably needed more sleep for his early trip.

Nghĩa woke and held her hands and asked, 'Why are you up?'

'I couldn't fall back to sleep,' she said. 'But you can. It's still dark outside.'

'I just dreamed we had a baby. A boy we named Tình.'

'Tình—*love*—that's wonderful! I know Tình will be just like you and become a great leader of the Nguyễn family.'

The couple got up and dressed, brushed their teeth, and sat down to breakfast. Hạnh watched as Mother Khiên quickly and skilfully rolled out several sticky rice balls.

'You're so good at that, Mom,' said Nghĩa. 'I remember you making rice balls the night the NVA soldiers attacked the Nationalist outpost.'

'Yes! I remember that night too, with Hạnh and her mother and Uncle Xung and Xeng's wife. The rice ball has to be really hot to be smoothed. Hold it too long in one place and it'll burn your hand.'

'Hạnh and I were just kids back then. I climbed to the roof of the lineage temple and saw the outpost go up in flames.'

Mother Khiên wrapped the finished rice balls in banana leaves and went out to wash her hands at the well. When she came back in, she asked excitedly, 'Did you hear that? Outside? Rats squeaking?'

'Rats squeaking? What do you mean, Mother?' asked Hạnh. She and Nghĩa ate breakfast while listening to Mother Khiên's answer.

'It's a good sign,' she said. 'When Nghĩa's father got up early to go fishing, I'd get up too and make rice for him. If I heard rats squeaking, he'd catch a lot of fish that day. But if I heard an echoing sound, it was a bad sign. I remember when the French attacked the village, all the women and children evacuated to Hồi Village. Father had to stay here and fight with the militia. That night, sleeping in Hồi Village, I heard a howling sound coming from the sky. I asked the other women and they said they didn't hear it. I got up, opened the window and heard the howling again. It was so strange! The next morning, I learned the French had arrested Father, Uncle Hinh, Uncle Dược, and Uncle Hòa. And if you ever hear a racket-tailed treepie* squawking, it's a really good sign. The morning after the arrests, I got up early to go to the Quai Market to buy some sweet potatoes, and when I reached the water tank, I heard rats squeaking. Then when I went out to the lane, I heard a treepie squawk from the roof of the lineage temple. When I got home from the market that afternoon, your sister ran out shouting,

* The racket-tailed treepie is a medium sized member of the crow family in Southeast Asia with green feathers, a small black mask, and turquoise eyes.

"Daddy's home! Daddy's home!" Your father and uncles had been released. Your father was tortured the worst by the French, and after that he could never do hard labour again. If his feet got muddy, he'd have a coughing fit. That's why he started fishing and always wore shoes when he fished. Some people found that strange.'

Nghĩa let Hạnh help him shoulder his rucksack. They took a shortcut so they wouldn't have to walk past the duck house and see Mr Nhương. The rice paddies glowed golden in the early morning sun. A flock of parrots flew across the sky. In the fields that had been recently harvested, the bend of the cut stems seemed to welcome the sunlight. In the others, a light breeze rustled the golden yellow rice stalks. Even the smell of the earth here was special. Every place Nghĩa went always made him see how Đông Village was different and how Hạnh was unlike any other girl. At the curve of the river, where they spent their wedding night, Nghĩa took Hạnh's hand. The sun rose, and the morning dew sparkled on the grass like jade.

'It's strange,' Nghĩa said. 'No matter how many times we've slept together, I'll never forget our first night here on the riverbank. I can still feel the grass tickling our bodies while we held each other. Right here! We did it right here on this grass!'

Hạnh smiled and playfully pummelled Nghĩa's back. He caught her hand and pulled her with him down to the ground. 'I want to see if you'll remember this.' Nghĩa hugged Hạnh and they kissed.

Hạnh pinched his ribs and teased, 'Now you can remember the moment I pinched you in the same place the grass tickled your ribs.'

Nghĩa laughed and squeezed his wife again.

'Time to go or you'll miss the bus,' said Hạnh.

'Don't worry! Squeaking rats mean I can't miss the bus!'

They laughed and joked all along the dike path. The sun climbed high into the sky, making the Linh Canal appear luminous in the young husband and wife's eyes.

PART III

Chapter 13

One evening, in patches of moonlight beneath the mango tree, a group of children were playing and singing 'Release the Leech'.* Old man Xung sat on the back of one of the old communal house's stone dogs listening to the children sing. Every now and then, he'd sing along loudly and wave his arms, but he tired quickly, his raspy voice mixed with wheezing.

Lately, Xung was allowed to go out in the evening under the supervision of Xeng's children. They had to keep an eye on him, otherwise he'd disappear and wander along the riverbank or dike. The cunning kids tied his ankles together beneath the stone dog's belly so he couldn't go anywhere and they could play without having to worry about him. He got used to this kind of treatment. But sitting for too long in one position made Xung's feet go numb, so he bent down, scratched his feet, and inadvertently discovered the knot. Then he loosened it and felt much better. And then he got up quietly and sauntered down to the riverside. Several young women from Đông Village had gathered there and were chatting and laughing loudly in the moonlight. The Silver Stone Bridge had two rails that had once been silver white but because of the war had been blackened with asphalt. People still called it the Silver Stone Bridge, though, just like they always called this part of the Đình River the Family River, despite the communal house of Đông Village having been torn down a long time ago. The only things left in the ruins were the two stone dogs snarling their teeth.

* A children's song and game a bit like tag

'Ladies, have you given up men? What's making you giggle like that?' cried Mr Đột, who was fishing in the river. 'Damn! You're scaring away all the fish!'

'How miserable Mr Đột's family must be listening to his nonsense!' said one of the girls.

'It's crazy that in the old days he was commune chairman.'

'Good thing he was chairman for only three seasons. If it had been three years, everyone in Đông Village would already be a reactionary.'

Then another girl said to Đột, 'You're so rude. We're just contemplating this beautiful moon, and you have to . . .'

'Contemplating the moon?' Đột said sarcastically. 'You girls are contemplating men! But with all the young men gone, you come here just to poke fun at old timers like me. So naughty!'

The girls knew Đột was just being grumpy, so they said nothing. In fact, what he said was true—not a decent young man was left in the village. All the able-bodied young men had volunteered to join the army when they were seventeen. Some even added a year to their ages to be eligible early. Only a few men remained. Nhiên, whose constant cough made him ineligible for enlistment, became secretary of the cooperative production team. One-eyed Tẹo guarded the rice paddy. Ngốc had a developmental disability and was his family's only remaining son left to help his father collect buffalo manure. He had just a few strands of hair on his big misshapen head and a red nose. No one could tell his age, and he grinned at everyone. Many of the girls in the village teased him, telling him they wanted to marry him, and because he thought they were serious at first, he became shy. But when he realized they were teasing, he said, 'If you want to marry me, let me kiss you first.' And he meant it. The girls got scared and ran away. The fourth was Hân, who all the village girls at first thought was tall, strong, and handsome, but was actually quite worthless. He was the village's first deserter. The day after he came home, the commune received a notification. That night, Miss Thao, who was Uncle Xung's youngest daughter and Hân's fiancée, returned all the engagement gifts to Hân's parents. The women in Đông Village would rather die alone than marry a deserter. They'd rather marry

Ngốc than marry a coward. Hân didn't dare leave his house after the commune told him he had to carry a sign on his chest any time he walked the village lanes that said, *If everyone were like me, we would lose our country*. He was scorned by the whole village. Even small children mocked him.

Since the day the Americans bombed the Linh Canal, no household in Đông Village dared to light their oil lamps at night. During the day, no one wore white clothes or hats. Schoolchildren wore straw hats and camouflaged themselves with leaves when they walked to school. All the bamboo groves got chopped down, and people used the bamboo to reinforce tunnels and bomb shelters. Everyone lived in fear. At first, when planes buzzed in the sky at night, everyone got up quickly and rolled into the trenches. But at some point, people got used to the sound of planes overhead and ignored the bombing. Life returned to something like normal. Everyone still had to live, work in the rice paddies, and attend weddings, funerals, and death anniversaries. Young women continued to sing folk songs. If they couldn't wear a white blouse during the day, they'd wear it on moonless nights. Young women got to wear bright and colourful clothes just a few times a year, and they wanted to dance in those clothes. In years past, they would have sulked if a man they liked made them unhappy. But now, there were no young men left to make anyone sulk, either happily or unhappily. Đông Village had become a village of women.

The moonlit night that group of girls and young women had gathered at Silver Stone Bridge, some elderly men fished from the riverbank, and old man Xung came down to the river to enjoy the cool breeze. Once he was free, he would rarely stay in one place. He waved his arms, stretched his legs, danced, and waded in the water. No one cared what he did any more, not even if he strolled through the village completely naked.

'Back in the old days, our ancestors never allowed girls to gather like this,' Đột said to his fishing buddies. 'Now the girls love to be out here. What a pity they're all so young and pretty, but still single.'

'Single, but some are still raising children like your sister,' one of the girls snapped.

'Mr Đột, if you have such compassion,' said another, 'why don't you find the guy who slept with Tý Hin so little Tươi can have a father?'

'If a guy ran out on my sister like that, my brother would tear him to pieces.'

These girls were so wicked, they seemed to really enjoy dredging up embarrassing stories to shut Đột up. As he tried to think of a snappy retort, he heard splashing in his net. The girls burst out laughing.

'Mr Đột, lift your net. There are fish in there!'

'Damn it!' shouted Đột. 'Who threw a rock in my net?'

The girls laughed and laughed. Just then, old man Quỳ's son, Huy, joined the group of girls standing on the bridge. Quỳ and Huy had recently relocated to Đông Village to avoid being bombed in the district seat. Old man Quỳ had started a photography studio and made a lot of money, and his son avoided army service because he had a lame leg. The two of them lived better than just about everyone else in the village because all the young girls flocked to his studio to have their picture taken. Kids spread the rumour that the father contrived ways to touch girls' breasts when he took pictures in the studio. The girls knew he was probably a pervert, but they also loved listening to his stories, especially the romantic ones.

'Pick the girl you like, Huy, and toss her into the river,' called Đột. 'Don't let them surround you like that.'

Hạnh and Uncle Vạn came to the bridge after leaving the new commune office and heard the girls' raucous laughter.

'You shouldn't be here!' shouted Uncle Vạn. 'You're breaking the blackout rules. Go home and sleep.'

The girls nudged and winked at one another and left. Uncle Vạn clicked his tongue at the way Huy leaned so cavalierly against the bridge. 'Just so you know,' he said, 'I'm watching you. You've been a bad influence on these girls ever since you moved here.' Then Vạn hobbled away without listening to Huy try to explain.

'Hạnh, you have to keep an eye on these girls,' said Uncle Vạn. 'That guy is trouble.'

Hạnh walked by Uncle Vạn's side trying not to cry. At the commune office, they had just learned her brother Hà had been killed in the South. Beside them as they walked, the skinny new bamboo trees planted alongside the road quivered in the moonlight.

'You have to be strong,' said Uncle Vạn. 'Sacrifices like these are our duty. Sometimes you have to put aside your feelings to do what must be done. Hà died a hero doing his duty as a revolutionary soldier, just like your father. But don't tell anyone about Hà yet so your mother can get another night's rest. At the memorial tomorrow, comfort your mother but try not to cry. You have to be a good example for the other women in the village. We have to accept Hà has been sacrificed for something greater than ourselves.'

The more Uncle Vạn comforted her, the more Hạnh wanted to burst out in tears, and the more she tried to hold them back, the more she felt she was suffocating. She gasped for breath.

'If you act like this, your mother will know,' said Uncle Vạn. 'Settle down.'

'I can't!' Hạnh said, now sobbing.

'Shh!' said Vạn. 'You'd better sleep at Mother Khiên's place tonight. And tomorrow morning go home early. If you tell your mother about Hà's death tonight and she screams and cries all night, it'll be your fault.' Uncle Vạn stormed off.

Hạnh stood still for a moment to wipe her tears before dragging herself to her mother-in-law's house.

'I thought you'd spend the night at your mother's,' Mother Khiên said as she unlocked the door. 'She was here earlier.'

Hạnh blanched. 'Did she say anything?'

'Your mother heard that the commune received some death notices, but we don't know if our hamlet has any. We didn't get any letters from Hà, Hiệp, or Nghĩa.'

'A lot of people have gone to war, but not many write home.'

Hạnh hurried into her bedroom. She felt so raw and on edge, she knew she might burst out crying and ruin everything. But she also felt bad for her mother, her mother-in-law, and Hà's fiancée, Hồng.

Near dawn, Hạnh finally dozed off but had a nightmare in which the commune received notice of Nghĩa's death, but didn't tell her. Hạnh screamed and wept in her sleep.

'What's wrong?'

The question startled Hạnh awake as Mother Khiên rushed into the room. Mother Khiên saw how distraught Hạnh looked and began to cry, assuming that bad news had come last night about Nghĩa.

'Mother!' Hạnh sprang from the bed and embraced her mother-in-law. 'My brother Hà died, not Nghĩa. The memorial will be later today. I got the news last night but was told not to tell anyone yet.'

Later, but still early in the morning, Uncle Vạn came to escort Hạnh to her mother's house. Hạnh was astonished that her mother received the terrible news with such composure, almost indifference, though her face paled as Uncle Vạn relayed the details. He spoke without daring to look at Nhân. 'He fought bravely,' he said. 'I'm glad you're taking the news so well. Hà followed his father's example to a glorious death. All last night, Hạnh and I were very worried about you.'

'So that's it,' said Nhân without shedding a tear. 'He's dead. My son Hà is dead.'

'A heroic sacrifice,' said Uncle Vạn.

'I'm his mother, so I've somehow known for a long time he would die, ever since he enlisted, but especially after going to several memorials for other sons from our village. Yesterday, I saw a couple commune officials pass by and peer inside the house without stopping or saying anything, so I knew something bad had happened. My premonitions were right.'

Hearing that, Hạnh realized her father's death from so long ago had been haunting her mother all this time. And her mother had grieved alone and in silence the whole night.

*

Everyone in Đông Village knew who owned the gun that they heard in the middle of the night. Nguyễn Vạn, of course, who else? In the evenings, Vạn carried his rifle out to a remote part of the riverbank. He lay on an abandoned brick kiln, looked east, and waited for low-flying American planes. The Americans were not easy to deal with. They had changed their bombing runs to fly in from the sea just over the surface of the river before reaching their target, and artillery Unit 37 didn't yet know how to deal with them. Now when American planes came flying in low, the villagers heard the stutter of Vạn's AK-47 and worried for him because these were American jets, not just a squadron of old French Dragonflies. A villager warned him, 'If you piss them off, they'll bomb the village and kill us all.' But Vạn was determined to bring one down and said to the coward, 'If you're afraid, just hide in a ditch, goddamn it! It's flying right above my nose—I can't just sit there and watch it go by.'

Vạn lay on the kiln and kept watch toward the sea. The vast night sky held towers of dark clouds blowing in from the east, which meant there would be rain. The river roared as the wind started to gust, chopping the surface. The sky went completely dark. Then came thunder and lightning and a drenching rain that lashed Vạn's cheeks. He packed up his gun, turned on his flashlight and shuffled back to the village beneath the lightning and booming thunder. Half a dozen snakehead fish had washed ashore and so he caught them and wrapped them in his shirt. When he reached the village, he decided to give Nhân some of the fish, though it was already late at night. He hobbled into Nhân's yard and then her kitchen, where he saw two buckets placed to catch drips from the roof. He smiled.

'Who's in the kitchen?' asked Nhân from the living room. Her loud voice full of bravado made him laugh.

'It's me, Vạn. Why aren't you asleep? I caught some snakeheads and came to give you a few.' He dropped the fish into the buckets and hurriedly put on his shirt. The fishy smell was not pleasant and the slippery fish mucus made his skin sticky, so he went to the well and rinsed his shirt and poured warm water all over himself. He felt a little less cold.

Nhân lit an oil lamp and poked her head out the door and peered toward the neighbours' houses, worried someone might hear them. She said, 'It's pouring. Why torment yourself like this? Come inside. Don't stand in the rain like that.'

Vạn was drenched from head to toe. He climbed the steps to the porch. Nhân went inside and then returned with a towel and some of Hà's clothes and gave them to Vạn. 'Here,' she said. 'Put these on. You don't want to catch a cold.'

Vạn came inside and put on Hà's clothes. Sitting at the table, he couldn't stop his teeth from chattering. Outside, the rain kept pouring down.

'The snakehead this season are really big,' he said. 'You might want to fry these tomorrow. Do you have a rag I can use to wipe down my gun?'

He can't just sit here, cleaning his gun and talking about fish, thought Nhân. The house felt warm and bright in the cool, quiet night. She looked at Vạn in Hà's clothes and thought he looked like a young man. Hạnh's words played through her mind. *He'll never marry because he's still in love with you.* Nhân loved Vạn's eccentric personality, but at times also hated it or was confused by it. She'd heard rumours about him. Some said he must like men because he never flirted with women. Some said he might have been injured down there at the battle of Điện Biên Phủ. Who knew? He had scars all over his body.

'Vạn, I don't mean to pry,' said Nhân, 'but ask sincerely, why haven't you married? These days especially, there are so few men in the village. Plenty of women would be interested.'

Vạn looked at Nhân like he didn't know her. Nhân's face flushed. She tilted her head, looked at him over one shoulder, and caressed her long, silky hair. Her face brightened and she smiled at Vạn. She was acting so strangely. Vạn had never known her to be flirtatious, but he could also never understand women in the slightest. He wondered whether Nhân ever felt like Công's widow, Hơn, so lonely and aching with desire that she'd do things she normally wouldn't. Vạn tried to regain his composure and asked, 'How about you? Do you ever think about marrying again?'

'Why do you ask?' Nhân batted her eyes coyly. 'My children are all grown, and if I were blessed, I'd have grandchildren by now. But you've never been with a woman. Don't you worry no one will burn incense for you when you're gone?' Nhân raised her eyes to glance at Vạn furtively. 'Or . . . are you gay, like some people have said?' She giggled nervously.

Vạn felt his face go hot. She really was losing it tonight. Could he tell her that he loved her, that he'd always loved her, that he'd love her forever if she dared? No way! The consequences would be too terrible. Their honour and reputations were tied to so many things, he couldn't do that to her. Vạn sat quietly for a while and then asked angrily, 'Who said I'm gay?'

Nhân watched as Vạn suddenly seemed immensely absorbed with cleaning his rifle, so she pretended to be angry and snatched the rag from his hand and threw it outside. 'Get some sleep,' she said. 'You can use Hạnh's room. I'll wake you early in the morning.' Then she gave him a conciliatory smile and said, 'I was kidding. Not that it matters.'

Nhân went into her bedroom and shut the door, leaving Vạn to sit alone by the oil lamp on the table. The rain was still pouring down on the banana garden outside. Nhân could not sleep. Even so, the rest of the short night flew by. Soon her roosters were flapping their wings and crowing. The rain had stopped at some point, leaving the atmosphere peaceful and cool. She got up to rouse Vạn so he could go home before the village was awake. If anyone saw him leaving her house early in the morning, they'd both lose face, especially her. She stood for a moment watching Vạn sleep. She felt aroused looking at him, but also some shame for feeling that way. She could hear and feel her heart throbbing in her chest. She sat on the edge of the bed and gently took Vạn's hand.

Her face felt flushed. Wondering whether it made her immoral, she leaned down and embraced him, her whole body shaking. Vạn woke and mumbled something she couldn't make out. The roosters crowed again. She felt Vạn return the embrace as his hands caressed her body. She had thought for years that her body had gone numb but now it seemed like a fire burned inside her. She panted as she struggled to escape his arms. Suddenly they both panicked and sprang from the bed.

'You can't be so reckless . . .'

'You're the one being reckless . . .'

Embarrassed, Nhân opened the door. Vạn staggered outside, and she stood in the doorway watching him go, until suddenly she said, 'The fish! You forgot to take the fish!'

'Right!'

Nhân hurried into the kitchen and picked up one of the buckets.

'Wow! Where'd you catch so many?'

'The riverbank. There's always so many there at the start of the rainy season.'

Chapter 14

Dâu bubbled with excitement as she and Hạnh prepared to go to their friend Thắm's wedding. Dâu wore a white shirt through which her bra could be seen.

'What about the blackout rules?' asked Hạnh.

'No one wants to look like an official at a wedding,' Dâu said. 'Let's find you something else to wear.' Then she pulled Hạnh into the bedroom, sat Hạnh down on the bed, and unbuttoned her shirt.

'Wear something colourful. It's a wedding, not a Party meeting. Planes flying up in the sky can't see what you're wearing at a wedding.'

Dâu took off Hạnh's brown shirt, rolled it up, and stuffed it into a drawer.

'Wow! Your breasts are so round and firm! Too bad Nghĩa's not here to enjoy them. What a waste!'

'You're terrible!'

'It's true! Your brother Hiệp and I aren't married yet, but you and Nghĩa are. A woman's youth doesn't last forever. You have to enjoy life as long as you can before you get old. If Hiệp doesn't come back in the next three years, I'm done for.' Dâu hugged Hạnh and spoke half pretending to sob. 'I'm ugly, but you're beautiful like Miss Ngần from the legend Grandfather Nghiên used to tell. I feel sorry for Nghĩa he's not back yet.'

Hạnh put on the blouse she'd made years ago for her own wedding, much to Dâu's approval. It had been such a long time since that night. Hạnh looked at herself in the mirror and knew she was still beautiful. They left for the wedding when firecrackers started going off. Đông Village had never had a wedding like

Thắm's, mainly because the groom was really different. Huy had a lame leg and yet he was marrying Thắm, one of the most beautiful women in the village. Even if a man had no legs, he'd still be able to marry a beauty like Thắm these days. The bride looked gorgeous in the wedding dress Huy bought for her. None of the other women in the village were as lucky as Thắm. She was eighteen, her eyes bright and clear, her beauty like a blooming flower. Huy really knew how to pick a wife. A lot of people said Thắm was especially lucky because, thanks to his bad leg, Huy wasn't eligible to enlist. Others said Thắm's parents married her off to Huy because of his family's wealth.

But just seeing Thắm's cheerful and contented face, Hạnh understood that Thắm loved Huy sincerely. Thắm had told her once, 'Not being able to enlist doesn't make him a bad person. He deserves to be happy like anyone else.'

'Do you think Thắm loves him?' Dâu asked in a whisper to Hạnh. 'I think the cripple's a pervert and a coward.'

'Don't be narrow-minded,' said Hạnh. 'Just because he has a bad leg, some people think he's somehow not a good person, but he actually has a handsome face. He's got a square jaw, a strong physique besides the leg, bright eyes, and a thick beard and eyebrows. It's not hard to believe Thắm loves him.'

'I don't think so. I think Thắm loves his crippled leg.'

After the ceremony, Thắm came to Dâu and Hạnh and asked, 'Will you take a photo with me and my husband? We can show it to Nghĩa and Hiệp when they come home.'

Thắm's rosy lips, bright smile, and happy face made Hạnh smile. 'Okay,' she said. 'I hope you two are very happy together.'

Thắm led Hạnh and Dâu into the studio. She winked at her husband, who hobbled over and stood next to her. Thắm placed one arm around his waist, and the other hand on Hạnh's arm. The photographer—Huy's father, Quỳ—danced around them, his camera dangling from his neck, a cheerful smile on his face. He patted Dâu's cheeks, lifted Hạnh's chin, and adjusted their posture.

'Okay, just like that! Smile! Wow, this town has so many beautiful people!' The photographer gave Hạnh a flirtatious look.

'I'll have to ask Thắm to be my matchmaker. What's your name, Miss?'

'Stop kidding around,' said Thắm with a giggle. 'She's married. Her husband is fighting in the South.'

'Oh, you poor thing! You're this gorgeous but have to sleep alone?' He placed Hạnh's hand on Dâu's shoulder and whispered, 'I'll come visit you tonight. We'll have a great . . .'

Before he could finish, Dâu jumped up and punched him in the face. She grabbed Hạnh's arm and they ran outside, leaving Huy, Thắm, and the photographer standing speechless in the middle of the studio.

At home, they went into Hạnh's bedroom. Hạnh threw herself onto the bed still feeling shocked at what had just happened.

'If I didn't love Thắm, I would've really taught him a lesson,' said Dâu.

'Calm down,' said Hạnh. 'It's Thắm's wedding day, and the couple didn't do anything wrong. It was that photographer!'

'I can't stand all his creepy talk. He made me so mad.'

'All photographers are like that.'

'I feel sorry for Thắm. How can she have a happy marriage?'

'Stop! No matter how happy we are, we should still sympathize with Thắm. There are no other young men left in the village.'

'You're in a mood today,' said Dâu with a laugh. Then quick as a snake she slipped her hand inside Hạnh's shirt and squeezed her nipple.

'Ow! What the hell are you doing?'

'Hee hee! I'll take care of you. You like it, right? Any time you want, give me a call. Don't let that pervert flirt with you . . .'

Not long after Dâu left, Hạnh's mother-in-law came home from the wedding, and the two of them sat down together to eat.

'You should've stayed at the wedding to hear what people said.'

'What did they say, Mother?'

'That you and Dâu are jealous of Thắm.'

'Ha! Well, that's not true. We left because that photographer can't control his hands.'

Several years had passed since Hạnh and Mother Khiên last received news from Nghĩa. Mother Khiên was starting to lose hope. Hạnh alternated between comforting her mother and her mother-in-law. Nhân was more resilient than Mother Khiên, who lived perpetually in fear and longed for news of her son every day. Whenever she heard any news of the war, she had to find out exactly what happened. She thought of the whole South as if it were as small as Đông Village.

'At the wedding, I heard a soldier in town just came home. Will you go see if he has any news about Nghĩa?'

'Of course, Mother,' Hạnh said to give her mother-in-law some peace of mind. Since the beginning of the year, Mother Khiên's personality had changed dramatically. She had a new *áo dài** made just to wear to go to the Buddhist temple with other elderly women in the village. Frequently at night, Hạnh would be startled awake by Mother Khiên muttering or yelling in her nightmares, which she'd tell Hạnh about in the morning. There were no stories of rabid dogs but some with rabid buffalo, stories of ghost mandarins commanding spirit troops to haunt her, and stories of disappearing ancestors' graves.

One morning, Mother Khiên met Hạnh in the kitchen and said, 'Last night, I dreamed Khiên came home to tell me Nghĩa had lost an arm. He said Nghĩa would be back on the 17th. Even if he comes back with just one arm, it'll still be lucky.' That was the 9th, and Mother Khiên calculated she had just about a week before Nghĩa would be home. That whole week, she anxiously counted down the days. Hạnh could not understand why Mother Khiên believed so adamantly in signs and dreams, but she also couldn't stop her mother-in-law's hopes from getting her own hopes up, so she found herself counting the days too. The 17th came and went, and Nghĩa did not come home, so Mother Khiên became sick and lay in bed refusing to eat. Fortunately, while she was sick, a Đông villager named Thành came back from the war. His whole body had been severely burned, and his face was swollen. Even his

* A traditional garment worn with pants by Vietnamese women, an áo dài has a long-sleeved, tight-fitting top with long panels in front and back that extend below the knee.

parents couldn't recognize him when he returned with a rucksack on his back.

Hạnh visited Thành privately and asked him to make up a story about meeting Nghĩa somewhere in the war zone to comfort Mother Khiên.

'Aunty, our Nghĩa has been promoted to major,' he told her. 'We met by chance while he was commanding an artillery unit. We hugged each other . . .'

Hạnh saw her mother-in-law's eyes brighten.

'Is he okay?' asked Mother Khiên.

'Of course! He's strong and healthy, Aunty. He's the best commander in the field.'

The whole village soon knew the story that Hạnh and Thành had made up, and wherever Hạnh went, people congratulated her. 'You should be proud! Your husband's a major now. So impressive!'

Hạnh didn't expect the whole village to respond that way, but Nghĩa's mother did get better. The neighbours came to congratulate Hạnh and her mother-in-law, and when Hạnh saw her so happy and serving special tea to everyone, she started to feel guilty and regretted making up the lie.

Later that day, Mother Khiên said to Hạnh, 'If you don't have a meeting tonight, I'll visit Uncles Xung and Xeng and his wife.'

After Mother Khiên left, Hạnh washed all the teacups and straightened the house, went to her bedroom, and lit the oil lamp. Hạnh looked up at Nghĩa's smile and gentle eyes in the framed photograph and smiled. 'Why, hello there, Major! How are you today? Even if you were just a corporal, I'd still call you major. The major of my heart! Ha ha! When you come home, I'll make clam soup with spinach for you because in a war zone there is no clam soup.'

Hạnh smiled at her daydream. She lowered the photo from the wall and wiped off the dust. Since Nghĩa left, she had tried to keep his zither and flute and books and other things exactly where he'd left them. Lamenting the fact that they never had a pillow to share, let alone a bedroom together, shortly after he had left, she made a pillow whose case she embroidered with a pair of birds and a red rose. One of the birds remained perched while the other took flight. The pillowcase had frequently been soaked with tears, and washed so many times that it was now worn, but Nghĩa had still not returned. It was white poplin, nearly a metre long, and when she washed it in the river, she did so at night because she wanted to keep it secret. She'd hang it to dry in the banana garden and pull it first thing in the morning.

She was hugging the pillow and thinking about Nghĩa when she heard her friend Cúc call out to her from the gate. Before Hạnh could get up, Cúc rushed in, fell into Hạnh's arms, and started to cry.

'I'm so unlucky!' wailed Cúc.

'What happened?'

'I just returned the betel and areca* to Thành's parents.'

'Are you crazy?' Hạnh held Cúc by the shoulders. 'Are you kidding?'

'I'm serious. I gave back ten times the amount they gave me and wrote a letter to Thành.'

'It's not about how much you paid back. Don't you see your honour's at stake?'

'I know, I know, but . . . I can't! I just can't love him.'

'You dope, it's only been three days! Why'd you take the betel and areca in the first place if you don't love him? Are you trying to kill him?'

'That's why I'm so miserable. I don't know why I said yes. When I see all those scars, I try to imagine how he used to be, but I can't. I keep having nightmares about how he looks.'

'That's terrible!'

'It *is* terrible. I'm such a horrible person.' Cúc nestled her head in Hạnh's bosom. 'I owe him and everyone an apology. I know everybody respects him and so do I. But you and others in the Women's Association talked me into marrying him, and then he proposed right away. Everything happened so fast and even though I wasn't sure I could love him, I accepted his proposal. But I should've told him I didn't love him, and that I couldn't love him. I just wasn't strong enough to say no. Now I have to bear the consequences.

* Betel leaves and areca nuts are traditional engagement gifts.

Last night he took me to the river, and in the dark I imagined his handsome face from before he went to war. I only heard his warm and charming voice. But when he came to my house this morning and I saw his face, that was it. I realized I couldn't get over it. If only I were blind and could just listen to him speak . . .'

Cúc lay her head on Hạnh's shoulder and sobbed. The dark night felt utterly wretched in the depths of Hạnh's heart. The sound of Mrs Khiên's clogs on the bricks came from the courtyard.

*

Towers of dark clouds loomed in a grey sky. The wind kicked up thick layers of dust that settled onto the hot earth, the rooftops, and the trees. Farmers working in the fields took fright looking up at the sky, worrying about the rice plants already in the ground. The gusting wind blew down dry tree branches and sent eucalyptus leaves into the irrigation ditches, fluttering like unstable birds. A few raindrops fell on Hạnh's shirt. People called to one another it was time to go home.

'A big storm's coming!'

Hạnh ran to her mother's house and found Uncle Vạn already up on the roof securing the thatch with ropes.

'You'd better go back to Mother Khiên's house,' her mother shouted. 'She needs your help.' Nhân threw a rope up to the roof for Uncle Vạn to catch.

Hạnh grabbed a hoe and ran. The wind roared in her ears. Plumes of dirt rose everywhere from the roads and lanes. Village children raced all over, picking up fallen lychees and other fruit. When she got to her mother-in-law's home, Mother Khiên was inside tying the kitchen door shut with twine.

Hạnh asked her, 'Mother, how can we use the kitchen if you tie the door shut like that?'

'It'll be a huge storm. I've already moved all the pots and pans into the living room. Go ahead and get some rice started. We need to be ready in case it floods.'

Mother Khiên filled the door cracks with straw from the back of the lineage temple. While they ate, the storm finally blew in, rattling the house with blasts of wind. Outside, tree branches creaked and cracked. The sky turned black. When a gust of wind blew out the oil lamp, Mother Khiên struggled to light it again several times without success. Hạnh groped her way to her bedroom. Rain came in under the doors and through the windows and splashed her face. Hạnh hung a poncho to keep rain from blowing in through the window and went to bed. The sea was roaring from afar. Human life truly seemed so frail in comparison to the forces of nature. At times like this, thought Hạnh, it would be better to have a man in the house.

She was also worried about her own mother. She wondered whether Uncle Vạn had stayed to help her, and that made her again want to find out if they still had feelings for each other. Uncle Vạn's eccentric personality and her mother's demure, traditional way of life kept them even from sharing their feelings, let alone acting on them. It was still always 'sister, sister this' and 'uncle, uncle that' with those two. Most people assumed they'd eventually move in together, but one, two, then more than ten years had passed, and they were still not together. They were like two shadows cast side by side, always close and yet always apart.

The storm grew even stronger. Somewhere, a gong began to ring repeatedly, so Hạnh sat up in bed and then heard Uncle Vạn shouting something from the lane. She took the rain poncho from the window and went to Mother Khiên's bedroom and told her, 'Stay here. I'll go see what's going on.'

'Put on warm clothes,' said Mother Khiên. 'That rain is freezing cold.'

Hạnh struggled to push open the door. A cold blast of wind and rain swept into the house and stung her face. Uncle Vạn's unsteady silhouette was barely visible, his voice drowned out by the gale. 'Attention! Attention! The dike is failing! Everyone except elderly women and children must gather at the co-op courtyard.'

He scrabbled onto old man Thiêng's porch and banged on the door. He ducked under a hedge and went to the Phús' house next.

When Hạnh passed the photo studio, she saw Thắm arguing with her husband at the front door. Thắm saw her and called,

'Hạnh! Huy doesn't want me to go. He said he'd pay a fine instead. I laughed at him and said, "If everyone paid, who'd save the dike?" At times like this, a basket of money is worth less than a basket of dirt, right?'

'Exactly! Plugging the dike, dousing a fire, and fighting the enemy are all top priority!'

Hạnh and Thắm locked arms as the wind blew them down the road toward the co-op storehouse. Broken branches lay scattered everywhere, and fallen leaves flew through the air all around them.

Inside the storehouse, torches had been lit, and the place was filled with people. Dâu shouted, 'Three cheers for brother Ngốc and sister Lùn for helping save the dike.'

Mr Đột laughed and waved a torch in front of Ngốc's face.

'Bang the gong!' Uncle Xeng shouted. 'Tao and Bống aren't here yet. Damn it! Don't they know the water's rising?'

'The flood mitigation committee should slaughter a pig to feed us all,' said Uncle Nhị. 'If the dike breaks, not even a dog will survive.'

'Let's go!' bellowed Uncle Vạn. 'We'll lose face if Đông villagers are the only ones late.'

Everyone carried hoes, spades, and bamboo baskets and hurried toward the Linh Canal. The surrounding rice paddies had flooded into a heaving black sea. The river roared like a kettle full of boiling water. From all around came the sounds of gongs, drums, and gunfire.

'Hey, Thành!' shouted Dâu above the wind. 'The women of Đông Village are really brave, aren't they? There aren't as many women on the battlefield in the South as there are here, right?'

'Southern women are still braver than you ladies,' teased Thành.

Dâu giggled along. 'When you were down there, did you conquer any women's hearts?'

'When you're fighting a war, there's no time for fooling around,' said Thành. 'Seriously! There were times when young men and women had to sleep in the same room and nothing happened.' Thành took Dâu's hand and teased, 'Before Hiệp left, did you let him get a taste of what to come home for?'

Dâu playfully thumped Thành's back and then ran to Cúc, saying, 'Hey, Cúc! I'm telling you, girl, you're an idiot if you don't think Thành's good enough for you. A guy like him's worth ten of Huy.'

Dâu's candour left both Cúc and Thắm speechless. Hạnh pinched Dâu's arm and Dâu started to change the topic. But then a powerful squall blew Hạnh, Dâu, Cúc, and Thắm into a heap, tearing at their bodies as if it would rip the clothes from their backs.

The villagers groped their way along the riverbank. At the big bend, Hạnh recognized the flat grassy spot where she had spent her honeymoon with Nghĩa, and where they had said goodbye. Memories rushed into her mind as if blown by the storm. At the Linh Canal return, the villagers held each other by the shirt and in a line crawled up the dike. On the river and in the canal, waves rose and fell and roared, splashing water everywhere. Lights bobbed all along the dike, sometimes flashing chaotically as people slipped in the mud. Hạnh followed the other villagers to a covered canal overlook where they could rest a moment, all of them just specks of dust amid the immense power of the wind. Waves pounded the canal diversion and shook the dike. Many of the people packed into the overlook were soldiers from the anti-aircraft unit helping to secure the canal from the storm.

'Everyone, listen up!' yelled Uncle Vạn. 'The flood mitigation team says the river will continue to rise. From now till morning, we and the soldiers will move all the rocks and dirt we can to shore up the dike.'

Uncle Vạn's words were nearly drowned by the roaring of the waves. All the strong, young men went to the canal return. On the dike, people lined up, passing baskets of dirt and rocks up and over the side to be swallowed immediately by the violent waves. Waves crashed relentlessly up and down. Soon everyone was exhausted. Hạnh felt pain in her arms and legs. By morning, several tons of rocks and dirt had been moved, and people were sprawled everywhere inside the covered overlook, their arms and legs trembling. In the dim light, Hạnh made out Dâu and Cúc sitting together in a corner.

'Let's get some sleep,' joked Đột. 'No flashlights, and no touching!'

'That hot air's got to be coming from Đột,' someone replied. 'Show some respect.'

No one had the energy for jokes. The storm continued to rage. Hạnh squatted near Thắm, her head resting on her knees. Within minutes, the overlook went quiet, with people leaning against one another and falling asleep.

'Are you tired?' one of the soldiers whispered to Thắm, who whispered something back. Hạnh smiled and fell asleep amid the sounds of roaring waves and whispers. When she woke, it was dawn, and Hạnh felt a little shocked to see the soldier asleep in Thắm's arms, his youthful face resting on her round, full breasts. Hạnh tapped Thắm's wrist. She woke and gave Hạnh an embarrassed look.

The wind continued to howl but the morning sky came bright. The river had crested at some point during the night and was now slowly going down. Still, the sky looked ominous. Waves endlessly pounded the dike, and choppy whitecaps filled both the river and the flooded paddies inside. In the distance, Dông Village could barely be seen behind a haze of rain. The mango tree in front of the communal house stood firm, an umbrella in the storm.

Chapter 15

Perhaps in the whole world, there are no other countries that have rolls of hay quite like those in Đông Village. About as wide as a flat bamboo tray and just as tall, they can be tied to the back seat of a bicycle. During a famine, even cows and buffalo have to be willing to share. Thirty workers from Đông Village volunteered to transport hay to Hải Hưng Province to feed the livestock starving because of the flood. The workers gathered in the co-op storehouse courtyard and were just about to depart when the photographer Huy hobbled in and grabbed Thắm by the shirt.

'Go home!' he hissed. And to the workers he said, 'I hired two people to do this job for her, but she insists on going. Go home, slut, and fuck yourself.'

Thắm blushed and tried to escape from Huy's grasp. Though he had a lame leg, he was still a strong man. He grabbed her arm and tugged, trying to drag her home.

'Let go and I'll come home,' said Thắm, forcing a smile. 'People are laughing at us.'

As soon as Huy let go, Thắm ran to a bicycle near the gate that had already been loaded with hay and hopped on. She stood on the pedals and rode swiftly out to the village road. Many of the workers in the courtyard laughed and mounted their bikes to pedal after her.

Huy stood there, speechless and seething. Then he hobbled over to block Hạnh's path and said, 'Listen, you, this is all your fault. You talked her into this. When she comes back, she's going to be sorry.' After venting his anger on Hạnh, he limped away toward home. Hạnh got on her bike and pedalled hard to catch up with the transport team. Thắm had stopped on the dike to wait for her. She grinned as Hạnh approached.

'Did I do the right thing?' she asked.

'When you get home, he'll tear your bones apart.'

'He wouldn't dare! After the night fighting the storm, someone told him I hugged the anti-aircraft gunner. Since then, he's been insanely jealous.'

'He's got a pretty good reason to feel that way! If I hadn't woke you, it could've been worse. People are saying the girl has a husband but acts like she doesn't care.'

'I told that soldier I'm married, but he didn't believe me.'

'Who would believe you? Look at your beautiful young face! And you flirted with him so much! Any man would fall for you.'

'I think that night was a once in a lifetime thing—meeting such a nice, handsome guy in such a crazy situation—so I gave him a friendly smile. He told me his unit's preparing to go South. Sunday morning, he's going to come to our village.'

'Really? That's a terrible idea! You're a married woman.'

'But I really haven't done anything wrong. I'll introduce you to him. His name's Thấu, and he's really nice.'

At the anti-aircraft battery, Thắm jumped off her bike and scanned the gun installations hidden beneath the banana trees that had been thrashed by the storm.

'Hey, Thấu!' Thắm called loudly. 'Are you in there?'

'You're acting like you know him pretty well.'

'I just want to tell him not to come to the village on Sunday.'

After a moment, Thấu climbed out of the bunker and stood in front of Thắm looking puzzled.

'Don't you recognize me? From the other night, during the storm . . .'

'Oh, Thắm! You look different today.'

'This is Hạnh. Her husband's in an artillery unit too.'

'Would you two like to come inside the bunker and see the battery?'

'We can't,' said Thắm. 'We've got to keep going. I came to tell you not to come to Đông Village on Sunday because we won't be there. We'll be gone several days.'

Thắm got on her bike and winked at Hạnh before pedalling away.

'Bye-bye, Thấu,' Hạnh said, standing on the pedals to follow Thắm. 'Nice to meet you.'

'Hey, Thắm!' shouted the young soldier. 'Drop by here when you get back. I want to tell you something.'

Thắm kept pedalling but was also giggling as Hạnh caught up. Hạnh asked, 'What's so funny?'

'Seeing him makes me smile,' said Thắm. 'And guess what? That night, I told him he could touch me wherever he wanted.'

'You didn't!'

'I did! But I don't know why. Everyone was snoring, and you dozed off. Only he and I were still awake, so we chatted. When he told me he'd go South soon, I thought we'd never meet again because none of our village men have gone South and come back, except for Thành, and look what happened to him. So, I took Thấu's hands and placed them on my breasts. I heard his heart beating like crazy, and felt his hands tremble, and I knew he'd never slept with a woman or been in love. Afterward, I wondered if he looked down on me for that, but now, I don't think so.'

It didn't take Hạnh and Thắm long to make it to Route 10, which was paved and passed through several shady casuarina groves. Here and there, a few trees had uprooted and fallen down during the storm, exposing their thick roots. Hạnh enjoyed riding through the shade but kept thinking about Thắm's situation.

At noon, the hay-transport team stopped at Đông Quan to rest and eat lunch. Thành urged everyone to eat quickly so they could catch the Triều ferry before it got dark. Hạnh strolled around the little groups of people eating balls of sticky rice. Ngốc had the best food—a ball of sticky rice like the others, but also a boiled chicken leg.

Dâu called out, 'Hey, Ngốc, want to share your food with me?'

'No way!' he said. 'I'll only share with Cúc.' He grinned at Cúc, who was sitting with some of the older men. After she returned Thành's engagement gifts, Cúc had changed a lot. Most of the villagers did not approve of her decision. Cúc's Aunt Nhị had told her, 'You're a fool. If you do this to Thành, you'll be single forever. No one will dare propose to you again. Don't even think a guy from another village will come for you. Even if you're as beautiful as a fairy, a guy like Ngốc will be your only option.'

Somehow, what Aunt Nhị had said reached Ngốc's ears, so whenever Ngốc ran into Cúc, he'd grin and say, 'Hey, Cúc, tell me when you're ready for me.'

Hạnh felt sorry for Cúc, who now lived like a quiet shadow, not daring to talk or laugh freely in public like before.

Dâu called out to her, 'Cúc *ơi*, come sit over here with me.'

Hạnh watched Thành lower his head and chew his food quietly. After a while, he said to the whole group, 'After we take the ferry, I'll take us to a house where we can rest.'

Dâu asked, 'Do you have a girlfriend there?'

'You've got it all wrong,' said Thành. 'When I was stationed there seven or eight years ago, an old couple kind of "adopted" me. Their youngest son was about sixteen then. I haven't been back since.'

By the time the team of hay carriers reached the Triệu ferry, the sun had already sunk down into the top of the nearby bamboo grove. The ferryman clanged his bell as he transported the hay carriers across the silty Luộc River to Hưng Yên. The lychee trees here all looked like they'd been severely battered by the storm. Many houses had been damaged and the farmers returning home from the paddies looked exhausted. Even the road was in poor condition, with potholes everywhere. Hạnh, Dâu, Thắm, Cúc, and Ngốc followed Thành off the road onto a trail, while the rest of the carriers waited. They came to a house whose roof was half thatch, half tile, with several new wattles of thatch having been recently installed. Thành led the team into the front yard. He called out, 'Father? Are you home?'

A woman about sixty years old tottered out and peered at Thành.

'Mother, we're bringing hay from Thái Bình to help feed livestock after the flood,' said Thành. 'May we spend the night here? We have a few more carriers out by the road. Where's Father?'

'Who are you talking about?' the old woman replied. 'My husband died years ago.'

'Oh, really?' said Thành. 'I'm very sorry to hear that.'

'Did you know my husband?'

'Mother, it's me, Thành. I was stationed here several years ago.'

'Don't lie to me. I'm old but not senile. I know the Thành who used to live here with us.'

Thành was moved. 'Mother, I was badly burned.'

'You were?' The old woman still seemed sceptical. Even so, she invited everyone inside, went to the kitchen, and came back with a large kettle of *vối* water* that she poured out into each guest's cup. Then she looked closely at Thành's face.

'Maybe my daughter Loan will recognize you,' she said, 'but I doubt it.'

'Where is Loan?'

'She's working now and will be home soon. Her husband died last year. Now she says she wants to live with me for the rest of her life without marrying again. My youngest son, Thăng, has been a soldier for a few years, but I haven't gotten any news from him. I wish he'd come home.'

Hạnh felt a lump in her throat as she drank the vối water. All the mothers in this country had the same feelings, just like her own mother and mother-in-law.

After a little while, Loan entered the yard, carrying a hoe. She looked about Hạnh's age and her pant legs were rolled up above her knees for working in the paddies. Seeing guests inside, she quickly rolled her pant legs down and greeted them.

'Loan, do you recognize this guy?' The old woman pointed at Thành. Loan stood silently. Her face flushed and then went pale. 'He says he's Thành,' the old woman said, 'who was stationed here before and who you often talk about.'

She shook his hand and held it. 'Are you really Brother Thành?'

'No, no, that's not me,' Thành said with a smile. 'I'm the person who fixed your flat tire and sandals so you could go visit your husband, who was stationed in Sao Đỏ. I'm the person who helped you set up the party to celebrate the friendship between

---

* *Nước vối* is a tea-like drink brewed with dried leaves of robusta, which is a flowering plant in the peach family.

our unit and your village youth association. Do you remember Tạo, who gave you the award for best farmer? He's been promoted to secretary of the union. And I have the Americans to thank for making my face so beautiful like this.'

Loan patted Thành's hand as he spoke. The old woman quickly ground some betel and areca with a mortar and pestle. Cúc's eyes turned red and she ran outside to the yard. Thắm looked at Dâu with teary eyes, and Dâu squeezed Hạnh's hand. As usual, Ngốc just giggled and grinned at everyone.

'Oh, Thành,' said the old woman, finally convinced. 'It's good you've come back. I bet we all need to eat. Loan will make some rice, but I'm sorry there are no vegetables because of the flood.'

'Don't worry, Ma'am,' said Dâu. 'We brought morning glory greens with us from Thái Bình. If grass couldn't survive the flood up here, how could vegetables?'

Ngốc ran back to the road and led the others to the house. He handed Loan's mother a bag, saying, 'Here's half a boiled chicken. My father said when I get married, he'll slaughter a pig.'

'You must come from a wealthy family,' she said.

'We used to be the poorest family in the village,' said Ngốc. 'We've been collecting buffalo dung for three generations.'

When dinner was ready, everyone ate together out in the yard. The moon shone brightly above the lychee trees. Frogs croaked from a nearby pond. Loan and Hạnh scooped rice into everyone's bowl. Hạnh suddenly thought about Nghĩa, feeling woefully certain he'd never come back.

'How many people who used to be stationed here have come home?' the old woman asked Thành.

'Just me, because I've been injured and can't do anything.'

'Were any promoted?'

'Not that I know of. Do you still remember Quách, who read a long poem at the dinner before we shipped out?'

'I remember him,' said Loan. 'The poem had a line like, "The battlefield urges us to march heroically."'

'Ironically, he was the first to desert.'

'Are you kidding?'

'It's the truth. He deserted before he even got to the war zone, but then he joined the *văn công* and now he's a professional poet writing about the war as if he'd actually been there. Soldiers fight with guns and bombs while Quách uses a pen as a weapon to write revolutionary poetry. My company originally had ninety soldiers, and two years later, only twenty are left. Some got killed by bombs, some by malaria, some drowned in the river, and some starved to death. A few even got killed by a falling tree.'

'Careful what you say,' said Dâu, 'or the local militia will arrest you.'

'Don't worry,' said the old woman. 'Loan is a member of the militia. I often tell her, if you're a coward, you'll be a coward wherever you go. If you're a hero, you'll go to war even if you know you're going to die. From this village, Loan's husband and many others died, but the younger generation, like my youngest son, is still not afraid.'

Loan let Thành and Ngốc sleep in her bed and joined the other women sleeping on mats on the veranda. The others strung hammocks between the trees along the path.

Before going to bed, the old woman said, 'Loan, I want you to carry the hay for Thành tomorrow. Let him rest and stay here with me for the day.'

Hạnh lay next to Sister Loan. Dâu and Thắm whispered to one another, giggling.

'When Thành lived here,' said Loan, 'my brother and cousins really looked up to him. You all should try to find him a wife. He's such a good human being.'

Cúc turned away and then suddenly leapt up and ran out to the yard.

'Where's she going?' asked Loan.

Hạnh said quickly, 'I think she needs to pee.'

After a long while, Cúc still hadn't come back, so Hạnh excused herself and walked out to the garden, where she found Cúc sitting under a lychee tree, sobbing.

'We're guests here, so behave,' Hạnh said. 'Go back to the porch and sleep.'

Cúc wiped her tears and sighed. 'I'm so miserable,' she murmured, and then followed Hạnh back to the veranda.

'The moon really is beautiful tonight,' Hạnh said loudly as they joined the others. She pulled Cúc down to the mat next to hers. The moon had risen high above the lychee trees and filled the courtyard with silver light. This hamlet felt very much like Đông Village to Hạnh. The night was so peaceful, the only sounds Loan's uneven breaths and Cúc's deep sighs.

Chapter 16

Lately, the Nguyễn lineage temple always smelled of fresh flowers and burning incense, thanks to Aunt Xeng who had begun to pray there several times a day. She looked perpetually miserable, her eyes either gloomy or terrified. If she ran into Hạnh or Mother Khiên, she'd give them a little nod and then hurry silently away.

'What's going on with Aunt Xeng?' Hạnh asked her mother-in-law.

'She's repenting.'

Hạnh knew Aunt Xeng was worried about her own family. Not long after great Uncle Xung finally recovered from his madness, her oldest son fell into a lime pit and suffered chemical burns from head to toe. They had to rush him to the emergency room at the district hospital. At the same time, her husband became ill with a strange mental illness. He became terrified of other people and would lie in bed, not speaking or eating, just glaring at the ceiling. If he heard someone approach, he'd shake with fear and turn his face to the wall. Then came a few nights when people walking home from production team meetings had to run as they passed Uncle Xeng's house because they were attacked in the dark with flung rocks and dirt. Some people blamed Uncle Xung, but he denied it. 'Screw you,' he said when confronted. 'I'm not crazy any more. And I'm too old for such childishness.'

Then, the same night someone chopped down all the trees in Mrs Kha's banana orchard, the new water cistern at Mrs Ngôn's house was smashed into a pile of cement and bricks. The next morning, Mrs Kha stood in the middle of her ruined orchard shouting, 'To hell with the bastard who did this! I've lived an upright life. Who would do this to me?' Mrs Ngôn heard the commotion and ran out, saw the ruined cistern, and said, 'I know who did it. All three generations of their family should be cursed for what they've done. The whole family's nuts.' Mrs Ngôn didn't name anyone, but everyone in the village knew she meant Xung's family. Everyone knew but no one had the heart to say anything else. Mostly people just felt bad for Aunt Xeng.

One night, after Hạnh and Mother Khiên finished dinner, Aunt Xeng came into the lineage temple carrying a large tray of fruit on her head.

'Today's the first of the lunar month,' Aunt Xeng said. 'This is for our ancestors.' Then she placed the tray on the altar. She lit and placed several sheaves of incense and then prayed in a quiet voice. Hearing her prayer, Hạnh realized she was praying to Father Khiên, and that Aunt Xeng apparently believed that his sudden death had made him a sacred spirit and a powerful mandarin in the afterlife who could determine the fate of the whole Nguyễn clan.

Aunt Xeng was still murmuring her prayers when Dâu suddenly came into the house with Thắm and pulled her into Hạnh's bedroom. Thắm threw herself onto the bed and sobbed.

'Stop crying!' Dâu said to Thắm. 'And stop being such a baby. Happiness and sorrow go hand in hand. Just give birth to your child, and if your lame-footed husband refuses to say he's the father, I'll do it. I'd love to be pregnant but can't.' Dâu laughed out loud. Then she said to Hạnh, 'You think I could become a man? Everyone says I look like one anyway. If Hiệp doesn't come back, I guess that's what I'll do.' Dâu flexed her arms and legs and then hugged Thắm brusquely. 'If anyone asks whose baby it is, tell them it's mine. Ha ha ha! It's Mr Dâu's baby! I mean, I have slept with you at least three times beneath the banana tree. Hee hee!'

The more Dâu tried to joke, the louder Thắm cried. Dâu pulled Hạnh outside and said, 'Can you let her spend the night with you here? Poor thing! She's still young and will have to live with this the rest of her life. I tried to talk her parents into letting her move back home, but they were angry and told her to go back to her husband. Thắm said she never wanted to see him again. We have to watch out for her. She's so upset, I'm worried she might try to drown herself in the river.'

Mother Khiên and Aunt Xeng came out of the lineage temple together and heard Thắm crying. They peeked in from the doorway and Mother Khiên said, 'Go to the altar and pray to our ancestors. They can ease your pain.'

'That's true,' said Aunt Xeng. 'May our ancestors bless you and give you peace of mind.'

Mother Khiên and Aunt Xeng left and Hạnh lay down next to Thắm and pulled up the blanket. The autumn night was chilly. In the bed next to Thắm, Hạnh still felt lonely. Tomorrow, Ngốc would marry Lùn, the dwarf, a couple Hạnh found quite cute and happy. Thắm had stopped crying but was still awake.

Hạnh asked, 'Did you sleep with that soldier?'

'I can't hide anything from you,' said Thắm. 'When I came back from the hay-carrying trip, that bastard Huy beat the hell out of me. I couldn't return to my parents' house because they'd just blame me for the beating, so I wandered along the riverbank out to Linh Canal. I felt like ending it all, just jumping into the current and never coming back, but then I thought about him—Thấu—so I visited him at the anti-aircraft battery and that's how everything happened.'

'You cheated on your husband!'

'That bastard doesn't deserve to be my husband.'

'Have you told your parents about the soldier?'

'They'd kill me if they knew.'

Hạnh sighed. 'All right. Get some sleep. We'll find a way to tell them about it later.'

She hugged Thắm and gently placed her hand on her warm belly. Hạnh wished she and Nghĩa had a baby.

The next morning came clear and sunny and beautiful. Thắm stood on tiptoe, trying to reach into the cistern to scoop up water to wash her face.

'Let me help you,' Hạnh said, pouring water into a basin for her. Thắm sat, cupped water in her hands, and washed her face.

'I'll get you a washcloth,' said Hạnh.

'No need.' Thắm blew her nose, smiled, and tilted her head to look at Hạnh. 'I have to get used to my new life. Nobody knows what the future holds. After I got married, I had everything

I needed. He'd scrub my back and kiss my neck. I thought I'd married the right guy and would be happy forever. He kept telling me, "You're my mermaid, my nightingale." Then I caught him with his girlfriend at the district studio. I actually heard him say the exact same words to her.' Thắm blushed, stood up, and rubbed her belly. 'Fortunately, this baby is not his.'

Mother Khiên sat at the breakfast table waiting for Hạnh and Thắm. She was very concerned about Thắm's pregnancy. She asked, 'Have you bought anything for the baby?'

'Not yet,' Thắm replied. 'But I don't care.'

'That won't do at all,' said Mother Khiên with a sigh. 'With your first child, you have to prepare. It'll be hard on you if you don't. It worries me you're so young and reckless.'

*

Hạnh had always been afraid of the part of the river where people went to bathe. As an adult, she was no longer scared of the river monster or the red-eyed ghost in the cemetery. She feared the temptation of No Man River.

Hạnh carried a hoe and stepped down into the new vegetable patch by the riverbank. She chopped and turned the soil until it became soft. Downriver, the buffalo boys and girls were calling to one another that it was time to go home. She wished Nghĩa would write her a letter like the one Thắm had received from the anti-aircraft gunner that said he had arrived in the South and missed her. She had held onto that letter all through the pregnancy and birth of her son, Linh, and would read it any time she felt overwhelmed. Just a few words from Nghĩa, like *I'm still alive*, would make Hạnh feel so happy. It had been eight long years since she had last seen him, and she realized that she felt stuck just living with memories alone and still waiting for the future to come. Her hopes were turning into hopelessness.

After turning the soil over and over until it was loose and fine, Hạnh cut a bunch of sweet-potato slips and planted them. The sun had gone down, leaving a stripe of red just above the horizon, and then the moon came up and lit the banks of the vast river.

Hạnh waded into the water to wash her feet and to take in the shimmering reflection of the moon, and for a moment it seemed she was lost in a world of fairy tales. Fleeting feelings of sorrow, loneliness, and regret rippled through her. She recalled her youth and the many moments of passion with Nghĩa, and desire seized her so strongly she felt her mind might burst. She plunged forward. She swam, kicked her legs, and stroked with her arms as if making love to the water, letting the current caress every part of her body. It felt so good. But then the current began to tug her down, and suddenly she feared she might drown, as if it weren't the current at all but the river monster who held her there. Terrified, she swam harder, struggling to reach the sandy shore weighted as she was by her wet clothes. She dragged herself up the riverbank.

Staggering to the spot where she had said farewell to Nghĩa, she removed her wet clothes and then lay naked on the grass. In the dark blue sky, thousands of stars glittered around the lonely moon. She drifted off to sleep gazing up at the heavens and shuddered in her dream when the moon seemed to grow big and red like the face of the ghost in the cemetery known for bewitching widows. She froze with a desperate fear as the ghost's face came close to her own. The ghost stuck out a long red tongue and licked her from head to toe and back again, as if this was how it would make love to her.

When Hạnh woke, the sun was already pouring its early morning light on the fields and river. She panicked when she realized she was still lying naked on the grass, so she dressed hastily and then ran back to the village. At the Silver Stone Bridge, she saw Ngốc with two baskets hanging from his shoulder yoke. He had already been out collecting buffalo dung and seemed surprised to see her wearing wet clothes so early in the day. Hạnh hurried past him and on to her mother's house, changed into dry things, and collapsed on the bed.

'What's wrong with you?' asked her mother. She lay a hand on Hạnh's brow. 'Heavens! Where've you been? You have such a fever!'

Her mother placed some medicinal leaves on Hạnh's forehead. Delirious with a high temperature, Hạnh announced she'd been raped by the red-eyed ghost.

Later, Mother Khiên said Hạnh had been possessed by an evil spirit, but Nhân said she thought she might have typhoid.

Uncle Vạn reprimanded Mother Khiên. 'Your praying all day to this or that spirit and all your other superstitions are a bad influence. Aunt Xeng too. Keep this up and I might have to drag you both to the commune office.' But privately he believed Hạnh missed Nghĩa so much that she had become lovesick. It was a common psychological problem for women during war.

*

Nguyễn Vạn's rooster often mounted Widow Hơn's hen.

After her son joined the army, Hơn tried repeatedly to seduce Vạn, but he knew what she was up to and kept his distance. To tease him, she set up a bamboo bed on the porch and lay on it during hot nights. She rolled her pants high up on her thighs to show off her ivory legs. He thought she seemed a lot like her female cat, which would climb up to the roof when it was in heat and yowl to be mated all night. Each time she heard its cries, she'd pretend it annoyed her and bang on Vạn's door, saying, 'Please get a stick and chase her away. That yowling is unbearable.'

She'd done this late one night and Vạn got up and looked at her through a crack in the door and saw that she had come over wearing only a thin, nearly transparent nightgown. If he opened the door, she'd swallow him alive. The next morning, as soon as Vạn opened his chicken coop, his rooster raced over to Hơn's hen, flapped its wings, strutted around, and then mounted it. The hen spread its wings and squatted with its tail feathers tilted high. It also reminded him of Hơn.

Watching the mating scene, Hơn called out, 'Oh, Vạn, look! Your rooster is "ruining" my hen.' Then she giggled and covered her mouth with her hand.

'I think it's the other way around,' Vạn replied. 'So naughty!'

'Don't be grumpy. I'm just teasing,' Hơn said in a sweet voice. 'We're next-door neighbours and see each other every day. We should have some fun! Even chickens know how to enjoy life.'

'No one's stopping you from having fun,' Vạn said angrily. 'Go ahead and find some fun for yourself.'

'Oh, nonsense! I mean us. You and I are like the sun and the moon, never together. You must know, at my age, not even a ghost would make love to me. There are too many virgin girls in the village who are not yet married.' Then she threw a handful of rice into the courtyard, and all the chickens, both hers and Vạn's, flocked together to peck at it. Hơn said, 'See, we share a courtyard, but the chickens don't divide it into your side and my side.' She smiled coyly at Vạn. 'What I'm really asking is, don't you ever feel lonely?'

'Such nonsense!'

'Normally, I don't feel lonely,' said Hơn, 'but when I see the Lang family doing so well, I feel a little sorry for myself. They've had a new baby every year. And every afternoon, when the parents line up all the kids at the river to bathe, I'm so jealous. I have only one person in my family now, Tốn, and he's gone to fight in the war.'

'It's good that he's a soldier. Aren't you proud of him?'

'I'm not complaining. I gave him lots of encouragement when he left. Looking at the war situation, do you think we're near the end? I hope when peace comes, Tốn will come home and date Mrs Đào's daughter, Hòa.'

Vạn was not pleased with Hơn's individualistic thinking. But she was the mother of a revolutionary soldier, so she needed some forbearance, and some education. He said, 'Sister Hơn, if you want Tốn to become a better person, you have to stop thinking so individualistically.'

Hơn smiled. 'Like you and me and the chickens in our yard?' She giggled. 'No really, I'm listening. A moral person will be blessed. Just like with Mr Khiên. He lived an upright life and after he died, he became a mandarin in the afterlife.'

'You're just as superstitious as everyone else!'

'You don't believe it's true? If Mr Khiên isn't a sacred spirit, then why did Mr Xung confess that he burned the lineage temple, and why did his son Xeng confess that he stole Mr Khiên's savings from under the oil lamp on the altar?'

'What?' Vạn grabbed Hơn's hand. 'Did Xung really admit he burned the lineage temple?'

'Go ask him if you don't believe me,' said Hơn, stroking Vạn's forearm until he let go and snatched his hand away. 'There are so many weirdos in the Nguyễn clan!'

Vạn hobbled to Uncle Xung's house. When he entered the yard, Xung was cutting bamboo into strips to weave into baskets, and Xeng was bent over a basket he was weaving next to a huge broken stone mortar.

'What are you doing here?' said Uncle Xung derisively. 'I thought you'd never come back to my house.'

'I have no choice. I came to ask you who set fire to the lineage temple.'

Uncle Xung glared at Vạn and tossed the blade he'd been using down to the ground.

'You're a nobody in the Nguyễn family. You have no right to interrogate me.'

'I'm the captain of the commune militia,' said Vạn.

'So you come as an official, not as a Nguyễn, I see. Well, I did it! I burned the temple. So what? I haven't admitted I'm guilty to the authorities but I confessed to Khiên's spirit.'

'Why?' asked Vạn. 'Why would you burn our family's temple?'

'Why?! You have to ask?' Uncle Xung threw down the bamboo. 'Because back then everything had completely gone to shit. I wanted to destroy the whole world, not just the temple. I hated the person who arrested me and locked me up. I hated the person who shot my sons, Xèng and Xình. I am not guilty. I was just a simple pig dealer. My sons Xèng and Xình only caught a few fish in the river and then were accused of blowing up Linh Canal. Only a fool would destroy the canal.' Then Uncle Xung cried.

Vạn turned to Uncle Xeng. 'Did you steal Khiên's money from under the oil lamp?'

'I did. I found it while cleaning the altar.' Uncle Xeng pulled Vạn inside the house. 'I beg you to leave my father alone. Let him enjoy the last few years of his life. He has confessed and been forgiven. Our ancestor has cured his madness, so please don't bring this up again. If you want to arrest someone, arrest me instead. But how many years must my family live in misery? My father lost his mind, my son fell into a lime pit and almost killed himself accidentally, and I've been punished by Uncle Khiên. When my son was in danger, Uncle Khiên appeared in my dreams and told me, 'You are a thief. If you don't confess, your son will die.' I was frightened and told my wife to take offerings to the lineage temple and to pray for forgiveness. My son was saved, and now I have peace of mind.'

'You're talking nonsense.'

'I'm telling the truth! Please forgive me.'

Vạn dusted off his pants and left for Aunt Khiên's house, but no one was there. He went to Nhân's place and found both women sitting by Hạnh's bed. She was pale and her eyes were unfocused.

'Let her rest alone for a minute,' Vạn said, leading them out to the kitchen, where he confronted the two women. 'You've been hiding things from me!'

'What things?'

'Is it true Uncle Xung set fire to the lineage temple and Xeng stole the money?'

'I don't know for sure,' Aunt Khiên replied. 'One night, Uncle Xung came into the lineage temple, lit incense, knelt, and then repeatedly muttered something like, "I'm guilty. I burned the lineage temple. I'm guilty." At first, I thought he was still crazy so I didn't take him seriously. But then, after that night, his madness was cured. It was so strange! Then Xeng's oldest son fell into the lime pit, and Xeng himself went crazy like his father. Not long after that, Xeng's wife placed a tray full of offerings on the ancestors' altar. She handed me some money and begged me to accept it, explaining that Xeng had been the one who'd stolen the money from under the lamp. I started to refuse to accept the money, but she insisted. She told me if I didn't take it, she'd have to burn it as an offering to my husband.'

Vạn refused to believe in anything supernatural. After Aunt Khiên went home, he told Nhân, 'Don't believe any of that nonsense. Hạnh is not possessed by any spirit. She's just lovesick. She misses Nghĩa.'

Vạn looked around the house to avoid Nhân's sad eyes. Since the day he'd given her the fish, he'd been feeling uneasy, as if he'd done something wrong. Fortunately, nothing had happened between him and Nhân. If society were to move forward, people had to learn to put their irrational fears and desires behind. If that meant Vạn had to be as chaste as all the virgin girls, so be it. And while Nhân seemed to him like forbidden fruit, Widow Hơn was more like a seductive flower with a deadly poisonous scent. To set a good example for the rest of the village, Vạn could not allow himself to fail. During war, women had to be so strong to live apart from their husbands for so long, and if he couldn't be just as strong, all the horny old men left in the village would cause a lot of trouble.

In the lane on the way back from Nhân's house, Vạn kept telling himself these same things. He stood for a moment on the Silver Stone Bridge and unbuttoned his shirt to feel the breeze coming in from the river. If every Đông villager acted as he did, with just the tiniest bit of proper restraint, there'd be no trouble. He felt angry about what old man Xung had done and how Aunt Khiên handled it, but Nhân knew too? And even Hạnh? That was really hard. He figured he'd lived half of his life so far and never put his own needs above others'. When he passed Commune Chairman Thới's yard, he heard people talking and laughing loudly amid the sounds of hammers and saws. Chairman Thới was building a new house. Vạn limped into the yard and stood there confidently, hands behind his back, watching the construction. But, of course, seeing Nguyễn Vạn, everyone stopped what they were doing to see what he wanted, and then quickly invited him to sit down and have tea. Thới climbed down from the roof and held Vạn's wrist.

'Please have some tea,' said Chairman Thới.

'No, thank you,' said Vạn, his eyes turning red. 'You should not be chairman of the commune. Our countrymen are off boiling in the hot water of war, and here you are building a new house for yourself. That's very selfish!'

Vạn finished his tirade and limped out of the yard. Goddamn it! If people didn't care about fighting the enemy, they wouldn't have even a bale of straw to sleep on, let alone a house. That guy needed to have been sent to the battlefield to know what bombs and bullets were really about.

Chapter 17

A few years later, in the middle of the most historical moment, the old loudspeaker on the roof of the commune office went dead silent. After Thành climbed a ladder to the roof to check the wires and bang on it a couple times, the loudspeaker buzzed and coughed and then finally announced the official news. 'Peace has come! The nation is reunited!' The news of the liberation of Sài Gòn cheered everyone. Farmers dropped their hoes and rakes and bamboo poles and baskets to the ground and stood in silence as they listened to every single, important word coming from the national radio broadcast. Peace! People had been yearning for it for so long they had begun to think it might just be an illusion. Now they cried with joy, 'Peace at last!' and 'The South is free!'

Hạnh ran as if flying to the Silver Stone Bridge and found people already gathered around the mango tree. They hugged each other, jumped with joy, burst into tears, and laughed. It was all so emotional. Thắm held her young son and ran to Hạnh and hugged her.

'I hope Linh's father will be back soon,' said Thắm. 'And, of course, that Nghĩa will be home soon too. Why are you crying?'

Through her own tears, Hạnh saw that Thắm was also crying.

Wearing only shorts, Mr Đột came up from the river with a bamboo fish trap strapped onto his shirtless back and a basket in his hand.

'Anyone want to buy fish to cook *riêu** to celebrate our victory?' Đột opened the basket to reveal fish flopping around inside.

---

* *Bún riêu* is a traditional soup with clear stock, tomato, shrimp paste, thin rice noodles, and various other ingredients such as banana flowers, crab, fish, vinegar, mint, and greens.

'Liberation!' he shouted. 'Buy some fish to celebrate! The dead are dead. The living must live meaningfully. Damn! I feel sorry for Tý Hin's daughter, Tươi. Her mother was afraid Tươi would have no one to marry, so she married her off to that old bastard Khôn in Hồi Village. What a waste! If Tý Hin hadn't been in such a hurry, Tươi could choose from dozens of guys when the soldiers come home.'

'Tươi made her own choice,' said Mr Dĩ. 'I feel sorry for Nhài. She'd been waiting for her husband faithfully for ten years with no news. Then, in a moment of weakness, she slept with old Đục, and her mother-in-law caught her in the act. Her husband will kill her when he comes back.'

'Spoken like you'd know,' said Aunt Nhị. 'But no one knew before today that peace would come. It's like they say about women and girls—wise for three years, but a fool in one hour.'

'Everything will be so great from now on,' said Uncle Nhương, sitting on one of the stone dogs while drawing a rake back and forth over the ground. 'Our village girls won't have to worry about finding husbands anymore.' Then he joked, 'Now the veterans can all have two wives!'

Hạnh hurried with Thắm and her son, Linh, to Nhân's house, not knowing yet whether her mother had heard the victory news. As they entered the gate, a terrible wail came from the house. Hạnh shuddered and raced inside. Nhân held her face in her hands, curtained by her long, dishevelled hair. Uncle Vạn paced back and forth, saying something to her. Dâu ran to Hạnh from the kitchen, hugged her, and sobbed something Hạnh couldn't understand. 'What did you say?' she asked. 'What's wrong?'

'Hiệp's dead,' wailed Dâu.

The news of Hiệp's sacrifice had come from Widow Hơn, who'd received a letter from Tốn. Hiệp had been killed just recently in the fighting to liberate Đà Nẵng. The letter had arrived a few days before, but Hơn couldn't bring herself to tell anyone until that morning, and even then, had done so at first accidentally. She'd shown the letter to Mrs Đào because she wanted Tốn to marry her daughter, Hòa, and even promised to slaughter a pig to welcome Tốn home and celebrate the engagement. Then Hơn started telling all the villagers about the party, and that Tốn had fought to liberate Đà Nẵng, and that's when she let slip the bad news about Hiệp. As soon as Mother Khiên heard, she came over to comfort Nhân, but since she hadn't yet heard anything about Nghĩa, she couldn't say a word. She was too afraid Nghĩa wouldn't come home either. So she just sat next to Nhân and held her hand while she cried.

'Let her cry,' said Aunt Nhị. 'She's been holding back her tears for too long.'

Cane in hand, Uncle Xung tapped his way into the house and sat quietly on a mat spread in the middle of the floor. Around noon, Widow Hơn also came by, probably because she finally felt bad about being the one who brought the bad news to Nhân. And out in the yard, all the young women and girls of Đông Village had shown up to comfort Dâu.

Of course, each and every person had their own complicated feelings at this moment, but certainly in all the village, Nhân was the most miserable.

A few days later, in the afternoon, Mr Phóng, the mailman, came into Mother Khiên's yard on his bicycle. Hạnh rushed out, unable to breathe. He handed her a telegram and said, 'It's happy news, Sister! Invite me when you slaughter a pig to celebrate.'

Hạnh could barely hold the telegram in her shaking hands as she read: 'I'll be home on the 17th – Nghĩa.'

'Mother! Mother!' she cried so happily she forgot to thank Mr Phóng. Nghĩa would be home on the 17th! Hạnh felt like she was dreaming, but no, the telegram was real, right there in her hand.

'What is it?' asked Mother Khiên as she emerged from the lineage temple, where she'd been burning incense and praying for Nghĩa's safe return.

'Nghĩa is alive! He'll be home on the 17th!'

'Oh, thank heaven our family has been blessed!'

Mother Khiên hurried into the lineage temple, knelt, and bowed repeatedly to the ancestors. Now she knew for sure that Nghĩa would be back on the 17th. The great ancestral patriarch had told her this years ago in her dream and had been watching over Nghĩa on the battlefield all along.

Hạnh took the telegram to her mother's house. Nhân was cooking. Smoke curled up in the air above the kitchen. Dâu was chopping bamboo near the pond, but stopped when she saw Hạnh and, as a joke, asked, 'Are you coming for rice leftovers?'

Laughing, Hạnh asked, 'What are you chopping bamboo for?'

'I'm making a few baskets for *Bu*.* I don't want to waste the old bamboo.'

'Can you weave a basket?'

'I'm going to try. Living here with Bu, I need to learn how to do men's work.'

Hạnh showed her the telegram and Dâu dropped the knife she'd been using and hugged her. Hạnh screamed when Dâu bit her ear.

'Bu ơi!' Dâu shouted as she ran into the kitchen waving the telegram.

The 17th finally came, and Hạnh and Mother Khiên rose early to boil water. When Nghĩa got home, the whole village would come to their house to celebrate. Mother swept the floor and cleaned the ancestral altar. Hạnh ran out to the edge of the village and back, over and over, anxiously checking the road to the province capital to see if a bus had come to drop off a passenger at the stop at Kilometre 3. But the nine o'clock bus didn't stop at Kilometre 3 that day, which worried Hạnh.

'Maybe Nghĩa's coming this afternoon,' she said. She looked apprehensively at Mother Khiên. 'I need to tell you something.'

'Tell me.'

'Thành and I made up the story about running into Nghĩa on the battlefield so you wouldn't worry. We also made up the story about his promotion.'

'Nghĩa's alive and coming home, that's all that matters. He'll be in charge of this place.'

---

* A term of endearment for Nhân that shows Dâu considered her like a mother

Hạnh hugged her mother-in-law and went into her bedroom. She'd gotten no sleep the night before but she didn't feel tired. She stood by the window, looked at herself in the mirror, and washed her face. Since the telegram arrived, she'd frequently gazed at herself in the mirror to see how much she had aged. It had been ten years.

The afternoon bus also came and went without dropping off Nghĩa. But then, near dinner time, an engine rumbled from the lane. Hạnh ran outside just as a jeep stopped at the gate. She felt her face flush as soon as she saw Nghĩa. Children rushed to gather around the vehicle as he and the driver got out. Nghĩa was wearing a uniform with a major's epaulettes and insignia pinned to the lapels. Hạnh stood there dumbfounded. She and Thành had made up the story about his promotion but it was true!

Nghĩa and Hạnh rushed together and held each other for a long time, as if convincing themselves the other was truly in their arms.

'This is my wife,' Nghĩa finally said to the driver. 'And this is Cường.'

'Nice to meet you,' said Cường. He shook Hạnh's hand and then plunged back into the swarm of excited children surrounding the vehicle.

'Where's Mom?' Nghĩa asked as he entered the yard.

His mother came out of the house and stood with tears streaming down her face as Nghĩa took both her hands into his own. Before he could say anything, Uncle Vạn hobbled in and gave Nghĩa a surprised look. Nghĩa hugged him too.

'You're a major, right?' asked Uncle Vạn, patting his shoulders. 'Wonderful!'

Thắm arrived with her son and stood before Nghĩa. 'Where were you stationed in the South?' she asked.

'She's asking about her gunner,' said Uncle Vạn.

'Oh, you got married and have a son, already?' asked Nghĩa. 'Who's your husband?'

'She married a photographer, but they divorced,' said Uncle Vạn. 'This little guy is the son of an anti-aircraft gunner who was stationed at Linh Canal. They sent his unit South years ago, and no one in the village has heard from him or his unit since.'

Soon the house was packed with visitors.

'Is it true Nghĩa is a major?' Uncle Xung asked as soon as he tottered inside. 'Damn! Just like I said, the Nguyễn family will be blessed from now on. Nghĩa's the first officer in the village, and he came home in his own jeep! Vạn has a lot of medals, but even he can't compare to Nghĩa.'

Nghĩa came over to Uncle Xung and held his hand, clearly surprised to see him healthy again.

'You thought I'd be dead, didn't you? Ha! I'll live for a long time, as long as it takes for the Nguyễn clan to be great again. Now that you're back, we'll throw a huge party on the death anniversary of our ancestor. Long live our ancestors! Long live our ancestors!' Uncle Xung shouted as if it were a slogan, which made everyone laugh until Mother Nhân and Dâu came into the yard.

'Nghĩa,' said Nhân, weeping. 'Both Hà and Hiệp are dead.'

Nghĩa comforted his mother-in-law and took in the faces of all the people gathered around. Everyone in the village had aged so much.

'Nghĩa, did you ever cross paths with my son, Tô?' asked one of the neighbours, Mrs Tang.

'My son was also stationed in Military Region 5,' said another neighbour, Mrs Chi. 'Did you see him?'

'You ladies are asking nonsense questions!' shouted Uncle Vạn. 'The South is a very big place!' Then he asked, 'Did you go to Sài Gòn and help liberate it? No? Then I guess you weren't as lucky as Mrs Sách's son, who got to go inside Independence Palace.* When we liberated Điện Biên Phủ—'

'Not Điện Biên Phủ again!' barked Uncle Xung. 'Điện Biên Phủ comes up in everything you say! Let's tell him what's been going on in the village instead.' Uncle Xung turned to Nghĩa, blinked, and said, 'Guess who the commune chairman is! It's Dương! That's really strange, right? He's not very well cultured, but he has a good spirit. All four of his sons joined the military. So he'll probably be re-elected a few more times. Did you happen to bring anything back with you?'

* The residence of the president of the Republic of South Vietnam

'What a question!' Aunt Nhị glared at Uncle Xung. 'You're asking like Nghĩa's just come back from the Soviet Union with a bag full of presents. It was a war! Poor Thành came back to the village with a burnt face!'

'Thành came back before liberation,' argued Uncle Xung. 'But now the South has been liberated, and victory and booty go hand in hand. Widow Hơn's son brought back many valuable things. He says he'll build a new house even bigger than his grandfather's. Hào may have been a landowner, but he didn't even have a bicycle. Tốn now has a cassette player and a motorbike. Coming back from a war like him is admirable. He says his grandfather and father became rich by owning lots of land, but he'll make a bigger fortune selling women's underwear. All the women and girls in the village will want to buy the bras and panties he brought home.'

Uncle Xung stood, went to the door, waved his cane, and yelled at the children horsing around in the yard and honking the jeep horn. When the kids ran off, he came back inside the house and, looking sad, spoke in an emotional voice. 'Nghĩa,' he said, 'I need to tell you something.'

The room fell silent.

Nghĩa's mother passed Mother Nhân and Aunt Nhị a plate of betel leaves and areca nuts. Dâu came in from the kitchen and sat down on the mat next to Uncle Vạn.

Uncle Xung lowered his head and futzed with his cane on the floor. 'Since you left, our village has never been peaceful. I've lived most of my life by now and have come to realize that our villagers are kind-hearted people but have miserable lives. Where does all this misery come from? Your mother and Hạnh's mother have been waiting for you for a decade. And many soldiers never return. Your Uncle Vạn has lived a lonely life as if being punished by Heaven. As for me, I committed a terrible crime—I was the one who set fire to the lineage temple!' Uncle Xung burst into tears.

Nghĩa wondered whether Uncle Xung was telling the truth or his mental problems had come back again. Looking like she was about to cry but pretending to need to spit betel, Dâu leapt up from the mat and ran outside. And then Thành came into the house and stood quietly at the door. Cúc came in a minute later, and when she saw Thành, she trotted into the kitchen to be with Hạnh.

'Nghĩa, can you recognize him?' asked Uncle Xung, wiping his tears. 'That's our Thành.'

Hạnh felt the way she had on the night of her wedding. Ten years was a long time but it also seemed like her honeymoon had been just yesterday. Since the wild night they swam together at the river, Hạnh had tried to keep her emotions in check around Dâu, but her friend knew her too well and could sense her excitement. Dâu squeezed her hand.

'Know what I'm thinking?' asked Dâu. 'You're crazy happy right now, and so am I, truly, because I'm suddenly single again. Plus, I'm a virgin, so I'm even worthier than you! I can tell Hiệp's spirit will protect me and help me find a good husband. So don't feel sorry for me. It's men's time during war, and women's during peace. And now it's peace! Ha! There'll be plenty of men now. Let's go for a swim!'

On the riverbank, Dâu looked around, took off her clothes and pulled Hạnh into the water.

'Stop! I don't want to get my hair wet.'

'Okay, sorry! I forgot you just washed it.'

A soft breeze rippled over the cool water. Hạnh tied up her hair and bent her knees so that the water reached her neck. The two riverbanks and village lights floated in the dark evening.

'This is so nice,' said Dâu. 'A few nights ago, Nhài had a little accident with Đục when they both showed up to bathe at the same time. I'm not sure if her husband will see it that way. If Hiệp and I had been more adventurous like Thắm was with the gunner, things could be better now. Our kid would be a big boy now, and Bu would be so happy. Do you think Thấu will come back for Thắm? I hope he will so she can take him and the baby to Huy's studio and have their photo taken. That would be hilarious!'

'Oh, Dâu,' said Hạnh with a sigh, 'when I think about all that's happened to Thắm and all of us, it seems so clear to me that our ancestral land really is sacred, and that none of it happened by accident. Uncle Xung and Uncle Xeng's illnesses and confessions and redemptions, Nghĩa's promotion to major and return on the 17th—all of it seems like it really has been orchestrated by a saint in the lineage temple.'

'You're right!' Dâu laughed and gave Hạnh a hug. 'You won't ever forget this date. You and Nghĩa will produce another "saintly son" for the Nguyễn clan and I bet your child will be conceived and born on the 17th too. Hee hee! Let's go home so Nghĩa won't worry.'

Hạnh felt so excited, like the whole village had turned out to celebrate her reunion with Nghĩa, and in so doing, they were finally celebrating their union as well. As she came up the lane, Cường was driving the jeep through the gate to park in the yard. He honked to tease the children, who cried out with glee and darted their hands towards the wheel to honk again. Inside the house, the neighbours were still talking, and Nghĩa's mother tittered happily, telling them all about her dream that Nghĩa would be back on the 17th.

In the bedroom, Hạnh touched Nghĩa's hand, and everything felt electric. He drew her into his strong arms. Her tears fell on his face. She imagined that to him she was still the same little girl, easily moved to crying. She ran her fingers through his hair. The terrible, turbulent years had now passed, and peace had returned. Her desperate longing for him was finally over. Her heart soared and her body tingled, an arid land finally drenched with rain.

Without hesitation, Nghĩa unbuttoned her shirt. Hạnh's heart beat faster.

'Nghĩa, did you hear something?'

'No, what?'

'Rats squeaking. There! Rats!'

'I can't think of that morning all those years ago without hearing those rats too. Mom says it's good luck, so what's your wish?'

'I want to have a baby. You named him already. Remember?'

'Of course! His name is Tình.'

Like the riverbank and village lights earlier, their bed floated on the night. All entanglements slipped away, leaving only Nghĩa's hands to glide over her body. Hạnh could hear him panting and see his shadow flickering both near and far. Nghĩa moved at times as soft and graceful as a cat, sometimes as ferocious as a tiger. But then Hạnh felt as though they were waiting for a thunderstorm that wouldn't break. She kept thinking they were close, but then nothing.

A rooster crowed. Hạnh climbed on top of Nghĩa and squeezed him. 'The rooster's crowing,' she said. Her face felt hot.

Nghĩa loosened his hold on Hạnh as if afraid of something. A long silent moment followed. 'Hạnh, sweetheart,' he said at last. 'I don't want you to be sad . . . but I can't . . . The doctor said I might have some trouble. I'm not yet completely healed.'

The thunderstorm blew over. The bedroom fell silent. Hạnh sobbed quietly, not for herself, but for him. His youth had passed so quickly.

Chapter 18

Many villagers looked at the jeep admirably as it sped down the road. Without Nghĩa, Cường drove a bit recklessly. 'When Nghĩa's in a good mood,' he said over his shoulder to Hạnh, 'please suggest that he let me borrow the jeep one day to visit my wife and parents. I haven't been home yet. I heard there's a rumour I'm dead.'

'Why don't you send them a telegram?' asked Hạnh.

'I want to surprise them,' Cường said with a laugh. 'If I drive this jeep home and park in my parents' yard, they'll faint. Then my wife will rush over and bite me. Do any of you ladies have any idea why she bites when she gets emotional? It's kind of scary!'

Hạnh and Dâu laughed from the back seat. Thắm sat up front with Linh in her lap. Every now and then the little boy got excited and squirmed in his mother's arms as he looked out the window at the roadside speeding by.

'Mama, will Papa come back in a car like this?'

'Your papa doesn't have a car but he has an anti-aircraft gun,' said Dâu. 'He'll come back with a big cannon trailer.'

'A car would be better,' said Linh.

The jeep ran under the shade of a grove of casuarina trees. They stopped in front of the gate of the district market.

'Since this is your first time here, you should walk around and see the area,' Thắm said, smiling at the driver. 'My son and I will keep an eye on the jeep.'

Cường went with Hạnh and Dâu into the market, and the boy clambered over and sat in the driver's seat, smiling and making motor noises and turning the wheel back and forth.

'Take it easy,' said Thắm. 'Be good!' They'd inadvertently parked across from her ex-husband's photo studio, and Huy was leaning in the doorway smoking a cigarette. Thắm shut the door of the jeep and slid low on the seat, afraid that Huy would see her. After a while, Linh got bored and asked her to let him out.

Thắm opened the door and gave him one đồng to buy a treat. 'Don't go too far,' she called.

Linh jumped down and wandered past the roadside stalls, peering into each and considering what he might spend his money on. Then he happened to stop in front of the studio to look at the large framed colour photos hanging on display. To his surprise, the woman in one looked just like his mother.

'Do you recognize her?'

The boy startled and then peered up at the man who was quietly standing right behind him. 'Come inside with me. I'll show you some more.'

The photographer led the boy inside, picked him up, and carried him upstairs. Then he showed the boy a thick stack of photos, all of his mother.

'I'm your father,' said the photographer. 'Look! Your mother and I have taken so many pictures together. Sit here and have a snack and I'll go get her.'

The photographer gave Linh a bunch of small bananas and went downstairs. When Huy got to the door, Thắm was already there, panicking.

'Where's my son?' Thắm grabbed Huy's shirt collar. 'Are you trying to kidnap him?'

'Calm down,' said Huy. 'We are still husband and wife. I apologize sincerely for what happened in the past. For a long time now I've been wanting to talk to you, but I haven't seen you come to the market.'

'We are divorced,' said Thắm. 'We have nothing to talk about. Give me back my son.'

'Thắm, don't worry! Come upstairs with me. He's fine.'

Thắm quietly climbed the stairs wondering what that bastard could possibly want to talk to her about.

Seeing his mother, Linh cried out, 'Mama! There's lots of pictures of you here.' Dozens of photographs of her with Huy lay scattered all over the table.

'Please take a seat and have some water,' said Huy.

Thắm sat and looked around at the little apartment above the studio. The room was painted light blue. The furniture looked clean and shiny. What surprised Thắm the most was the enlarged, framed colour photo of her on the wall in the adjacent room. Did Huy still love her? She really had been in love with his square jaw and thick beard, and they had made many sweet memories too, despite the bad ones.

'Why haven't you remarried?'

'Thắm, you misunderstand me,' said Huy, bowing his head. 'I'll never marry again because I'll love you until the day I die. It was all my fault. I know you know I wasn't faithful. But now I see everything clearly. None of the women who came to me could compare to you. Only you are my wife.'

'Were you injured in the war?' Linh pointed at Huy's bad leg.

'I had a bad accident when I was about your age. I fell out of a tree.'

'You were a bad boy.' The boy smiled. 'My mother says any boy who climbs trees is bad.'

The boy sat on Thắm's lap and showed her several pictures of her with Huy from their wedding day.

'Mama, is he really my father?'

'No! Your father is a soldier.'

'If he's not my father, then why did you take so many pictures with him?'

'Stop asking foolish questions. We're going home.'

Thắm stood to leave, but Huy caught her hand and said, 'Please, I beg you. We're not divorced. Come back and live with me. We'll start over from the beginning.'

'You're wrong! I'm married to someone else.'

'You're lying. I know you've been living alone.'

Thắm yanked her arm free and hustled Linh back out to the street and into the jeep. She slammed the door.

'Mama, why are you crying? He didn't do anything.'

'Linh!' Thắm yelled. 'Not another word! You may not talk about what just happened.'

The boy couldn't care less. He climbed into the driver's seat and turned the steering wheel and pressed the horn.

After a long while, Hạnh, Dâu, and Cường came back with lots of things and put them into the vehicle.

'Do you want to do any shopping?' the driver asked Thắm.

'I don't need anything,' said Thắm. 'It's just nice to get out of the village once in a while.'

Cường started the engine and drove the jeep away from the market and out of the district seat. Linh climbed into the back to sit with Dâu, who offered him a banana.

'I don't want a banana,' he said. 'That man gave me a banana earlier and showed me pictures of my mama. She took lots of pretty pictures with him.'

'Did you take him to see that bastard?' asked Dâu, shocked.

'No!' Thắm's face flushed hot. 'He kidnapped Linh. I had to go in there to get him.'

'That's not true!' said Linh. 'I went by myself. He asked if I wanted to live there with him. His rooms are really high above the street and really nice.'

'Did you like him?' asked Cường.

'Yes. He has a beard but doesn't look scary. He didn't yell at me or spank me. He grabbed Mama's hand and tried to hug her, but she got scared and pulled me outside. He didn't hit her, but she cried.'

'Linh, stop! You're being very naughty. When your papa comes back, I won't take you with me.'

'You're lying! You always say Papa will come, but you never bring him home.'

'Your papa will be home soon.' Hạnh held the little boy in her arms and comforted him. 'He'll bring you a cannon trailer. He's a big, brave, tall and handsome soldier. Not like that guy, who might seem nice, but isn't.'

'He also gave me this to buy new clothes to go to school.' Linh pulled some paper bills from his pocket.

Thắm turned in the seat, glared at him in disbelief, and yelled, 'Who gave you permission to accept that money?' She slapped his hand and snatched away the money.

Terrified, Linh bawled and held Hạnh's neck.

'That's enough!' Dâu snapped at Thắm. 'You let him wander in there and now you hit him.' Then, to Linh, she said, 'Shush now, and come sit with me.'

The boy climbed into Dâu's arms and sobbed, his innocent cries sounding utterly pitiful and sad.

As she held the little boy and nuzzled his head and smelled his hair, Dâu felt an ache deep inside her, a painful regret for having refused Hiệp at the riverbank all those years ago. He'd wanted her so badly, but back then she imagined it wouldn't be so long before they'd be together again, married, and having their own child. 'I'll wait for you,' she had said. 'Five years, ten years, however long it takes.' But Hiệp never came home.

The jeep sped along the dike. Bright sunbeams lit the rice paddies all around with gold. To break the heavy atmosphere that had settled inside the jeep, Cường asked, 'Mrs Hạnh, what do you think I should bring my wife when I go home? I've been thinking about it but can't decide. What do women like nowadays?'

'It kind of depends on the person. I think I'd like anything my husband gave me.'

'In my unit, some guys bought their wives clothes, others scarves or watches or sunglasses. One guy named Duệ said he'd give his wife the shiny, pointed knife he'd made himself and kept in the bottom of his rucksack.'

'Damn!' said Thắm. 'Who gives his wife a knife?'

'He had his reasons. He heard his wife cheated on him.'

Alarmed, Hạnh asked, 'Is he going to kill her?'

'Oh, no! He's innocent as dirt, the sweetest guy in my unit. Sensitive too. He can actually read people's minds. He's got a warm voice and bright eyes and is really charismatic. Near the end of the war, he was captured by the enemy, but he said he wasn't worried. Instead, he said he was worried about the puppet soldier* who'd been assigned to stay up all night guarding him. He told the guy, "I won't try to escape. If you don't believe me, you can tie me up and get some sleep or you could shoot me so I'll die, and then you won't have to stay up all night guarding me." The puppet soldier didn't dare shoot him, so he tied Duệ's legs together with a rope and then went to sleep. While the puppet soldier slept, Duệ untied the rope but didn't run. I think even if he had run, he wouldn't have been able to get very far. But you know what he did? He snuggled up to the puppet soldier and went to sleep. When the puppet soldier woke the next morning and found him untied, he asked why Duệ didn't try to escape. Duệ just smiled and said, "Now you know you can trust me." And you know what? It was the puppet soldier, a few days later, who helped him escape. When liberation came, our unit was the one who accepted the puppet soldier's surrender. He told me the story himself.'

Hạnh was confused and asked, 'If Duệ is so noble, why would he give his wife a knife? Is it a threat? Or does he want her to kill herself?'

'No,' Cường said and laughed. 'Duệ's not so simplistic. He said he planned to give her the knife and say, "Darling, I made this knife myself. Its steel will never rust, and it's all yours. Our love will always be as true as its blade."'

'What would you do if your wife cheated on you?' Thắm glanced nervously at the driver.

Cường scratched his ear. 'I think I'd buy a mirror and a beautiful comb and give them to the man who took care of her while I was away.'

'Liar!' Dâu said with a pout. 'If it were me, I'd punch the guy in the face.'

---

* A derogatory term Northerners used for soldiers in the Army of the Republic of Vietnam

'Thắm, I can tell you how to make your man come home based on my wife's experience,' said the driver. 'Not long after I enlisted, I got a really strong feeling one day that something was wrong at home, so I got permission to take a leave. But when I got there, everything was fine. When my wife saw me, she giggled as if she somehow knew for sure I'd be back that day. In bed that night, I told her I didn't know why I felt so unsettled the day before. She laughed again and told me, "I missed you so much I cooked your shirt in a frying pan."'*

'But Thắm doesn't have Thấu's shirt,' said Dâu.

'Didn't you keep anything from him?' asked the driver.

'He gave me a scarf,' Thắm said. 'But it was brand new.'

Cường laughed. 'Think it will fit in a frying pan?'

Thanks to the driver, everyone was back in a good mood as the jeep arrived at the village gate. Children ran out to the lane, calling out, 'Aunty Hạnh, let us ride in the jeep with you!'

Cường parked the jeep in Mother Khiên's yard. The late afternoon sun brightened Hạnh's rosy face as she carried the groceries she had bought for a party the next day into the kitchen. The major smiled happily when he saw his wife. Mother Khiên smiled too, her lips bright red from chewing betel. Hạnh felt elated. For so long she and her mother-in-law had lived with so much missing from their lives, like two silent shadows. And now everything was different. She felt, for the very first time, the gravity of who she now was, the wife of the head of the Nguyễn clan, the biggest clan in Đông Village.

* An old superstition held that if you heated something that the person you missed had worn, they'd know you were longing for them.

PART IV

Chapter 19

It was the first time a two-storey house had been built in Đông Village. Located on the site of landlord Hào's old kitchen, its owner was Tốn, Hào's grandson. Fortunately, Widow Hơn had managed to preserve the last and only drop of the bloodline of the former richest landlord in Đông Village.

Old man Hào had been executed, and Tốn's father had swallowed his tongue and committed suicide, which left Tốn and his mother living in the kitchen on the property now occupied by Nguyễn Vạn. After eighteen years, the kitchen of a former landowner once again became the residence of a bourgeois family. Tốn's new house looked like a French chateâu in the middle of a poor countryside, a modern Western girl amid the rustic Đông villagers. The windows on the second floor had fluttering blue curtains, and its ostentatious balcony and wrought iron railing had been extravagantly designed. None of the villagers had ever seen a house like this one.

Since Tốn had come back to Hơn's house, Vạn had felt uncomfortable and often woke in the middle of the night. Tốn hired a truck that unloaded construction materials in the yard all day. Vạn got startled each time Tốn turned on his stereo. The speakers blasted deafening sounds like thunder and the voices of both Western and Vietnamese, male and female vocalists. Sometimes their voices sounded like laughter, sometimes like moaning. '*If I die tomorrow, will you be sad*?'

When Tốn played music at night, Vạn often had to get up to pee. In all his life, Vạn had never been in a relationship with anyone, so he had no idea what joy or sorrow might come from love. The closest he ever came to joy was the one rainy night he gave Nhân some fish. Nothing happened between them. And it was only that one time that he placed his hand on her body—the body of a widow. Sometimes he felt aroused when he couldn't control his instincts and stared at Hơn's white thighs after she rolled up her pants and lay like a cat in heat on the bamboo bed in the middle of the yard.

Tốn's presence destroyed the tranquillity of Vạn's soul. Everything turned upside down. Vạn never imagined the person who could cause him such turmoil would be Tốn. He was a descendant of the exploiting class, and it was Vạn who had rescued him from the other children's torment. And now, he was the bourgeois owner of a mansion. Some of the villagers said Tốn inherited a stash of secret gold from old man Hào. But Uncle Xung said Tốn's wealth came entirely from selling women's underwear. The house got built so fast, it seemed to Vạn he just woke up one morning and it was already there, right in front of his eyes, as garish and indecent as Hơn herself.

Vạn's house, which used to be landowner Hào's, was nothing compared to Tốn's mansion. Part of the roof had collapsed. Moss grew in patches on the walls, and plaster flaked from other places to reveal the bricks beneath. His bed, which he'd been using for eighteen years, and which he tried to forget had been Hơn and her husband's nuptial bed, got wobblier as the tenons loosened. The ceiling had blackened with soot and was full of cobwebs. When Vạn moved in, he had divided the place into two sections, and the kitchen was where he stored both rice and clothes. Tốn's building a mansion next door made Vạn realize his house was in ruins, and that made him see his lonely old man's life was a ruin too.

But in Vạn's opinion, the worst thing was that Tốn's bourgeois lifestyle disturbed the village's tranquil atmosphere. Young men and women gathered at Tốn's house to sing sentimental songs. If Tốn had not been a soldier, Vạn would drag him to the commune and condemn him for his bad influence on the youth. A power line had been extended to the village to run irrigation valves, and, even though only the commune secretary and chairman had been authorized to have electricity, somehow Tốn had bribed someone and his house got electricity too. And once he had it, he used it a lot. In the evening, when the whole village was dark, his house was bright with lights, and music played all night, which he arrogantly called ' healthy form of entertainment after a hard day's work'. Vạn did not find the music entertaining or healthy. Instead, it felt like torture because it kept him from his sleep. Only Hơn knew about Vạn's disgruntlement, so if she saw him at home at night, she'd tell Tốn, 'Choose a cassette with progressive songs, so Mr Vạn can enjoy them.'

The young people gathering at Tốn's house covered their mouths and giggled, saying, 'What does Mr Vạn know about music? He only listens to one song, "Liberate Điện Biên"'. When Vạn heard that, he got angry and yelled over to the new house, 'Screw you, punks! If there'd been no Điện Biên victory, you would not exist! Without Điện Biên, there'd be no peace. You wouldn't have chairs to sit on while getting so fat! Only reactionaries would plant such bourgeois seeds.' But despite Nguyễn Vạn's fury, he never criticized Tốn directly because he'd also sacrificed by fighting on the battlefield for their country. He had heard that the fighting in the South was even fiercer than at Điện Biên Phủ.

A barrage of firecrackers kicked off the day of Tốn's wedding, startling Nguyễn Vạn awake and filling his house with smoke. Later, Vạn sat in a corner at the reception, grumbling quietly about the music that played as the groom brought the bride into the room. Widow Hơn came over to him, her smile red with betel, and whispered into his ear, 'Will you help me, Vạn darling? Everyone knows you're my closest next-door neighbour. Will you make a speech for me?'

Vạn looked aghast. 'I can't represent the groom's family!'

'Pretty please?' Hơn poked Vạn playfully in the ribs. 'Everything's different these days. You don't have to be a relative, and you're so good with speeches. Besides, Tốn wouldn't be who he is today without your help.'

Vạn didn't know what to think about Hơn's request. All around him amid the cigarette smoke were familiar faces from the village.

Could he stand up and give a speech to his fellow villagers for the benefit of an enemy of the proletariat? No way! Hơn knew nothing about social class. Or was she playing another trick?

While the MC spoke, Vạn panicked that he might get called upon, so he stood and quietly stepped outside. On the village road, he saw Uncle Xung coming down the lane from Nghĩa's house. The old man stopped and whacked crossly at a fallen leaf with his cane.

'Is that you, Vạn?' he said. 'It's all over. Nghĩa could even be a colonel, but he's gone too far now. He doesn't give a shit about our ancestors. I heard he plans to bring in a crew to tear down the lineage temple and build a new house. I hope he doesn't have the guts to go through with it.' He shook his cane and without waiting for a reply, stalked away.

Vạn limped to Nhân's house and saw that she and Dâu were preparing to have dinner. Cheerfully, Dâu got an extra bowl and chopsticks and invited him to join them.

'Thank you,' said Vạn. 'Hơn invited me to her son's wedding party but I couldn't bear being there.' Then he tried to act natural as he sat down on the mat beside the dinner tray. Dâu had been living with Nhân since Hiệp's death, so Vạn no longer felt hesitant to visit her like before.

'Dâu caught all the crabs and made this delicious soup,' said Nhân as she ladled some into Vạn's bowl.

'Tốn's wedding is much bigger than that photographer and Thắm's,' said Vạn. 'And Hơn's family seems to have gotten back some of their lost reputation.'

'Don't be mean!' Nhân gave him a look. 'Her son came back from the war, built a house, and found a wife. Why shouldn't they be happy?'

'Uncle Vạn,' said Dâu, 'I heard that after the wedding, Widow Hơn wants to get married again. Maybe you could get in on that?'

'You're crazy! I'm already over fifty, and even just considering it would make me lose face with the village.' Vạn took a breath to regain his composure. 'What about you? Have you considered Thành? His face is ruined but he's a very good man.'

'I volunteer to stay single.' Dâu laughed. 'I'll stay right here with Bu.'

'She's crazy, right?' Nhân said to Vạn. 'She even told me she wants to adopt a child. I told her not to adopt because she can still have her own baby. Since the day she moved in, I've felt sorry for her. Hiệp's death has made this house unlucky, and she's the one really suffering.'

'Bu, you don't need to worry about me. Hạnh and I are like sisters. She's married, so I get to come live here with you.'

'I know that,' said Nhân. 'But my time and Uncle Vạn's time has passed, and nothing more needs to be said about that. But you still have your youth—don't waste it!'

Outside, the sky turned dark. Dâu lit the oil lamp, casting yellow light onto their faces, and Nhân spoke again. 'Dâu, I'm serious. You never know what's going to happen, so you shouldn't take anything for granted. Look at Hạnh. Nghĩa's been back two years, and they try every month, but she's still not pregnant.'

'You worry too much!' Dâu said with a smile. 'Once their house is built, they'll have a baby, a whole horde of them, one after another, and then you'll have lots of grandchildren.'

'Uncle Xung's angry about the new house,' said Vạn. 'It won't be pleasant.'

'The Nguyễn clan is so backward,' said Dâu. 'What's the point of always giving each other such a hard time? Nghĩa fought in the war for ten years, and now that we have peace, he needs to renovate. No ancestor would scold him for doing so. Hạnh told me they don't have much money, but Nghĩa's friends saw the poor condition of his house, so they gave him the cement to build a flat roof. But to make that work, he'll have to tear down the temple walls and reuse the bricks.'

'Nghĩa is being dumb,' said Vạn. 'He's a major in the People's Army but he still has an individualistic mind. Now it's peacetime, and soon rural areas all over will be rebuilt and restructured. Our village also will be completely torn down and rebuilt. There will be rows of townhouses. And no one will be able to keep their lineage temples then.'

'When will this happen?' asked Nhân sceptically.

'Soon. Our country was occupied by imperialists for scores of years, so we had to devote everything to fighting them. Now we live in peace, and everyone has to maintain our solidarity to rebuild the country. What we should really be worried about is the rise of selfish bourgeois people like Tốn and his mother. They have no place in a socialist society. I'm their neighbour, and I can tell you, their way of life is not good.'

Dâu carried the dishes out to the well and washed them.

Nhân picked her teeth clean with a toothpick and then said, 'Dâu is really hard-working. She taught herself to weave baskets as skilfully as men. If only Hiệp were still alive . . .'

'You can't change the past,' said Vạn. 'So what's the point of *if*?'

Nhân said nothing. Of course she understood the point of *if*. For years, she had gone to each house in the village and persuaded young men to join the army and had comforted their mothers and wives as well. She understood losses were inevitable in war, but she had not imagined she would have to suffer so many. She had lived through her life getting smaller and smaller as the men she loved disappeared from it. Somehow, because her husband and Hà went first, she fooled herself into thinking for sure Hiệp would come home. But no, now she understood all too well. Her husband was dead. Hà was dead. And Hiệp was dead, never to return, and with him gone, her last hope was dead too.

Most days she felt as if she'd fallen into a bottomless abyss. For months now, at least once a week in her sleep at night, she'd dream that the three dead men from her family had come back to rake her over the coals. Her husband's eyes would burn like fire as he said, 'You wicked woman, you murderer. I was already dead from war. Why did you let our sons die too?' Then it was Hà's turn. 'Dad and I were already dead. Why didn't you keep Hiệp at home?' And then Hiệp would join in, saying, 'Did it make you happy to send me off to die?' Nhân would wake terrified and screaming, 'No! I'm not wicked. I'm not a murderer. It's not my fault. The French and the Americans were the murderers. Forgive me, Hà and Hiệp, I beg you, please forgive me!'

After each nightmare, she thought she wouldn't be able to survive, and yet she had to try to continue a normal life. She was the wife and mother of martyrs. But she was also Hạnh's mother, and it was in Hạnh that she now had to place all her hope for the future. Nghĩa had come home, bringing honour and glory back to the Nguyễn clan, to Đông Village, and to her daughter.

Nhân gazed intently at Vạn and suddenly she needed to say it all out loud so *he* could finally understand. 'I'm like an old leaf about to fall from the tree,' she said. 'I was born during war and I have learned to bear many hardships, but now we have peace, and all I want is happiness for the next generation. Even when a leaf falls, it's still good for the roots.' Nhân lowered her head and sighed. 'Vạn, I don't know why I've been thinking so much about this. I'm a lone woman, and that's okay, but I can't bear to see Dâu like this. She's a strange girl—sometimes very quiet, sometimes very hot-tempered. It's like Hiệp is somehow holding her back. I've also suggested making a match with Thành, but she keeps saying no. Do you think they have some kind of personal, hidden conflict?'

'I don't think so. They definitely don't hate each other.' Vạn looked at Nhân hesitantly. 'Just like you and me, we don't hate each other but . . .'

Nhân said nothing.

Drums and children's laughter came from the co op storehouse courtyard. The moonlight stretched Dâu's shadow along the hedge as she came into the kitchen. Out on the veranda, a black cat slept along the rail.

*

Hạnh and Nghĩa ambled side by side beneath the bright moon. They had spent the whole day visiting every Nguyễn household seeking permission to tear down the lineage temple and build a new house. Nghĩa squeezed Hạnh's hand. His voice was emotional. 'It makes me sad thinking about the old lineage temple before it burned down. Do you remember anything about it? Those big, black ironwood pillars, and the couplets with gold letters written on the red background that hung from the two columns in the main hall, all looked so solemn and elegant. And the two long wooden pall-bearer poles with hand-carved dragon heads on the ends and the throne with colourful, carved flowers. And the white funeral flags with black edges and yellow fringes. All those things burned too. I don't know if we'll ever have things like that again.'

They'd saved the hardest visit for last, and both Nghĩa and Hạnh took long calming breaths as they turned into Uncle Xung's yard. Hạnh's heart beat fast. She'd always been afraid of Xung's quite complicated family, and maybe more so since they married because so many of them had such strange personalities. Uncle Xung was really hot-tempered and not at all tactful. Uncle Xeng, on the other hand, was very cunning. And his sister, Aunt Thao, was just plain arrogant and unfriendly. Ever since she returned the engagement gifts to the deserter Hân, she'd been living alone waiting for Heaven to send her the perfect man. Unfortunately, even after the war, there were fewer men around and she couldn't find one she liked. Only Aunt Xeng was truly kind to Hạnh, and that was because she believed Hạnh's father-in-law was a sacred spirit. Aunt Xeng often said that everyone in her family was doing well thanks to the ancestors' blessings they received after she prayed in the lineage temple.

On the front step, Aunt Xeng was shaking a bamboo tray to husk rice, her back bent, her head slightly tilted away. Aunt Thao sat on the porch weaving a straw mat. Uncle Xeng and his oldest son were sawing a log by the pigsty, with his youngest son standing unsteadily on the log, probably and ironically to keep it from moving. Above them, a lantern dangled from a tree branch, lighting their work. Inside, two little girls were doing their homework next to an oil lamp. Uncle Xung sat on the porch with his legs crossed, weaving a hammock.

Everyone stopped what they were doing when Nghĩa and Hạnh approached. Uncle Xung dropped his hammock. Uncle Xeng and his oldest son came over to the porch and sat down, panting. Aunt Thao went into the kitchen and came back with a pot of tea.

'So, you've decided to bring in a crew to destroy the lineage temple, haven't you?' said Uncle Xung. His acerbic voice sent a chill down Hạnh and Nghĩa's spines. 'When you came home from the war, I was delighted to see you'd been promoted to major. But now I see how you're using your rank to launch an attack on our ancestors.'

Nghĩa had been fearless in battle, but Uncle Xung's words still made him feel nervous. 'I'm asking for the whole clan's permission to tear down the lineage temple so I can build a new one, a much bigger and better one.'

'I don't need big,' said Uncle Xung. 'Our ancestors prefer to keep what they built while they still lived. You have to understand the lineage temple is the soul of the Nguyễn clan. You were busy fighting the war, so you don't know all that happened. Ask your wife and she'll tell you. My family is doing well now because we've come clean with our ancestors, been forgiven, and are now blessed.' Uncle Xung gazed at Nghĩa with genuine concern. 'I love you, Nghĩa. That's why I'm telling you this. Xeng and I have been punished, and if you're not careful, one day it'll be your turn.'

'He's right,' said Aunt Xeng. 'Our family takes great care not to do anything that might offend our ancestors.'

'That's enough,' said Uncle Xeng. He slapped the leg of his oldest son who had fallen asleep lying in the courtyard. 'He'll have to decide.' The boy got up and followed Xeng over to where they'd been cutting wood and got started again. Aunt Thao took up the mat she'd been working on.

Hanh and Nghĩa headed home, skirting the edge of a pond. Fish snapped at insects on the surface and frogs chirped from the shallows. The reflection of the moon quivered under a slight breeze. Hạnh leaned into Nghĩa.

'What are you going to do?' she asked. 'Everyone agrees except Uncle Xung's family. If we rebuild and something bad happens to them, will it be our fault?'

'Tearing down the lineage temple has nothing to do with Uncle Xung's family. They work hard and will be rich again soon. Nothing bad's going to happen. I feel sorry for them because they work really hard but always credit the ancestors for their achievements.' Nghĩa squeezed Hạnh's hand. He didn't want to think about Uncle Xung any more. He kissed her when they reached the bamboo grove.

The young soldiers from his unit helping Nghĩa with the construction were sleeping in hammocks strung in the yard, so Nghĩa and Hạnh carefully tiptoed past them and into their bedroom inside the house. In bed, Nghĩa hugged Hạnh and asked softly, 'After last time, have you felt any different?'

Hạnh nuzzled her head into his chest. She didn't want him to feel disappointed. She whispered, 'I hope I'll get pregnant this time. Everything will be so much better once the house is built and we have a baby. Do you think we'll have a son?'

'Of course! And he'll look like me. The country's finally at peace, and he'll live happily. He'll be a poet when he grows up.'

'You have a lot of ambitions!'

'Know what my grandfather wanted my dad to be? He made him study the old Chinese characters, hoping Dad would become a mandarin, but instead he became a fisherman. Dad wanted me to become head of the clan and I turned out to be a soldier. And so, I want our son to be a poet.'

'You're a soldier but you're romantic like a poet.'

'Poems came to me often on the battlefield, but I couldn't write them. Sometimes when I'm in a good mood, I think if everyone were a poet, the world would be a much more peaceful place, because poets never want to have war and they are all gentle people.'

Hạnh gave him a tender squeeze.

'I've heard it's harder for women over thirty to have babies. Is that true? Is it more painful for women that age?'

'I don't know. I've never done it.'

'From other things in my experience, if I think positively about something else when I'm in pain, it helps. So, when you are pregnant and are in labour, think about our son and use your imagination.'

Hạnh thumped Nghĩa's chest and giggled.

Nghĩa continued, 'When you're in the delivery room, think about our son, but not as a newborn. Imagine him as a three-year-old. Maybe that will help you forget the pain.'

'You're so good at imagining things! When I'm in pain, I can't imagine anything else. Soldiers have a great sense of humour. Remember Cường? He told us his wife loved to bite him! That she bites him every time they're together.'

'Oh,' said Nghĩa. His face clouded over. 'She's gone. He bought all those gifts for her, but when he got home, he found out she'd been killed in the last B-52 attack on Hà Nội.'

'Oh no!' Tears rolled down Hạnh's cheeks. 'I thought she had moved out to the countryside.'

'His mother was very sick, so his wife went back to Hà Nội to take her to the emergency room. It's terrible—his healthy wife died, but his sick mother is still alive.'

Hạnh said nothing for a long time, imagining the awful scene in which the driver returned home and learned he'd never see his wife again.

After a while, Nghĩa asked softly, 'Are you asleep?'

Hạnh hugged Nghĩa. 'I don't know why but any time I lie next to you, I can't sleep.' Her hands floated gently over the scars on his ribs. The scars were strangely smooth. Each time after they made love, he'd fall asleep, and Hạnh would stay awake, tracing his scars and listening to the beating of his heart.

Nghĩa said, 'These scars represent the patch of grass that poked me.'

'A ha! The scars are the official stamp of our honeymoon. With them we'll never forget that night.'

'That's right. You're very smart.'

As Nghĩa unbuttoned her blouse, she whispered, 'You're tickling me! If you make me laugh, people will wake up and laugh at us. You'll be embarrassed if they tell everyone you came home on leave and made love to me all night.'

'Well, my men are probably more experienced than me about this.'

'Do you know if any of them are unmarried? Any we can introduce to Dâu?'

'Who knows if they already have a girlfriend waiting at home. Why not ask her to come here and see if she likes anyone?'

'I just don't want Dâu to end up like Thắm. She's been waiting for Thấu to come home but he hasn't, and she can't go back to Huy. What if she did and one day Thấu just showed up? Wait! Hear that? Rats squeaking!' Hạnh squeezed Nghĩa.

After breakfast the next morning, Hạnh took the tray of dirty dishes outside to wash. Mother Khiên was getting ready to go to the market. Nghĩa and the soldiers held sledgehammers and crowbars in their hands about to tear down the lineage temple. One soldier was so excited he had already climbed up to the roof. Suddenly Aunt Xeng came into the yard carrying a tray on her head full of sticky rice, bananas, paper offerings, and incense. She looked happy and smiled.

'Good morning, Aunty and Nghĩa and Hạnh. Hello, "skilled American fighting" soldiers!' she said and smiled again at them all. 'Our ancestors have blessed my family. One of our pigs has reached one hundred kilograms, and my father-in-law told me to make these offerings to our ancestors to show them our gratitude.'

Then Aunt Xeng stepped into the lineage temple while Mother Khiên looked terrified and the soldiers looked stunned. Nghĩa had already removed the incense bowl, candle holders, and throne. Aunt Xeng screamed, and the items from the tray spilled to the floor. She knelt and cried, 'Oh our ancestors, oh our village! Nghĩa and his wife have already destroyed the altar!'

Nghĩa rushed inside. 'No need to cry, Aunty. Just wait a month and the new lineage temple will be finished. Then you can come back and pray.'

Aunt Xeng left and a little while later, Uncle Xeng and Aunt Thao and several neighbours rushed into the courtyard and stood outside the lineage temple and screamed and cried. Uncle Xung tap-tapped in with his cane and stood in the yard. He glared at everyone and then shook his cane and raised his head up to the sky.

'May Heaven witness this! Everyone! You see what's happening. Nghĩa and his wife have violated the great great grandfather's teachings. He thinks because he's a major he can bring soldiers here to destroy the lineage temple. He has taken an enemy Vũ as his wife. The ancestors will punish him for these evil deeds and his bloodline will be extinct. Hạnh will never get pregnant!'

Old man Xung limped away, tapping his cane.

Hạnh ran to her room, fell to the bed, and covered her face with her hands, sobbing.

Chapter 20

No vestige of the ancient Nguyễn lineage temple remained after Nghĩa built a large, airy, three-sectioned, flat-roofed house on their ancestral land. The middle section held a beautiful new altar to the ancestors that had been carved with dragons and phoenixes. Instead of facing the river like the old one, the new house faced south to catch the cool breezes that blew in from the Diêm dike.

Not long after they finished the house, Hạnh bolted upright in the middle of the night. She had never wanted so desperately to have a baby as now. Her longing to be pregnant had troubled her occasionally, and like tonight even haunted her sleep, but it had gotten worse after she received a letter from Nghĩa asking again, *Any sign yet*? He was stationed in the province capital, and his letter also told her his unit would soon be deployed to the border at Lạng Sơn and Quảng Ninh, where the situation had gotten intense.*

Hạnh couldn't believe that the American War had just barely ended, and another one had already begun. She, and everyone, once again lived with daily anxiety and fear. She got up and paced her newly built bedroom that still smelled of fresh plaster. If only she had a baby, everything would be different. She returned to bed and eventually fell asleep again, only to dream about Nghĩa dying in battle, and then that she was raped by the red-eyed ghost from the cemetery, which made the village shun her, leaving her

* In February of 1979, China launched a surprise invasion across the border into Vietnam as a retaliation for Vietnam's occupation of Cambodia to dislodge the Chinese-backed Khmer Rouge and end the genocide. The war ended after a month of heavy fighting when China withdrew its troops. Both sides claimed victory.

feeling terribly lost and lonely. She dreamed again about being cursed by Uncle Xung, who called her a devil for seducing Nghĩa and ruining his family. She yelled in his face, 'No! I'm not a devil. I'm Hạnh, daughter of Nhân. My father and brothers Hà and Hiệp are war martyrs.' Then she ran out to the rice paddies. The tale of the Fairy's Eye and others that Nghĩa's grandfather Nghiên used to tell flashed through her mind. She took off her clothes and jumped into the pond to wash away her misfortune. 'I'm not a devil,' she shouted. 'I'm Nhân's daughter, Hạnh, and I have been wronged!'

Mother Khiên tapped on her bedroom door. 'Hạnh, dear, what's the matter?'

'Oh, Mother, I'm sorry,' said Hạnh, now awake. 'I had a terrible dream.'

Hạnh could not go back to sleep. At dawn, Mother Khiên was already up and busy preparing breakfast. From her window, Hạnh saw her mother-in-law quietly plucking gooseberry leaves in the garden. Recently, she'd noticed that Mother Khiên had aged a lot and her attitude toward Hạnh had changed slightly. Sometimes she caught Mother looking at her and sighing, and she wondered whether Mother's worries had to do with Nghĩa's upcoming trip to the border or Hạnh's trouble getting pregnant. Human patience was limited. Mother was also a daughter-in-law of the Nguyễns, just like Hạnh. With Nghĩa away again, Hạnh had watched Mother's sorrow grow, and it weighed on her that she might be one of the causes.

Back in bed, Hạnh heard the sound of clanking dishes and bowls and then Mother Khiên's footsteps. And then a sigh.

'Breakfast is ready,' Mother Khiên said, tapping at the door. 'Come eat while it's still hot.'

'I'm very tired, Mother. Please go ahead without me.'

Mother Khiên quietly stepped away. The long silence that followed made Hạnh imagine some terrible disaster loomed over them all, about to strike. Ever since they had renovated the old lineage temple and moved into the new house, the villagers and especially some Nguyễn clan members had treated her less warmly than before. Their wary eyes and a mean-spirited rumour that the major's wife had gone deaf and couldn't be spoken to kept her from having good relations. It all made Hạnh feel exhausted, like she was drowning in a sea of illusions.

Her throat felt dry, so she got up to drink some water. Mother Khiên had left. The house was empty, the tray of food on the table untouched. Her mother-in-law had taken just one scoop of rice from the pot to feed the cat, who blinked at Hạnh from where it lay on the front porch. Even the bright light from the garden felt like too much, so she shut the door and went back to bed.

A dim light passing through a vent in the wall shimmered on the ceiling, which Hạnh imagined looked like a small grey cloud hovering over her trembling body. She felt a burning fever rising inside her and it seemed as if the bedroom itself would dissolve into ashes and dust. Maybe this would be the way her passionate relationship with Nghĩa died. She was exhausted, but, as her husband had so frequently suggested, she tried to bring some sweet memory with him to mind. The grass, the breeze, the riverside . . .

A car engine rumbled outside. Would Nghĩa be coming home? Why now? As usual when thinking of her husband coming home, her heart began to beat wildly. She rose and opened the window. The familiar jeep came into the yard through the gate and screeched to a stop. And there he was! Tall and proud in his uniform decorated with chevrons and medals. His hard-soled shoes tapped on the brick steps. Hạnh smoothed her hair and rushed to open the front door.

Nghĩa leapt to embrace her and then stopped short. 'Oh no!' he said. 'Are you sick?'

Hạnh wondered just how awful she must look. She hugged him and said, 'Just a little headache.'

'Where's Mom, darling?'

'I don't know.'

Hạnh set the tray of food on the mat and from the doorway called to the driver to invite him in for tea. She'd never seen him before.

'You two go ahead,' said the new driver, smiling. 'I just want to walk around a bit and get some fresh air.'

Disappointment showed clearly in Nghĩa's eyes. And then she understood everything all at once. She leaned into Nghĩa's chest and cried as he wrapped his arms around her.

'I had a meeting at the district military headquarters this morning already, and have another one later in the province capital, so I thought I'd swing by. I have to go soon. I've been ordered to the border.'

'I'm glad you came home,' she said.

Nghĩa pulled Hạnh into the bedroom.

Afterward, Hạnh felt sorry for her husband's necessary haste. She satisfied his desire but felt nothing herself, leaving him clearly stunned by her lack of excitement. Trembling in his arms, she realized suddenly how thin she'd become.

'You've gotten so skinny,' said Nghĩa, noticing the same thing. 'I'm worried about you.' He gently squeezed her pale, bony hands. 'Get some rest, and if you don't feel better soon, you should go to the district and see a doctor. I need to go find Mom now.'

It was midday, and the neighbourhood was empty, the adults having gone out to work in the fields. Only a few children had gathered around the jeep this time to ask the driver questions. Nghĩa skirted the pond to Uncle Xung's house, where he found his mother talking with Uncle Xeng, who was saying, 'I want to say very clearly, it is sacred.'

Uncle Xeng slapped his own thigh when he saw Nghĩa. 'I just mentioned you, and here you are.'

'You're back.' His mother gave him an anxious look. 'It's good you're home. Hạnh is sick, and Uncle Xung hasn't eaten in several days. Nghĩa, I'm worried something bad's about to happen. Sometimes Hạnh acts like she's lost her mind. I'm afraid she's gone a bit mad like Uncles Xung and Xeng did.'

Inside the house, Uncle Xung writhed in bed and gazed up listlessly, his eyes unfocused. Nghĩa had set aside his own misgivings about Uncle Xung, wondering often whether it was he himself who had caused all his family's problems.

'Sit down,' said Uncle Xeng in a quiet voice. 'I need to talk to you.' Uncle Xeng took a long draw of tobacco from the water pipe. 'You're always gone, busy with your military duties, so you don't know what's going on with the family. Your father's dead, so you have to be responsible for the family, solve the problems between you and your wife, and make sure your mother isn't upset. If I can speak frankly, the longer you live with Hạnh, the more you and your mother will suffer. Hạnh will never be pregnant. That's the simple truth. You have to consider the Nguyễn clan's future as well as your own.'

'Thank you for your advice, Uncle,' said Nghĩa. 'But with the border war, I can't deal with these things right now.' He turned to his mother. 'Let's go home. I don't have much time.'

'That's exactly what I'm saying,' said Uncle Xeng.

On the walk home, Nghĩa's mother tugged his sleeve and said, 'Please, son, think about what Uncle Xeng said. I have nothing against Hạnh. I love her too, but you have to think about the future.'

Nghĩa had never thought about betraying Hạnh. He did not expect their marriage to turn out like this.

Leaving the village, the jeep passed the Linh Canal, and Nghĩa still felt dizzy and confused. After his meeting at the province military headquarters, the office closed for the afternoon. As Nghĩa strolled to his jeep, a man walking the opposite direction seemed familiar. It turned out to be his old comrade, Biển. It had been nearly fifteen years since they said goodbye at the bus station.

'Is that you, Biển?' asked Nghĩa.

Biển stood motionless in front of Nghĩa, his face brightening as he saw the major insignia. He reached out as if to embrace Nghĩa but at the last second stopped short. 'Oh, Nghĩa!' he exclaimed. 'You look so imposing in your uniform, I almost didn't recognize you. Who would've guessed you'd end up in command!' Biển shook Nghĩa's hand with both of his. 'I thought the war took away everything, but then we get to meet again.'

'How are things?'

'Just so-so. Did you think I deserted that day? No way! I'm no coward. But, wow! Seeing you here brings back such memories!'

Biển invited Nghĩa to come to his house to have a drink. The driver followed Biển's directions to guide the jeep through town.

'Thanks to my father, I have a house in town,' said Biển. 'I'm worthless now, but my wife is wonderful. I guess that's life! Rarely is there both a good husband and a good wife.' He pointed and said to the driver, 'My house is right over there at the curve. You can park in front.'

As soon as the car stopped, an adolescent boy rushed out of the house and stared at Biền and Nghĩa. He looked about thirteen or fourteen and his face was dirty.

'Bad boy!' said Biền. 'You didn't greet our guests or your father. Where's your brother?'

'He's taking a nap.'

'Please come in,' Biền said to Nghĩa and the driver. They entered the house and saw a toddler asleep on the floor. Biền took a chair that had been upside down on the bed and set it on the floor, and then invited them to sit. The rickety wooden table held three brown cups and a teapot with a chipped spout. Biền poured hot water from a thermos into the pot and stirred in some tea leaves.

'Okay, no need for more invitations. Everything's here in front of you.'

Biền gently picked up his sleeping son and laid him on the bed.

'This is my younger son,' he said, joining them at the table, 'born after the war, and the older boy over there was born after we visited this place together all those years ago. My wife, who wasn't yet my wife, sent me that telegram to get me here, and so a lot of good came from that trip home. She was beautiful back then, but now she's fat and sells vegetables at the market. It's a hard job, so she's not home very often. How about you? Any children?'

Nghĩa shook his head.

'In this one area, I've had greater success than you,' he joked. 'But no big deal, I'm kidding. The real accomplishment is earning that star and two stripes on your shoulders. You can have a son whenever you want. You're a man, and there's plenty of women out there. That's why it's a blessing to be a man.'

Biền stood, opened his son's schoolbag, and tore a sheet of paper from a notebook. He wrote something, handed the paper to the bigger boy, and whispered in his ear. The boy ran outside. Nghĩa looked at the toddler on the bed, who every now and then smiled in his sleep.

'He's probably dreaming about his mom,' said Biền. Then he turned to the driver and said, 'Have some tea. You're welcome to take a nap on the bed there. Major Nghĩa and I have a lot to catch up on. It's been such a long time!'

'Why didn't you come back to the unit after that visit?' Nghĩa asked. Then he smiled. 'Did you go AWOL just to keep satisfying your girlfriend?'

Biền patted Nghĩa on the shoulder and grinned. 'You have a sharp tongue now, huh? Your guess is partly true. I stayed longer than allowed because I had slept with her the night you were here, and the whole leave, and I realized I had to marry her. Not because I just wanted to have fun with her. I'm a pervert, I can have fun anywhere. It was because I realized I really did love her. She's such a good and lovely woman. I knew I didn't want to be the kind of guy who never settles down, especially since it seems all I have to do is blink and a girl gets pregnant. Even with the chaos of the war, I had to get married first. Then I returned, but they assigned me to another unit. Like I said, I'm no coward.'

'So you're not afraid of death?' Nghĩa asked.

'I don't think anyone born in this world likes the idea of death. But millions of soldiers go to war knowing they might die and still do it anyway. That's the important thing. Let me tell you a story I'll never forget that proves when people face death, they reveal their true selves. I had a friend about our age, in my new unit. He had a beautiful girlfriend, and I thought he seemed like a good guy. But before we fought the dry season campaign of '72, he told me, "I have a feeling I'm about to die." I asked what he was talking about, and he said, "I had a premonition that I'll die if I fight in this battle. So if you truly love me, stab me here right now, and I'll go to the field hospital instead." He pointed at his arm and handed me his knife. I told him to stop being a coward, and he said, very calmly, "You're right. I'm a coward. I slipped away from camp last night to go to the village nearby and pick papayas so I could drink the resin and make my body swell, but somehow it didn't work. I realized if I had to choose between death and my girlfriend, I'd choose her. I want to make love to her at least once, and then if I die, I'll have nothing to regret. I tried to talk her into letting me sleep with her the day I left, but she refused. She hugged and kissed me, and told me, 'We should wait until you come home after the war.' Now I know I'll never go home if you don't stab my arm." I told him I wouldn't do it, and he said, "It's up to you."'

Nghĩa listened attentively to Biển's story. Suddenly, Biển grabbed his hand and continued, 'You know what happened after that? He couldn't stab himself, and so he fought in the campaign, bravely in fact, but in the end, he was right and died a hero. What really makes me think about it a lot is that he got the wound that killed him while saving me and our company commander.' Biển bent forward to put out the cigarette that had burned down between his fingers. 'There's only a thin line between bravery and cowardice. Human instinct generally is to do good things, and if people do evil, it's because of things outside their control. That's what makes people heroes or cowards.' Biển struck a match and lit a new cigarette while peering through the smoke at Nghĩa. Suddenly he slammed his fist on the table and said vehemently, 'It's been fifteen years since we last met, and I feel I have to tell you, I'm really happy for your success, but I'm also ashamed of myself. No one knows how long they'll live. If we're too serious, we can ruin each other. My father ruined me, and I ruined him. He was very hard on me. Once, I started a fight with another kid in the street, and my father said, "He was a bastard." But then I skipped class to take an injured friend to the hospital, and my father called me worthless. He often scolded me, telling me if I kept studying so poorly, I'd end up a farmer. So, being a farmer is bad? If that's the case, there are a lot of bad people in this country! For sure, cowards are more dangerous than bastards. This gets really obvious during a war. A bastard will still be brave enough to save his comrades, but you should never count on anything from a coward. A bastard rarely earns a promotion, but a coward becomes a boss easily. A bastard probably wouldn't kill a person, but a coward kills thousands by letting them down. You probably think I'm splitting hairs, but that's human nature. Some people can only see things from afar, some from the middle, and others only what's right in front of their noses.'

'Is your father still working?'

'As I said, I ruined his career. I was a bad student, and he didn't want me to enlist, so he bribed someone so I could stay home. But then the bribe was discovered and he was forced to resign. You remember my sister, Thủy? She was so embarrassed that I "deserted" to get married and that Dad lost his job, she left the văn công and volunteered to join the Youth Brigade. She never married or had kids. After I got married, I realized I couldn't stay home while my sister went to fight, so I got my rucksack and went back. Look here!' Biển unbuttoned his shirt and showed Nghĩa the scars all over his chest.

'What happened with Thủy? Where does she live now?'

'The same house I took you to back then. My father lives there too. He visits my mother in the countryside every now and then. He tried to persuade her to move to town, but she says she's old and won't live much longer. She considers her ancestors' land the best place on earth. People have different preferences, so it's not easy to force them to change their minds. When my wife gets home, I want to invite you to dinner. In the meantime, I've told my son to go tell his aunt to cook for us.'

Nghĩa didn't know what Biển had written to Thủy, but when they arrived at her house, a tray full of delicious foods—roast chicken, spring rolls, rice and vegetables, and a bottle of rice wine—was already on the table. Thủy's eyes brightened seeing Nghĩa.

'Oh, hello!' she said. 'My brother said a friend from the army would visit but I didn't expect it would be you.' Her cheeks turned rosy. Her mischievous mannerisms had gone and her voice sounded more mature. 'I always knew you were a talented man. I said that from the beginning.' She didn't dare to look up at Nghĩa as she spoke.

'I'm not so talented,' Nghĩa said with a smile. 'It's just luck.'

'If you're not talented, how did you become a major? My brother was only ever an average soldier.'

'I admit I'm worthless. Where's the driver? Let's all sit down and drink some wine.'

'Thủy, where's your father?' asked Nghĩa.

'He's gone to visit Mother for a couple days. He's supposed to be back today.'

Biển said, 'Let's not wait for him because we don't know when he'll be back.' He poured rice wine into the glasses. Thủy sat next to the driver.

'You look so different,' Nghĩa said to Thủy after two glasses of wine.

'I've aged a lot, haven't I?'

'So it goes, we all get old. It's been nearly fifteen years. You look more mature now, in a good way.'

The driver ate quickly and excused himself to go out and keep an eye on the jeep. It had been a long time since Nghĩa had drunk like this, but both Biền and Nghĩa were delighted to see one another again, and happily made toast after toast. Seeing Nghĩa a bit tipsy, Thủy signalled to her brother not to make Nghĩa drink more. From Nghĩa's questions about Biền's sons and toasts to family and their wives, it became clear Nghĩa was unhappy that he and Hạnh had not yet had children. When they finished the bottle, Biền helped him lie down on his father's bed to rest.

'He drank a bit too much today,' Biền said to Thủy. 'Let him rest. He has to leave early tomorrow for the border. Poor guy! He fought for so many years and only got a few years of peace. Now he has to fight again. Our country is always at war, one after another, probably because we have lots of generals, but few outstanding majors like Nghĩa. In my unit, he was the best, always calm, smart, honest, and kind. Can I leave it to you to clean up, Little Sister? I've got to run home.'

Thủy cleaned up the table. The unexpected meeting with Nghĩa was such a surprise. In front of Biền and the driver earlier, Thủy had to suppress her overwhelming emotions as her memories with Nghĩa came rushing back. In this very room, she had held his neck and kissed him! She had been so naïve! When she joined the Youth Brigade, she assumed she was emotionally weak, but it turned out she was the strongest one. She overcame every obstacle and had no trouble avoiding temptations. After six years in the Youth Brigade, she came back, studied hard, and got into medical school. After graduation, she got a job at the province hospital. She was no longer an impetuous person. In fact, she had become quite contemplative. She often sat with her thoughts quietly for hours. As she washed the dishes, she wondered whether fate had brought Nghĩa back to her. Her father had still not come home, so she locked the door, turned off the light, and went to bed. The room fell silent.

The more she tried not to think about Nghĩa, the more visibly he appeared in her mind. She couldn't figure out why the first night they met, she had kissed him. It was unusual, even for the dramatic, mischievous girl she'd been. It had been a naïve, platonic kiss rather than a romantic one, but later, any time she was lonely, she would think about it. At this very moment, she could feel her lips on his. She ached to kiss him again. She tossed and turned, unable to sleep, until suddenly she heard Nghĩa calling for Biển. She got up and turned on the light.

'Oh, Thủy, hello. Where's your brother?'

'He went home. You slept all night. It's almost dawn!'

'I'm so thirsty! I can't believe I drank so much.' Nghĩa sat at the table and downed a whole glass of water. 'I'm sorry I woke you. Go back to bed. But can I take a shower before I leave?'

'Of course. Let me open the door for you.'

She got the key and opened the apartment door. She showed him the bathroom down the hall, gave him soap, a towel, and a basin, and then she went back to bed. She pulled the curtain to block the light coming from the dining area. A little while later she heard Nghĩa's footsteps as he came back into the apartment, and the click of the lock. Through the thin curtain, Thủy could see his silhouette standing quietly for a moment before lying back down. The room became quiet. Thủy tried to lie still, but her mind could not stop thinking about Nghĩa. She wanted desperately to rush out, lie down beside him, hold him in her arms and kiss him like the first time. Thủy tried to find inside herself the bold, naïve girl she used to be, but it was not so easy to do. If she took a risk and lay down beside him, he'd probably think she was loose. Maybe he already thought that about her anyway, given how forward she'd been back then. Thủy suddenly felt sad and tears poured from her eyes. She got up and tiptoed to the other room.

'Miss Thủy, why aren't you asleep?'

'I . . . I wanted to turn off the light so you could sleep.'

'No need. Soldiers can sleep and wake in any condition.'

Thủy felt embarrassed and went to the table to pour herself some water. She rarely drank water at this time.

'You leave for the border this morning, right?'

'I didn't plan to stay. If I hadn't run into your brother, I'd be with my unit already.'

'How long will you be stationed there?'

'I don't know. It's military duty. It could be a few days or it could be years. It's been great to see you again, by the way. Please let me know when you get married. I . . . I've never forgotten you.' Nghĩa lay still in the bed without looking at her.

Thủy's face flushed hot. She couldn't utter a word. She should've run back to her bed but some crazy idea made her edge closer to Nghĩa. Some part of her wanted to revisit the same coquettish play from the past, but her limbs trembled, and her heart beat fast. She stood motionless in front of Nghĩa unable to speak.

Nghĩa's face looked dreamy. Then he opened his eyes and looked at her intently. He gazed at her ivory neck and her round breasts hidden beneath a white nightgown spotted with tiny flowers. Nghĩa looked like he wanted to say something but his lips just quivered. Only a stone heart would allow Thủy to turn away. In life, rarely are there moments as electric as this. He trembled as her body fell into his. She caressed his body and her breasts heaved against him and she felt the desire rise in him. She kissed him wildly, and he kissed her back, each feeding on the other's heated passion. These were not the playful kisses of the past.

Everything happened quickly and ended quickly too. Thủy pulled her nightgown back on, intensely satisfied, her whole body thrumming with sweet exhaustion. She had given him her virginity without regret, and now she felt elated that not only someone else on earth, but *Nguyễn Nghĩa* understood her completely. Only he knew she was still a virgin after so many years in the Youth Brigade, and that was enough. Meeting her eyes and then letting his gaze roam over her body, he looked a little scared, and then a little chagrined.

'Why didn't you tell me?' he asked. 'Why stay a virgin so long and then give it away to me like this?'

Thủy smiled. 'It just seemed right. I've given you my virginity freely, so don't imagine you've stolen anything. I don't regret what we've done.'

'Still,' he said, placing her hand on his chest, 'I shouldn't have . . .'

'It's all right. If I didn't tell you, maybe you'd think I'd been with someone before. But it's okay—I feel lucky that I've been with you instead of anyone else.' Thủy pulled Nghĩa's face against her chest. 'Can you see anything to regret from there?'

Nghĩa laughed and kissed her. 'No.'

'I'm so happy. It must be Heaven that brought you to me. No one knows what war will bring. I hope sister Hạnh won't mind letting me have some fun this time, but don't worry, I won't say anything and no strings attached. I've lived through bombs and bullets and know I'd never be selfish to a soldier about to leave for the front.'

'What are you saying? I'm not about to die!'

'That's not what I meant.' She kissed his lips. 'I gave myself to you freely because I have nothing to save myself for. I've been miserable for years worrying someone who doesn't deserve my virginity would just take it. I've given it a lot of thought. Virginity's only important to young people. A young man would never want someone like me. Maybe one day I'll marry some widower, but no old man is going to care if I'm still a virgin.'

'Thủy, please stop talking like this . . .'

Morning came, and with it, up from the street, the noise of traffic. Thủy kissed Nghĩa and got out of bed to prepare breakfast so he could leave before the weather got hot. They said a quiet, quick goodbye, and then Thủy bicycled to the hospital to ask for the day off. Back at home, she slept until noon. When she woke, she had the strangest feeling, and after some thought, realized it was because over the last night she had finally, fully become a woman. She wrote in her diary: *Last night, I gave away my virginity to a married officer, bound for the front. I promise myself never to come between him and his beloved wife in Đông Village.*

Chapter 21

For days after their night together, Thủy lived anxiously, feeling like something big was about to happen. Maybe she'd become pregnant or maybe another man would suddenly find her irresistible. She felt nervous and excited all at the same time. On Saturday, Thủy asked her father's permission to visit her mother in the countryside, hoping to hear some news about Nghĩa. After lunch with her mother, she bicycled out to Đông Village, which took a little longer than usual because the main road was under construction. She tried as she pedalled to recall which of her former classmates originally came from the village. At the top of the hill above a stone bridge, she hopped off her bicycle and took in the view of the lush green paddies and silver river threading through them. Her face felt hot not only from the climb but also from wondering whether it was crazy to have come all the way out to the countryside like this. She coasted down to the bridge and, as a few men watched from the commune headquarters' courtyard, she washed her feet in the river. On the pier, a woman was soaking jute fibres strung over a stick by repeatedly dipping them into the water. The river sparkled with light from the bright sun. Thủy rolled up her pants and approached the woman, who peered intently at Thủy.

'Is that you, Thủy?' asked the woman.

Thủy couldn't remember the woman's name, though she looked very familiar.

'I wouldn't blame you if you don't remember me,' said the woman, sighing. 'I look so old now. I was a bad student and will have to live here my whole life, but a smart girl like you can go anywhere you want.'

'Oh, Thao!' Thủy exclaimed, taking the woman's hand. 'I'm sorry! It's been so long.'

'What are you doing here?'

'I'm looking for Xoan's house,' said Thủy.

'Xoan's not here. She lives in Hồi Village.'

'Oh no! I thought this was her village.'

Thủy squatted on the dock and took the other end of the stick to help Thao soak the jute. She was glad it was Thao she'd run into.

'Do you have a husband or kids?' asked Thủy.

'No, but it's okay.'

Thủy tied the jute to her bicycle and walked Thao home. They hung the fibres in the yard to dry, and then Thao introduced Thủy to her father, Mr Xung. 'Dad, this is my former classmate, Thủy. She's a doctor at the province hospital.'

'Wonderful!' said Mr Xung. 'Please come in and have some tea.'

As Thao caught her up on their classmates' lives, Thủy's mind wandered, trying to think of a way to ask about Nghĩa. When the opportunity arose, she said, 'I remember there was a guy a class above us from your commune who won the best student award. What was his name again?'

'Nguyễn Nghĩa,' Thao answered proudly. 'He's my cousin.'

'Oh, right. Nghĩa. I remember now.'

'He's a major in the army and has his own jeep and driver. Unfortunately, his marriage has been troubled. He and his wife have been married since before the war, but they still don't have kids. Not only is a married, childless woman miserable, she also brings misery to her husband and his family.' Thao seized Thủy's hand, and said excitedly, 'Hey, you're a doctor! Maybe you can help us! His mother has been sick for days and won't eat. Do you think you could help them figure out what's wrong? She talks in her sleep too, all kinds of crazy things. I've been sleeping over there a lot to help take care of her.'

'Where's his wife?'

'She's also really sick. She moved back in with her mother.' Then Thao turned to her father and said, 'I'm going to take Thủy to see Aunt Khiên.'

'No one can cure her,' said Mr Xung. 'Look at me and Xeng. No doctor helped us and we got better.'

'You never know,' said Thao. 'Let's see if my friend can help.'

Thao took Thủy to Nghĩa's house. Mrs Khiên lay on the bed, her eyes half closed. A wiry, intense looking man with short grey hair sat next to the bed talking to Mrs Khiên but stopped when he saw they had a guest. Thao introduced him as her Uncle Vạn.

'My friend's a doctor,' said Thao. She lifted the mosquito net and sat on the bed next to Mrs Khiên. Thủy said hello and sat beneath the netting next to Thao.

'I don't have my stethoscope with me,' said Thủy. 'I ran into Thao and she asked me to come.'

Nghĩa's sister, Duyên, came in from the kitchen and Thao introduced her to Thủy. The sister's eyes brightened and said, 'What luck you ran into each other! I hope you can figure out what's wrong with Ma.'

Thủy held Mrs Khiên's wrist to check her pulse. She used the lamp to check her eye dilation and gently probed her abdomen. Thủy asked whether she had any pain and when Mrs Khiên said no, she thought she might literally be sick from worrying so much. Her pitiful face looked haggard, her body emaciated. Thủy controlled her emotions so she wouldn't cry, feeling quite surprised at Nghĩa's dire family's situation. She discreetly looked around the house and yard. Nghĩa's sister poured tea for everyone.

'You should take her to the hospital,' said Thủy.

'I told you,' Mr Vạn said to Mrs Khiên. 'Did you hear what the doctor said? You have to go to the hospital. I'll take care of the house.'

Duyên and Thao walked Thủy to the gate. She told them what to expect with the hospital paperwork and gave them a few names in case they needed help.

Thủy bicycled to the stone bridge still feeling shocked. Suddenly she felt very attached to Đông Village and Nghĩa's family.

Only now did she really see the charm of his hometown, with its clear cool river meandering through green bamboo groves and sunlight dancing on its surface. Even the bridge's worn stones had a kind of charm, thanks to so many people having trod upon them.

*

That spring, Nguyễn Vạn joined a tree-planting group with some elderly men and could only rarely be found at home. He got up early every morning and cooked rice, ate some of it, and put the rest into a bag along with a bowl and chopsticks and another little bag of uncooked rice to make later. Then he'd take his machete and leave the house, often stopping at a neighbour's for morning tea before going to work. The women in the neighbourhood would see him hobble by with his bag and machete and scold their children and husbands, 'Hurry! Get up! Here you are still sleeping, and Mr Vạn has already gone to work!'

Vạn had recently come to believe it had been a terrible mistake to accept Hào's house as his residence. Wouldn't he have been happier if he had built his own home? He lived alone and didn't need such a big place. Cleaning it was so time consuming! Each morning, he left his house quite happily, knowing he wouldn't have to see Hơn or her son all day. When one vegetable is wormy, so are the rest. After Tốn brought home all those bourgeois items and built a mansion and married a beautiful wife, both his mother and his wife got pregnant at the same time. It was so embarrassing, the two women hardly dared to look at one another. At meals, there were two protruding bellies around the tray. In brief, it was the bourgeois items to blame. Tốn sold sexy red lingerie that he brought back from Sài Gòn, and Vạn didn't know whether Tốn gave his mother some to wear, or she stole them, but however she got them, she hung them to dry after washing in the banana garden behind the house so no one but Vạn would see them.

He discovered them one night when he went out to pee and saw something red that he thought at first was a bunch of banana flowers. He touched them and felt surprised to find they were soft like a woman's flesh, and only then realized it was Hơn's bra.

This happened about the same time Hơn started craving sour star fruit. Vạn thought she used them to braise fish, but she was going through a lot of them. One day, after she'd taken a bath with scented soap, she came over to Vạn's house holding a star fruit and smiled coyly at him.

'Do you have any salt?' she asked. 'Can I borrow some to eat with this star fruit?'

Vạn was surprised because he knew she had salt at her house. She went into his kitchen looking for the salt, which was right there but she said she couldn't find.

'Did you hide your salt jar?'

'It's in there.'

'Where exactly? I'll pay you back a whole bowl tomorrow.'

Annoyed by whatever game she was playing, Vạn rushed into the dark kitchen. Immediately, she fell into him, either intentionally or unintentionally. His hand accidentally brushed against her breasts.

'Oh, you naughty boy! You like them, don't you?' Then she clasped his hands and placed them on her chest. 'Here, feel them if you want. You're a man and should know how it feels to be with a woman.'

Hơn panted and Vạn lost control of himself. The softness of the bra had some disorienting power over his mind. Seemingly on their own, his trembling hands started to knead her breasts. When she put her arms around his neck, he could smell her scented soap and then her armpits, which brought him to his senses. Terrified, he ran into the next room and sat down on the mat. A burning oil lamp without a shade wavered across his vision. Hơn covered her mouth and giggled as she followed after him with the lamp. She had unbuttoned her shirt, showing off the pink bra Vạn had seen in the garden.

'Close it!' Vạn barked.

Hơn was about to close the door behind her when Vạn shouted, 'I mean close your shirt!'

Hơn shyly lowered her head, looked at her breasts, and buttoned up her shirt. 'Don't you like them? That's odd—it seemed like you did! Listen, you're old and have no one to take care of you, and this breaks my heart. I can give you a baby. Haven't you ever thought of having one? Since Tốn married, I've felt so lonely because he spends all his time with his wife and loves her more than me. I want to have my own baby, my own joy. You'll feel the same when you have one. Imagine your own little one jumping up and down, holding your neck, saying "Daddy, Daddy!" It's really fun to have a child in the house. When he grows up, he'll rebuild this place, just like my son rebuilt mine. Tốn will help us . . .'

'I'll never depend on your degenerate, bourgeois son! Get out of here!' Vạn leapt to his feet and dragged her by the arm outside. How dare she insult him like this, a Điện Biên veteran!

Later, when Vạn looked back at what had happened, he was glad he didn't fall into her trap, or she would have told everyone she'd slept with him and the baby was his. Hơn's belly was getting bigger and she lowered her eyes any time she saw Vạn. But if someone made her mad, she'd vent her anger on him, and he dared not retaliate, because he worried she'd make a scene about him touching her breasts. He hated the coward who had slept with her but was too afraid to admit it.

Sometimes he'd hear a noise at night and get up to see who was visiting her, but never found anyone. It's better to ignore her, Vạn thought. On the days Vạn planted trees far along the new road, he contributed the rice to cook for lunch. When he worked near the hamlet, and the other people went home for lunch, Vạn did not. He just took a nap under the mango tree. When it rained, he sat in the commune headquarters. Sometimes he rested in a hammock hung in the commune storehouse or under the Silver Stone Bridge.

Aunt Khiên had been hospitalized for over a month, and Vạn was still looking after her house. He no longer dropped by neighbours' houses like he used to. Several members of the Nguyễn clan had been saying recently that Hạnh and Aunt Khiên were sick because Nghĩa had torn down the old lineage temple. Vạn was not a spiritual person but seeing Aunt Xeng burn incense and pray every night worried him. Uncle Xung had been crazy and Uncle Xeng too—would Aunt Khiên be okay? Hạnh's condition had improved somewhat and she'd begun to take care of her mother-in-law a couple days a week so Nghĩa's sister, Duyên, could take care of her own family at home.

The border war was intense, and in the past, Nghĩa had gotten leave to come home after his father's funeral, so it seemed likely he hadn't received the news that his mother was not well. Vạn was glad that Hạnh's condition had improved, but it saddened him that her life with Nghĩa had been so troubled. He knew she wasn't happy that his extended family had caused them so much grief, and worse, the situation seemed to be making Nhân sadder and lonelier too.

Vạn sighed as he entered Hạnh and Nghĩa's courtyard. Inside the new lineage temple, Aunt Xeng and a few women were kneeling in front of the ancestors' altar and praying. Otherwise, the night was quiet, and the incense smelled fragrant. Duyên arrived just after him, dropped her bag on the veranda, sat down inside, and breathed a sigh of relief.

'How's your mother?' asked Vạn.

'Thank Heaven she's getting better.'

Aunt Xeng and the women rushed into the kitchen from the lineage temple. Aunt Xeng asked, 'Has she recovered? When will she be back?'

'We hope she'll be home in about a week,' said Duyên. 'She's lucky that Aunt Thao's friend, Dr Thủy, has been helping with her case. I've never met anyone as kind as her. When Ma kept passing out, Dr Thủy donated blood for her transfusion. She even let me sleep at her house, which is close to the hospital and really nice. Whatever help I need, she gives. When Nghĩa comes home, he needs to do something to repay her kindness.' Then she looked at Vạn and said, 'I've got to go. Would you please look after the house for a few more days? I really miss my kids.' Vạn assured her it was no problem and she hurried home.

'She's so rude!' complained Aunt Xeng. 'She just raced in and out and didn't bow once to the ancestors.'

*

Hạnh felt caught in a whirlwind. She had marshalled enough strength to come to the hospital several times over the past weeks to help Thao and Duyên with Mother Khiên's care, but on the afternoon Mother Khiên would be discharged, the doctor could see how sick Hạnh really was. She had nothing left to lose except her feather-light body, which felt completely exhausted from being blown here and there by the torrents of life. The doctor kept lingering in front of her. Framed by her white collar and her beautiful face, the doctor's gentle but powerful black eyes kept peering very intently at Hạnh. She could sense the woman's tremendous capabilities hidden beneath the white coat and expressed by her soft hands and beautifully long, delicate fingers. A country girl like Hạnh couldn't compare herself to a woman like that, both a goddess and a ghost with such a strange, haunting power.

'You shouldn't go home with Mrs Khiên,' the doctor said, holding Hạnh's wrist to check her pulse. 'Your heartbeat is very weak. You should check into the hospital so we can treat you. Let me go get you some milk.'

The doctor exited the room and closed the door, but her warm voice echoed in Hạnh's mind. The woman unnerved her. Suddenly Hạnh panicked and bolted out of the room, down a back stairway and out of the hospital. The street was crowded with people but it felt to her like she was the last person left on earth. At the bus station, Hạnh searched for her mother-in-law and Aunt Thao, who had left not too long before to catch the last afternoon bus back to the village. At last, she saw Aunt Thao about to board, and she ran to catch them, but then the doctor appeared out of nowhere and again held Hạnh by the wrist. She felt powerless beneath the gaze of those beautiful black eyes, incapable to resist those long, delicate fingers. The doctor was saying, 'Really, Sister, you should come back to the hospital. Your heart . . .'

The driver started the engine, which rattled the bus and broke the spell.

'No!' Hạnh insisted. 'I'm not going with you.' Her legs and arms felt like they weighed a thousand pounds. With enormous effort, she escaped the long, delicate fingers and climbed the steps into the bus. The driver's assistant closed the door and the bus rumbled away. Hạnh peered out the window and saw the doctor still standing there, her white coat brilliant in the afternoon sun.

'You're acting so crazy,' said Aunt Thao. 'Dr Thủy told us you needed to stay at the hospital.'

'She's so kind,' said Mother Khiên. 'You don't find many like her.'

Hạnh sat in silence. The potholed road jarred the bus up and down, left and right.

The driver's assistant tapped Hạnh on the shoulder. 'Pay for your bus ticket please.' Then he saw her face and asked, 'Are you sick?'

Aunt Thao paid for the ticket. Behind Hạnh, some passengers began to talk about the war at the northern border and up the Mekong.

'My son just wrote me that he was being sent to Cambodia soon.'

'The only thing our country is good at is fighting invaders,' complained someone loudly.

'When invaders come, we have to fight. We can't just sit here and let them cut our throats.'

'Damn it! Our country's like a beautiful girl all the men want to have.'

'Human beings are really smart and really stupid. We're stupid because we work so hard to protect life and then we just destroy it. The smarter we are, the more destructive weapons we create. Terrible! In a flash, everything dies, not even an ant or a worm can survive.'

Chapter 22

One of Hạnh's few wedding gifts was a wooden trunk. When new, it had been stained with a dark red varnish, but now the colour had faded to a pale brick-coloured red that resembled the colour often used to paint coffins. Inside the trunk, along with some clothes and a silk scarf, Hạnh kept the old handwritten book that contained the Nguyễn family genealogy and the great great grandfather's words of wisdom. Mother Khiên had given the book to Hạnh when Father Khiên died so she could read it and pass it on to the next generation when the time came.

One evening, Hạnh invited Uncle Xung, Uncle Xeng, and his wife to come to the ancestors' altar. They burned incense while Mother Khiên sat quietly on a mat off to the side. Hạnh placed the crimson-covered book on the altar with trembling hands and said, 'I've been lost, and Heaven has helped me find my way again. I've made Nghĩa and our family suffer. I've kept this book for years without fully appreciating the great great grandfather's words. I accept responsibility for everything.'

Then she opened the cover and took out a letter that had taken her many nights to write. 'Mother Khiên,' she said, 'this is my formal request for divorce. When Nghĩa comes home, please give it to him. From now on, he's free, and I ask for your permission to move back to my mother's house.'

Great Uncle Xung and Aunt and Uncle Xeng stood in front of the altar, stunned and speechless. For a moment, the house was totally silent, and then Mother Khiên burst out crying. Hạnh knew she wouldn't be able to control her tears so she hurried outside. It was an autumn night, the weather a bit chilly, and a drizzle splashed raindrops on her face. She shivered as she made her way home in the dark. She went into her mother's house and sobbed on the bed.

'Have you gone crazy?' Nhân sat next to Hạnh and held her hand. 'Why do something so foolish? You've already gone through hell, why divorce now? No one beat you. No one threw you out. For heaven's sake!'

Hạnh wiped her tears, hugged her mother, and forced a smile. 'That's right, no one kicked me out. It was my choice. Don't you want me to come home and live with you? You've been living all by your lonesome for so many years, and now that I'm back, it'll be better.'

'I don't want your pity. You need to take care of yourself. In all my life I've never heard of a girl getting married and then ending up like this.'

'Ma, please don't make a big deal out of this. You don't understand.'

A cold wind blew in, and the oil lamp's sputtering yellow light flickered over their pale faces. Her mother sobbed. Hạnh wanted to say something to comfort her mother but nothing would come. No one could understand her. She had said nothing about Nghĩa's secret affair with Thủy.

One night, while Mother Khiên was still in the hospital and Dr Thủy was working, Aunt Thao had taken Hạnh to the doctor's house to rest. Hạnh knew it was not polite to read Thủy's diary, but she was so curious about the beautiful doctor with the magnetic, dark eyes, she couldn't help herself. And suddenly the doctor's unusual special interest in her family and extra care made complete sense. Strangely, Hạnh felt no resentment toward the doctor or Nghĩa. She just felt sad, and later, when she went to the district clinic and consulted with a chubby female doctor about her inability to get pregnant, she felt even worse.

'You're lucky!' said the doctor while writing down Hạnh's information. 'Most women these days are trying to have fewer children. How long have you been married?'

'Over fifteen years.'

'Have you ever had mumps?'

'You're asking me about mumps?'

'Yes. Have you had mumps?'

'I think so, when I was little. Why?'

'Mumps can cause ovarian failure, or if your husband has had it, it can cause some fertility problems for men too. But whatever the cause, if you can't get pregnant after normal sexual intercourse with your husband for fifteen years, you might consider adoption. There's a lot of abandoned love children in the orphanages these days.'

'What do you mean?'

'You're kind of a slow thinker, aren't you?'

After she moved home, people in the village found Hạnh's completely changed personality rather surprising. No longer a gentlewoman in public and easily angered, she now spoke with an acid tongue. Then at night, she'd hug a pillow and weep. She had decided she'd rather have people's hate than pity. Though she'd announced the divorce, she still loved Nghĩa—in fact, maybe now more than ever. For a while, she tried to curb her feelings of weakness by blaming Nghĩa for all the bad and sinful things that had happened. But the more negatively she thought about him, the sweeter and more handsome he appeared in her mind. All the lovely memories they'd made together now burned her withered heart to ash.

One day, as Hạnh harvested duckweed at the pond, Thắm and Linh came and told her that they'd heard Nghĩa had returned. Hạnh dropped the knife into her basket and said, 'You can't believe everything you hear.' Then she snatched up the knife again and continued to work. Her heartbeat quickened. Her mind whirled. She almost cut herself.

'Aunty Hạnh!' said Linh. 'Will you let me sit in Uncle Nghĩa's jeep again and drive with you to the market in town like last time?'

Hạnh forced a smile. 'It's not my jeep, sweetie. You'll have to ask Uncle Nghĩa. I don't live with him anymore.'

'Why not?' the boy asked innocently.

'Don't be rude,' said Thắm.

'I'm not being rude,' said Linh. He told Hạnh, 'If you won't let me sit in the jeep, I won't let you sit in my father's tank when he comes home.' Then he sulked off to the other side of the pond to catch dragonflies.

'Thắm, please tell Dâu to come over tonight,' said Hạnh with a big sigh.

'What's wrong?' asked Thắm.

'You won't understand.'

Thắm and Linh left. Hạnh continued to harvest duckweed, oblivious to what she was doing. Her knees shook. Her eyes blurred. Her feet sank into the mud and when she stumbled and fell into the pond, the duckweed she'd harvested floated out over the surface. Hurriedly she gathered it all back into the basket and then walked home, shivering in her wet clothes.

'Good heavens!' exclaimed her mother from the kitchen. 'Why are you soaking wet? Better go towel off and put on dry clothes or you'll catch a cold.'

Hạnh went into her bedroom and got changed. Then she returned to the kitchen and warmed her hands by the cooking fire. Her clumsy shivering knocked over the kettle, spilling water onto the fire and sending up a plume of ash.

'What is wrong with you today?'

Hạnh said nothing. Thinking about meeting Nghĩa later was like knowing an earthquake was about to happen. She felt light-headed and disconnected from everything. At dinner, while sitting with her mother, Hạnh started to feel as lost and powerless as she did as a young girl, like when she had followed her brothers Hà and Hiệp to set traps to catch birds. And, at the same time, she felt so old, her limbs stiff, her face weathered like an old crone's.

'You look like you've lost your mind,' said Nhân, glancing anxiously at Hạnh between bites. 'Be careful or you'll get sick again. Here, eat more of this hot soup. It'll warm you up.'

Hạnh tried to finish her bowl of soup and then went into her dark room without a lamp. She groped through the trunk for different clothes to put on. She found the purple Hong Kong–style shirt and black silk pants outfit she'd bought when she went to the district market in the jeep with Thắm, Linh, and Dâu. It had been just two years, but it seemed like so long ago. She'd worn these nice clothes each time she went to the hospital to visit Mother Khiên. Now she couldn't recognize herself in them. She sat on the bed and combed her hair in the dark, realizing for the first time how much it had thinned because of her illness.

Since moving back in with her mother, Hạnh had been trying to forget her sorrow. She worked hard in the fields all day and was also raising two pigs, so that when bedtime came, she'd be exhausted and could fall asleep easily. She dreaded having insomnia and took sleeping pills if she couldn't fall asleep on her own right away, especially on days when she didn't quite tire herself out.

Hearing her mother and Dâu talking, Hạnh came out to the yard. Dâu saw Hạnh wearing the purple shirt, winked at her, and said, 'Oh good! I worried you might keep wearing the same messy clothes as usual. I was just at Nghĩa's house. They're talking about you with great Uncle Xung, Aunt Thao, and Aunt and Uncle Xeng so I snuck out to come here. I overheard Uncle Xeng say you've been keeping company with raucous women. Ha ha ha . . . looks like they've been keeping an eye on you all along.' Dâu giggled at her own joke.

Hạnh's mother came in from the kitchen with the kettle in her hand. She started to say something but stopped. She took the tea-stained cups and saucers outside to wash them.

'Bu is so thoughtful, preparing to welcome the special guest,' said Dâu. She unscrewed the soot-stained oil lamp chimney. 'I'll clean it so you can see the major's face clearly.'

'How is he?'

'Handsome as ever.' Dâu grinned and poked Hạnh in the ribs, whispering, 'Let him have a good time with you tonight. He has travelled all the way from the border just to see you.'

Hạnh thumped Dâu's back with her fist. Her face flushed hot. When Hạnh left Nghĩa's house and moved back in with her mother, Dâu had moved out. But she still came over and stayed late every night. When there was a movie or a play at the co-op courtyard, Nhân would babysit Linh so Thắm, Dâu, and Hạnh could go out. The three of them remained close friends, despite their very different personalities, and never hid anything from one another.

Nhân came in with the cleaned cups and saucers and placed them in the middle of the table. She gave Dâu a sly look. 'Where'd you go last night that you didn't come over? Could it be you're dating someone?'

'Maybe?' Dâu giggled. 'Last night, Mr Ba Chương took me to the riverbank to enjoy the view.'

'What? That's crazy! You went with him? In cold, wet weather like this?'

'I know, it's hard to believe. I had just left my house to come here last night, and apparently Mr Ba Chương was hiding in the banana garden waiting. He followed me and flirted with me. He was wearing nice clothes—a white shirt, dress pants, and leather shoes. I asked him where he was going, and whether he dressed up so nice like that every evening. He laughed and told me he was glad to see me and that he had a story he wanted to tell me. I suggested we go to the Silver Stone Bridge, but he said, "Dâu, you are a romantic woman, but I'm afraid my step-daughter, Tươi, will see me sitting on the bridge with you and then tell her mother, Hin, about it. I don't want to get either of us in trouble." So I suggested we go to the riverside, and that's where he told me about his plan to dig a pond and raise fish. Then he told me to guess what else he had planned. I said he probably wanted to hire labourers to help dig, and he said, "Silly girl! It's not about the pond! I could say one word and the whole village would volunteer."'

'You should stop teasing that old man,' Nhân said, laughing. Hạnh cackled too.

'Let me finish,' said Dâu. 'Mr Ba Chương pulled me down to sit next to him and look at the river and then he asked if I knew why he built such a big house. He was freezing. His teeth chattered, and I moved closer to him to keep him warm. Then he stammered, "I built such a big house for you." He said Tý Hin gave him permission to marry and have a second wife because she can't give birth again, after having Tươi and then marrying him and having three more daughters. He said I was the only woman in the village he was attracted to. I slugged him on the shoulder and said, "What a pity! You should've said something sooner. I already accepted another proposal." Mr Ba Chương let out a long sigh and looked so pitiful. I told him I'd try to make a match for him with Thắm, but he said no because he was afraid Thắm's son would grow up and take over his property.'

Just as Dâu finished her story, Thắm and Linh walked in.

'Speak of the devil.' Dâu smiled at Thắm and Linh. 'I was just saying I want to make a match for you. He's rich!'

Linh came to Nhân and showed her the candy Nghĩa had just given him.

'Let me adopt you,' said Dâu, 'so your mommy can move in with Mr Ba Chương.' She pulled the boy into her arms and kissed him.

'Send your own mommy to Mr Chương! My mommy's waiting for my daddy to come home and then she'll give me a little sister.' The boy bit Dâu's thigh.

It was already quite late, and Nghĩa had not yet come, so Dâu left with Thắm carrying her sleepy son on her back. The house was quiet again. Nhân snuffed the oil lamp and went to bed. Hạnh lay in her own bed, listening to the sounds outside. A wind blew through the banana garden and rustled the leaves. A firefly careened through the air of Hạnh's bedroom, circled lazily around, and then landed on the mosquito net. Hạnh pulled up the blanket to cover her head, wondering if Mother Khiên would think the firefly was a good sign or a bad one. The question about the firefly haunted her all night. When she woke that morning, she felt like she hadn't slept at all. Nhân had already eaten breakfast and gone out to the fields to work. Hạnh looked at the breakfast Nhân had left for her on the table and knew that her mother understood she hadn't slept.

Hạnh washed her face and was patting it dry when Nghĩa finally arrived. He looked the same—tall, strong, and handsome. His bright eyes still mesmerized Hạnh. She shuffled across the floor and sat down at the table, trying not to meet his gaze.

'Please, sit,' Hạnh said flatly. 'There's not much to say. Everything's over. Now that you're back, did you sign the divorce paper?' She had already planned her sentences and memorized her lines so she could be like a tape deck that only needed to be set in front of Nghĩa and the PLAY button pressed.

Nghĩa came to the table and stood there speechless, as if unable to believe that those words had come from her mouth. And yet, she was sitting right there, glaring at him with her fiery eyes. He jumped a little when she shouted, 'Speak up! Just tell me the date we have to go to court.'

'Have you gone crazy?' Nghĩa exclaimed. 'Where did you get such an idea? Have you forgotten all our good memories?'

'Good memories? I don't think you're seeing things clearly. Our past has nothing but sorrow and humiliation. We have no choice but to follow our own paths. I'm sure you can find a better life with someone else.'

'I want to know what caused all this.'

'What caused all this?!' Hạnh tried to remain calm and poured tea into the cups. 'We've been so wrong thinking love is all that matters, and now we have to pay for our mistake. You're always gone and have no idea about all the cruel things I've had to put up with. Your ancestor's curse is ingrained in the flesh and blood of your thousand-year-old family and will never be forgotten. There's no point in talking. Everything's over.'

'Sweetheart, please reconsider. I've been transferred to the province military headquarters. Now that we won't have to live apart, everything will be fine.'

'The province military headquarters?' Hạnh looked straight into Nghĩa's eyes. 'Good for you. I'm sure you'll be very happy living in the province capital. But between us, it's over.'

Chapter 23

Major Nghĩa's decision to sign the divorce paper and give Hạnh full ownership of the house he had built on his ancestors' land created quite a stir in Đông Village, with many villagers saying he was being generous to her to compensate for her lost youth. Then he announced he would take his mother to the province capital to live with him, which shocked Mrs Khiên tremendously, but she had no choice other than to live with her only son, her last refuge. Nghĩa took only his mother's clothes, a blanket, a mosquito net, and a few other necessities with them.

Some people didn't understand her feelings and said, 'You're lucky to get to live in an exciting place like the province capital, so you shouldn't regret leaving the boring countryside.' Of course, Mrs Khiên didn't regret leaving everything behind to Hạnh. But she felt empty because she had lost something very important—something a thousand times more important than the house. Her life as a daughter-in-law of the Nguyễn clan was not entirely happy because so much of it involved hardship and sorrow, but her emotional attachment to the land on which she had given so much could never be broken. What would life be like living on land to which she had no such connection? She noticed Nghĩa now avoided his ancestral homeland and duty as head of the clan. When Nghĩa gave Uncle Xung the crimson family ledger, Uncle Xung said, 'Nghĩa has given away the ancestors' sacred land and lineage temple to a Vũ woman—our great great grandfather's mortal enemy,' and those words haunted Mrs Khiên. She got into the jeep and cried. Uncle Xung, cane in hand, stood on the porch as the jeep taking the head of the clan to the province capital left columns of dirt rising from the road.

Suddenly, the colour of his face changed, and Uncle Xung announced, 'As long as I'm alive, Hạnh will never live on Nguyễn ancestral land.'

But Hạnh knew already she would never be able to live in the house built on the Nguyễn ancestral land. Her life there was ruined. She regretted that Nghĩa felt he and his mother had to leave and hoped that he would find new happiness after the divorce and start a new family on his ancestral land. Hạnh felt like she had somehow committed a crime.

Days and months passed, and no one lived in the house. The door was kept shut, the garden abandoned. Sometimes, Aunt Xeng would come and open the door to burn incense. When Hạnh had to pass by, she couldn't look at the house. It was like a thorn piercing her heart, a symbol of all the Nguyễn family's wounds and hidden resentments, just like Hạnh's lonely life. The door began to crack, and some kids snuck inside and graffitied terrible things on the walls. Hạnh once suggested that Uncle Vạn move there to live, but he immediately replied, 'Never!'

It was true Uncle Vạn would never even consider living in the ancestors' house, at least not since he had volunteered to help take care of the tree nursery. When the co-op's duck farm went bankrupt, the commune leadership gave the farm to the tree-planting team to build a nursery, which would grow casuarina, eucalyptus, margosa, lychee, longan, and many other kinds of trees. The only vestige left of the duck farm was the eighteen-year-old clay house the Youth Association had built for Hạnh and Nghĩa. It had been eighteen long years, and the house still stood there. Only its roof needed to be repaired.

Uncle Vạn readily volunteered to move to the nursery because he detested living next to Hơn's family. It was said she had eaten a lot of fatty food during her pregnancy, and so her four-kilogram baby boy had to be born caesarean. The baby wailed and screeched all night, so a rumour circulated that the father was a pig castrator in Hồi Village. Others said the baby looked like the mason in Hạ Village. One of the elderly men on the tree-planting team joked, 'Vạn, why don't you be the father since no one else wants to? You could have both the baby and his mother, and that would save you from having to buy betel and areca for the wedding.'

Vạn kept his face blank. 'No thanks!' Never would Nguyễn Vạn mess around with her, the former wife of a colonial collaborator!

Before he moved, if for any reason Vạn stayed at home for the day, Hơn would ask him to watch the baby so she could wash clothes or do other chores, saying, 'Damn it! My son and daughter-in-law never help. Please give me a hand.' Then she'd press the baby into his arms and hurry away, so Vạn would have no choice but to babysit. The one time Vạn refused her request for help, she gave him a nasty glare, and Vạn feared she'd make a scene about him touching her breasts, so he relented. But now that he lived in the nursery, he no longer had to put up with her.

His nursery house was quiet with good light and lots of fresh air. Vạn got up each morning and enjoyed the serene greenness of the place surrounded by trees. On hot days, he'd discard his shirt and go for a swim in the river. He came to feel as if he were living in a completely different world, one that finally allowed his personality to mellow. At night, the old duck shack was completely quiet, and no one knew what he did or where he went. The Đông villagers almost forgot about Vạn because they hardly ever saw him hobbling along the village road or stopping by neighbours' houses for tea.

The nursery property was separated from the noisy outside world by a bamboo fence. In the afternoon, buffalos and their calves, children, old people, young men and women swam and bathed at the river, and after a long day of hard work, none of them cared much about Vạn, if they thought of him at all. He tried not to pay much attention to the activities at the river, but when women showed off their bodies while swimming, he couldn't stop himself from feeling some lustful desire. He lived a lonely, secluded life, but outside, the world was still lively.

Only now had Vạn begun to regret not marrying when he was younger. He rarely thought about himself and ate simple foods just to survive. He seldom went to the market. If he was hungry, he went to the fields and got sweet potatoes or beans. If he went to the paddies, he'd find crab or crawfish to make soup. He ate just two meals a day, and they cost him almost nothing.

Days turned into months and years. Vạn nearly forgot he had once been a soldier. His soldierly life as a Điện Biên hero was now far in the past. Occasionally, something would make him recall the day of the final victory at Điện Biên Phủ or the time he had carried his rifle out to the old kiln to try to shoot down low-flying American planes, but those were fleeting moments, like meteors streaking in the night. The only war souvenirs he kept were a few medals he stored in a bag hung in a corner and the patched uniform jacket he wore occasionally to remind himself and the other villagers who he was. The little kids who'd never known war couldn't imagine why anyone would wear such an old rag like that and told him to throw it away. Only Major Nghĩa understood Uncle Vạn. Before he left Đông Village, he gave Vạn a new pair of combat boots, which Vạn had not yet worn.

Each year, on 27 July, the commune invited veterans and their families and the families of war martyrs to attend a memorial at four in the afternoon. Gauging by the sun, Vạn guessed it was about three, enough time to strip off his clothes and jump into the river to bathe. Then he put on the new shirt to which he had pinned his war medals, and the boots Nghĩa had given him, even though the weather was hot. Vạn always observed this day with respect, and he felt excited as he strolled from the riverbank to the Silver Stone Bridge. People came and went from the commune headquarters, and he recognized familiar faces that had aged like his as time went by. Most of the disabled veterans had been injured during the American War. Some had lost an eye, others an arm or a leg and had to walk with crutches. Among the veterans who had fought against the French, Vạn had the most medals. The commune office set up two rows of tables and filled them with flowers, candy, cigarettes, and lemon wine. They made Vạn the guest of honour and seated him at the first table. That's where he was when he saw Nhân sitting at the far end of the room, looking old and frail and sad.

He guessed she was sad because Hạnh had become so ill-tempered and frequently stayed out late at night. The last time Vạn had run into Hạnh, she had gone from laughing one minute to sobbing the next. The villagers said she was possessed by an evil spirit because sometimes her eyes were white, sometimes red. Nhân told Vạn that it had gotten worse after Hạnh went with Thắm to Hà Đông, seeking information about the gunner, Thấu, because Thắm was worried he'd died in the war and would never come back. But the gunner hadn't died. After liberation day, he had moved his whole family to the South and lived there since then without telling Thắm. Some villagers also claimed he'd married a woman from a bourgeois family. Life was like that sometimes.

Vạn emptied his glass of wine and sat down next to Thành. He tapped Thành on the shoulder and asked, 'Between Dâu and Thắm, who would you marry?'

'Uncle Vạn, you're drunk,' said Thành, looking at Vạn hesitantly. Then he whispered, 'Mr Ba Chương is very rich, but Thắm doesn't want him, and I'm a nobody with a ruined face. I think Thắm might have fallen in love with the photographer again, and Dâu has become a devout Buddhist and goes to the temple with the elderly women every day to pray.'

'Really? I guess they've lost their minds.'

It had been a long time since Vạn had drunk wine. He felt exhilarated as he staggered home along the riverbank. Up in the sky, clouds shaped like an old man, a cow, and a dog floated lazily around the red sun on the horizon. The river looked pink in the sunset light. Footsteps came from behind him. He turned and found Hạnh standing there, quite close.

'Uncle Vạn, you look great today!' she said, her smile beaming a bit too intensely.

Vạn saw the red blood vessels in her eyes and wondered if she really had been possessed. Her laughter sounded so weird, and she couldn't stand still. Instead, she fidgeted like a madwoman.

'Where are you going out so late?' asked Vạn.

'Going . . . for a swim . . . a swim . . . ha ha ha!' Then she danced down toward the pier. Her shadow gradually vanished into the dark.

Vạn opened his house at the nursery and looked for a match to light the oil lamp. It was still hot outside, and the nursery was quiet. He took off his boots and lay down on the bed. Thunder rumbled in from a long way off, heralding a heavy rain. Vạn shivered, his face flushed hot, his temples pounded. The wine he'd drunk had started to have some effect. Then a gusty wind roared in, and waves crashed onto the riverbanks and the pier. The storm hit with a torrent of rain, followed by more lightning and thunder and gusts of wind that put out the lamp. Outside, someone screamed, and then Vạn heard heavy footsteps. The door suddenly banged open, and in the doorway he saw the silhouette of a woman rushing inside just before she pounced and he was pinned to the bed.

'That's him!' the woman shouted. 'That's him!'

'What?' said Vạn. 'Who?'

'The ghost!' she shrieked. 'The red-eyed ghost!'

Vạn panicked, unsure whether he was dreaming or awake. The wine was making his head spin and inflaming his lonely heart. His skin came alive with the woman's hot, naked body against his, her breath heavy on his neck. In the midst of the wild, stormy night, and more aroused than he'd ever felt before, Vạn let himself lose control, let himself joyously and gratefully believe that Nhân had finally chosen to be with him. At long last, he let his body do what it had ached to do for so long. The two bodies entwined. Sparks flared in his eyes and dissipated into the most serene and blissful feeling he'd ever felt. And then, too soon, booming thunder filled his room with blinding white light, and Nguyễn Vạn realized he was no longer Nguyễn Vạn. The woman moaning in his arms was Hạnh.

For her whole life, and most of his, he had loved her like a father. He was happy when she was happy, and he was heartbroken when she suffered. He had been by her side through so many things and had never thought of her this way, never imagined that her misery could push her into his arms. Was she so desperate? Had she gone mad?

'You miserable, pitiful man,' Hạnh said as he recoiled. 'No one will know. Or are you scared I'll only bring you sorrow?'

No, thought Vạn immediately. That wasn't it. But before he could speak, she had sprung from the bed and was out the door, back into the raging storm and pouring rain. And that was when Vạn realized that what she had always brought to his lonely life was life itself. Whether with sorrow or happiness, at least with her he had always felt alive. Even so, after that night, Vạn felt ashamed and could not bring himself to meet the gaze of anyone in the village, including little children.

For days and days, he hid himself away in the nursery house, tormented by his thoughts. With one indiscretion, he had destroyed both Nhân and Hạnh's pure and sacred love. He had also destroyed the pride he'd held for himself, and now was stooping so low as to consider using his rifle to put an end to it all. He cursed himself and cursed his shame, knowing he'd turned himself into an even worse human than old man Xung or that tramp, Widow Hơn. His whole adult life, he had imagined that he carried himself with the dignity of a Điện Biên veteran. Now that dignity was gone! Even worse, he was the bastard who had ruined Hạnh's dignity as well. After that rainy night, he could tell she was avoiding him. He felt sorry for her and he loved her. Her courage and kindness had brought the only joy into his miserly life. And now the sound of her moaning on that night kept echoing in his mind.

Even after more than a month had passed, there were whole days when Vạn could do nothing but pace back and forth inside the house. On one such day, it was nearly dark, and he realized he hadn't yet made dinner, so he washed and cooked a handful of rice. The fire illuminated the whole house, and while he gazed attentively at the coals under the pot, Hạnh came and stood in the open doorway with a small cloth bag slung from her shoulder. A terrible dread came over Vạn. Her worried eyes peered down at him from her pale, thin face. To his surprise, she ran to him, knelt beside him, and took his hands in hers.

'Hạnh, you shouldn't come here again,' he said. 'I'm a bastard. A real bastard!' In the stillness of the house, he could hear his heart beating fast and the crackling of the fire. The rice pot boiled over and water hissed as it hit the coals.

'I'm leaving the village,' said Hạnh. 'I'm leaving right now and never coming back. I came to say goodbye.'

'No! Please forgive me, Hạnh. It's all my fault. You don't have to go anywhere. You have a long life ahead. You have to stay on this land, your mother is still here . . .'

Just as suddenly as she'd left the last time, Hạnh stood and—before Vạn could say anything else—was out the door. He stumbled to the doorway and watched as her unsteady shadow disappeared into the dark. Trembling, Vạn realized his crime was even more serious than he first imagined. It was he who had raised her. And now it was he who had backed her into a corner and forced her to leave the village. Where would she go? The question repeated endlessly in his head.

Terrified, Vạn left the cooking fire burning brightly and ran to the pier. His mind went blank as he groped his way along the shore in the dark. Splashing came from the inky river, making Vạn panic that Hạnh had been swallowed up. 'Hạnh!' he shouted. 'Hạnh!' He hobbled as fast as he could over No Man River's uneven banks. For the first time in his life, Vạn felt a horrible, sickening fear.

Chapter 24

It broke Thủy's heart every time she saw Nghĩa's mother's sad and miserable face. Mother Khiên drank some water and went to her bed to lie down. Nghĩa read a few lines from his newspaper before putting it down to gaze at Thủy affectionately. She could read his mind—he was again thinking about her giving birth to a son. Soon after the divorce, she had accepted his proposal, and they had married quickly and quietly. All along the walls of their bedroom, he had hung pictures of adorable children. She loved to see him so taken by a picture of a little boy with black eyes and a cute smiling mouth.

'Do you have to work tonight?'

Thủy kissed his lips, and she could feel deep in her heart how much she loved him. She squeezed his hand and said, 'Yes, I've got to go, dear.'

She carried a handbag and walked out to the street, her heartbeat thumping loudly in her ears. There was always a lot of traffic in the evening. Young couples held hands and laughed as they strolled along the sidewalks. They looked so happy. Thủy's youthful years were long gone, but she still felt as giddy as a young girl when she was with Nghĩa. Crossing the street at an intersection, she stepped out right in front of a motorbike. The young driver squealed his brakes, cursed at her angrily, and sped away. At the bus station, Thủy stood beneath a tree and observed the chaotic scene. People bustled in every direction. Others sat or lay on the ground alone or in small groups. At the station window, a crowd of people stood waiting to buy their tickets. This was the third time Thủy had come. The first two, she'd given up and run home after only five or ten minutes because the men who approached her looked dirty and dangerous, and they frightened her. Those nights she told Nghĩa they didn't need her at the hospital after all and then began to kiss him passionately to prevent him from asking any further questions. It wasn't hard, which is what worried her most.

'You want to buy a ticket to Hà Nội?' a bold-looking black-market ticket seller asked as he approached her under the tree. 'Five đồng, no line.'

'No.'

'Where are you going?'

'Nowhere!' said Thủy. She wished he'd go away.

'Then why are you here? Oh, I get it. You're new to the profession.'

'Leave me alone!'

'Hey, who do you think you are? You look old, but even the pretty, young ones need my help getting clients.'

Thủy ran from the bus station, feeling utterly embarrassed. He'd called her a prostitute! But wasn't that what she was trying to become? A free-of-charge prostitute? This part wasn't easy.

After walking a little while, she regained her composure. Not far from the station, she noticed a neatly dressed man drinking tea at an old woman's sidewalk stall. He looked healthy with a kind, simple face. He had a wide mouth, big eyes, and thick eyebrows. Thủy sat down next to him.

Thủy chose the biggest apple from the woman's basket, smiled at the man, and asked him, 'Have you tried this kind of apple before?' Then she asked the old woman, 'Are they sweet or sour?'

'Sweet,' said the old woman. 'They taste really good.'

'My treat,' Thủy said to the man, handing him the apple. He looked at her with surprise. She continued, 'Are you going to Hà Nội?'

'No, I just got here from there. I missed the last bus to the district.'

'I'm going to Hà Nội,' said Thủy. 'Waiting for the bus all night will be so boring!'

'We have no other choice,' said the man. 'None of the hostels have rooms left. I checked already.'

Past midnight, Thủy was able to cajole the man into strolling to a flower garden with her. The stone benches were empty and wet with dew. The grove of trees was quiet beneath the streetlights. She panicked when suddenly he grabbed her hand and asked, 'Do you have a raincoat?'

'A raincoat?'

'A condom! I don't mind a little fun but I don't want to catch anything.'

He pulled her to the grass behind a bush not lit up by the streetlight. She nearly leapt away, but he caught her quivering body with his strong arms, and said, 'Oh, I'm sorry, don't run. I won't . . . I thought you . . . I must've misunderstood.'

The man was embarrassed. He unslung his duffel bag and dropped it by the bush. Thủy steeled herself. 'I'm not a prostitute,' she said. 'Just lonely.' Then she gave herself to the man, letting her body dissolve in his arms. Looking up at everything from the dark spot where she lay, she felt the whole world spinning around her. She closed her eyes when he heaved onto her on the grass. Thankfully it ended quickly and Thủy rolled him off and leapt up and ran away without saying goodbye or even once looking back. Streetlights poured pools of light into the otherwise empty street.

For a week after the incident in the park near the bus station, Thủy felt extremely anxious. She monitored her body for anything unusual. Five days, ten, then twenty passed without any noticeable effect. Only her disappointment and severe self-scorn exhausted her. She couldn't take another risk and realized how stupid she'd been, even though as a doctor, she knew better. She shouldn't have run after sex with that stranger because it impaired conception.

Thủy had decided she would do whatever necessary to maintain Nghĩa and everyone else's trust, even if it meant deceiving them. She had to restore the clan's faith in him. She wanted a baby as desperately as he did, but Nghĩa and everyone else had to believe the baby was his. Thủy's donor needed to be a complete stranger who would never know her identity. She knew all too well how men would keep coming back for more after they'd had fun once. Hence, the bus station and the one-night stand. Just one time with a stranger and that was it, she had told herself. She wouldn't allow herself even to think about that guy again. But she was sure she'd spoiled his 'donation' with her nervous flight and that thought nearly compelled her to return to the bus station. At this very moment, though, she just couldn't do it. She felt worse than a prostitute. Instead, she stormed to her office at the hospital, threw herself onto her day bed, and lay there feeling terrified about what kind of person she might be turning herself into.

*

At home in their bedroom, Thủy looked around and saw everything, the pillows and the blanket, the clothes on the hangers, the pictures on the wall, everything shining brightly in the electric light. Nghĩa had just put up a new photo of a mother and baby breastfeeding. Looking at the baby's cute mouth on its mother's nipple, Thủy felt sorry for herself. She had begun to feel tormented by Nghĩa and her mother-in-law's expectations, and she felt she couldn't continue to lie.

'That's a really beautiful one, isn't it?' Nghĩa came into the bedroom and hugged and kissed her.

She had already made up her mind to tell him the truth, but how would a person even begin to tell a story like hers? Her heart thumped in her chest. She hugged Nghĩa, and then held him and said, 'I need to tell you something.'

Nghĩa gave her a worried look.

'I'm very sorry, sweetheart, but I've kept a secret from you.'

'About what?'

'The lab results after we went to the hospital last time. I thought maybe there was still a small chance we could get pregnant, but it's not working. We'll have to adopt.'

Nghĩa's eyes suddenly went blank and he collapsed onto the bed. She hurriedly took his hand and said, 'It's not your fault. It was the war, your injury, the years and years you spent on the battlefield.'

Nghĩa shivered as if a needle had pierced his heart. 'All along,' he said, 'it was my fault. Not yours. Not Hạnh's.'

Chapter 25

Mrs Khiên died one morning of a heart attack. Nghĩa buried her next to his father in the village graveyard. After the funeral, he applied for retirement and stubbornly filed for divorce, just as Hạnh had done before. He returned to his ancestral land and to the empty house he had built on the grounds of the old lineage temple. He intended to repent for all the wrongs he'd done to the Nguyễn clan. He repainted the house and repaired the ancestral altar. He carried bucket after bucket of fertile mud from the pond to the garden, planted banana trees and fertilized the two rows of tall areca trees, whose leaves had begun to yellow from lack of nutrients. At night, he lay on the bed in the quiet three-section house, reflecting upon himself and all the people in the village who had lived similarly sorrowful lives.

Uncle Vạn now rarely left the nursery. When Nghĩa visited him the first time after moving back to the village, he was shocked at Vạn's aged appearance. He had the bony face and thin, white hair of an old man. Thành remained a bachelor all his life because of his deformed face. After Cúc returned Thành's engagement gifts, she had hoped she'd find a better husband, but instead, she ended up being Mr Ba Chương's second wife. Dâu had always been so ornery, but now she was living a peaceful life and going to the Buddhist temple every day. And Thắm, one of the most beautiful women in the village, remained a single mother. Hạnh's mother hardly spoke now. Nghĩa had heard that after Hạnh left the village, Mother Nhân had become very ill and almost died. Ever since he came back to the village, he had helped Nhân all he could, and they both tried to learn what caused Hạnh to leave, but to no avail. One rumour said she'd gone to Bắc Thái. Another that she'd gone to Hà Nội, or south to Hồ Chì Minh City.

Nghĩa looked at himself in the mirror every day and saw that his hair had started to grey. He busied himself with plans to throw a huge party on the annual death anniversary of his great great grandfather, hoping both to rival the tributes his parents used to put on and also to thoroughly fulfil his duty as last head of the Nguyễn clan. Back in the days of his parents' care, the lineage temple had truly been magnificent. Back then, Hạnh had still been a little girl, as pure and gentle as a dove.

One spring day, Nghĩa went to the district market and bought flower seeds and trees that his father had cultivated when he was alive. Nghĩa was growing old and had decided to devote himself to revitalizing the ancestors' land. He was busy planting when Thắm's son came into the yard with a schoolbag on his back. Linh was now a teenager, and handsome like his mother and father.

'Hey, Uncle Nghĩa!'

'Linh, my boy, what's up?'

'Aunty Hạnh has just come back!'

Nghĩa stood up straight, shocked, then held the boy's arms in his dirty hands. 'Are you sure?'

'Yes, for sure! On my way home from school, I saw her walking toward her mother's house and holding a little girl's hand. The little girl's very cute in her flowery dress.'

Nghĩa felt thunderstruck. Hurriedly, he washed his hands and feet, changed his clothes, and ran to Nhân's house. He stood speechless at the door when he saw Hạnh sobbing by her mother's side. The little girl was sitting in Mother Nhân's lap and telling her grandmother something. From the girl's face alone, he knew for sure she was Hạnh's daughter because they looked exactly alike. Seeing Nghĩa, Hạnh stood abruptly and wiped her tears. Nghĩa noticed her taking in the grey in his hair.

'You're here too!' said Hạnh. 'Please have a seat.'

Nghĩa sat down, unable to utter a single word.

'Mama, is he my papa?' asked the little girl. She slid down from Nhân's lap and ran to Hạnh and wrapped an arm around her mother's leg. She looked back and forth between her mother and Nghĩa.

'No, he is not,' said Hạnh. 'This is Major Nghĩa. He bravely led a whole battalion against enemies at the fronts of two wars. He is a talented leader.'

The girl pouted and said, 'Why did you tell me we would see my papa? I want to see Papa.'

'Behave! Let me speak with Major Nghĩa.'

Leaving Nhân's house later, Nghĩa staggered as if he had heatstroke. Memories of their past together burned through his mind like shooting stars. At home, as he scraped rice from the bottom of a pot, he heard footsteps in the yard. It was Aunt Xeng. Nghĩa set the pot in the basin and invited her to come in.

She shook her head. 'My father-in-law wants to talk to you,' she said. 'It's important.'

Nghĩa followed her back to the house where great Uncle Xung lay on his bed scratching his temples and twisting his ears. He sat up when Nghĩa came in and said, 'I'm sure you know why I asked you here. Hạnh is back, and she has a child. Did you know that? We've treated her wrong.' Uncle Xung's voice quivered as he stood and walked shakily to the altar. He handed Nghĩa the great great grandfather's crimson ledger. 'I kept this while you were away, but now that you're back, you should have it. You need to apologize to Hạnh and invite her to live with you or everyone will laugh at us. You're the sterile one, dummy, not her. Our family's been wrong all along. We have to fix our mistakes.' Uncle Xung blinked and continued, 'On the death anniversary this year, as head of the clan, you have to speak on behalf of the whole Nguyễn family and announce once and for all that the curse is lifted forever. No more hatred. You're a major, so you know what to say to convince people. I'm ancient already, and when I think about all that's happened, and all we've done wrong, I . . .' Uncle Xung choked up, unable to continue.

*

Hạnh took her daughter to the Silver Stone Bridge to see the river sparkle beneath the moon. The whole riverside was bathed in glittering light.

'Where does Papa live?' asked the girl.

'We're almost there.'

Excitement swelled in Hạnh's chest as she strolled with her daughter along the riverbank. The moment felt very precious. Throughout her married life, she had wished to have a child but it had always seemed impossible. Then she was pregnant after she and Nghĩa divorced, so she felt she had to leave. But living far away from the village for a few years taught her that she could not escape reality forever. Đông Village was an important part of her, and her daughter needed a father.

Hạnh pointed out the lush, green nursery above the river where there was a little clay house glowing with the warm light of an oil lamp. A breeze blew through the trees, rustling the leaves and carrying the pleasant smell of burning casuarina and eucalyptus wood. Hạnh knocked, and then she and her daughter stepped inside. Uncle Vạn sat quietly on the bed, hunched over and white-haired like the old man he'd become. Hạnh fell into his arms and burst into tears. She cried without knowing whether she was happy or sad for Uncle Vạn.

'Mama, why are you crying?' asked the little girl. 'Where's Papa?'

'Right here,' she said, pointing at Vạn. 'He's . . . your father.'

Nguyễn Vạn trembled and gazed bewildered at Hạnh and her daughter. 'Oh, Hạnh . . . what are you saying?'

'You don't understand?' Hạnh held Vạn's thin, shaking hands. 'This is your daughter. I've brought her here to meet you. Can't you guess why I had to leave the village all those years ago?'

Vạn sat frozen on the bed, still as a statue. Hạnh pulled her daughter onto her lap and caressed her hair. A quiet moment passed. Suddenly Vạn startled back to life, as if he'd been lost in a dream. He took Hạnh's hand and said, 'Now I understand everything. I am guilty, Hạnh, I am guilty. I've committed a terrible crime.'

'What are you mumbling about? You're not a criminal.'

'Yes, I am. I'm guilty. You have to get back together with Nghĩa. He divorced the doctor and moved back to the village. Please let yourself love him again.'

Hạnh hugged Vạn and felt his ribs and bony body. His face brightened for a second and then turned dark. He held Hạnh's hand with one hand and caressed the little girl's hair with the other.

'She's our daughter,' said Hạnh. 'Aren't you happy to meet your child?'

'You don't understand me,' said Vạn, 'but I understand you very well. Don't pity me. There's nothing left in this life for me. I'm old, and you and Nghĩa are still young. If you don't go back to him, you're guilty too. Oh, people are so stupid! We've all done so many stupid things.'

Vạn lifted the girl onto his lap. 'Is she really my daughter?' He lowered his head to peer closely at the little girl. In all his life, this was the first time he was a father. The girl opened her eyes wide and peered back at him, probably because she didn't yet believe this old man could really be her father.

The cool night was peaceful and quiet in the nursery. It was the dry season, so the shallow water in the river made it easy to see the white sandy bottom glittering beneath the bright moon. Moonbeams lit the steps and the entryway. With the fragrant little fire in the hearth, Uncle Vạn's home felt quite cozy. The familiar oil lamp glowed on the windowsill. Hạnh closed the door, her daughter already fast asleep on her father's lap.

'Please don't stay, Hạnh,' begged Vạn. 'Take your daughter back to your home with Nghĩa.'

'Never!' she said. 'I'll live here with you the rest of my life. It's the only place I ever want to be. Is that so scary?'

More than anything, Hạnh wanted this little house, the one built for her, the one that would be her joy and her daughter's future, to be her family's home. She wanted to sweep the floor every morning with a broom, and to make fires to cook rice for Uncle Vạn as she had when she was young. She wanted Vạn to teach her daughter how to cook rice properly by measuring with her finger. Every trivial memory from her childhood now flooded through her mind. She would not let him live a lonely life any longer. Being away from the village had made her realize all human beings need a family. It would make no sense when we wanted to make life better to go around blaming ourselves and feeling guilty all the time. And her own loneliness helped Hạnh realize no one in this life was as miserable and lonely as Uncle Vạn. She would take care of him in his old age, like a daughter taking care of her father or a wife taking care of her husband. Without intimacy, they were basically the same anyway, just doing things with love for each other.

Hạnh gently took her sleeping daughter from his arms and tucked her into the bed. Uncle Vạn sat beside her, saying nothing. Hạnh blew out the oil lamp and hugged him. This felt like the first completely happy and peaceful night she'd had in a long time, free from worry, longing, heartache, or desire.

She fell asleep, and slept soundly, and when she woke, golden sunbeams were shining through the window and the cracks in the door. Vạn had already risen and gone somewhere. She woke her daughter and together they went down to the river to wash their faces. Groups of people stood on the Silver Stone Bridge and waded in the river shallows at the footing, searching for something.

Instinctually, she knew something bad had happened. She held her daughter's hand and they ran to the water's edge. Just then, Nghĩa jumped from the bridge into the middle of the river. Hạnh stood watching numbly as Nghĩa surfaced, pulling someone behind him to the shore. Hạnh and her daughter ran to them, knelt beside Uncle Vạn's waterlogged corpse and wept.

*

For many years, Nguyễn Vạn had lived his isolated life at the nursery, and now the suddenness of his death forced the villagers to consider how it had come to pass. Nghĩa volunteered to host the funeral at the renovated Nguyễn lineage temple.

As the white mourning headbands were torn from a large cloth and distributed, old man Xung stood on the veranda, blinking at the crowd that filled the yard. Many Đông villagers were quite surprised simply to see him still alive, not to mention that he looked as good as he did at such an old age. He was probably the longest living Nguyễn of all time. Shakily, he fit the white mourning band around his head. He felt something boiling in his heart, and tears filled his eyes. His tears fell not only for the man in the coffin but also for all the sorrow and pain of the past. He cried for Vạn, for his two dead sons, and for himself having gone mad with grief and being locked up in the lineage temple and in his own home. He tore a mourning band with his teeth and handed it to Nghĩa, who stood next to him. Then he glanced at Hạnh, who stood behind Nghĩa, holding her daughter's hand. He passed her a mourning band too.

Hạnh placed the mourning band around her daughter's head. Old man Xung felt uncomfortable as he caught Hạnh's fiery eyes blazing straight at him. He hurriedly bent down and tore another mourning band and gave it to her.

Behind Hạnh stood Uncle Xeng and his wife, Aunt Thao, and old man Xung's three grandchildren. He tore six more bands and gave them to Uncle Xeng. He felt a bit embarrassed those six mourning bands were bigger than the others, but he didn't do it on purpose.

Dâu, Thắm and Linh, Cúc, and many others also wanted to wear the mourning bands, but they were not closely related. Old man Xung handed each of them a band anyway and announced, 'Anyone who wants to wear a mourning band, please come help yourself.'

No one seemed to notice that Nhân had come up and stood right in front of the coffin, still as a stone. She pulled an old mourning band from her pocket and tied it around her head, and then stood still and silent again. Over the course of her life, she had stood beside three empty coffins mourning her husband and two sons. This was the first time she stood in front of one with the corpse of a loved one actually inside. The dead hero in the coffin was not related to her, but he had been her best friend, someone who understood her better than anyone else.

Everyone was astonished when Hơn insisted on wearing a mourning band too. She stepped forward and tore two pieces of white cloth, one for her and one for Tốn.

'Put this on,' she said to Tốn softly. 'Without him, you wouldn't be here.'

No one wailed, no one made a show of their sorrow, but every person there knew their hearts were breaking. They felt sorrow for a lonely soul and for the tragedy of a human life. Their grief mixed with the mournful sound of old man Khoái's funeral trumpet.

'Damn! Old man Khoái is playing the trumpet so beautifully today, even better than Lý and his son in Hồi Village,' Uncle Phỏng whispered in Uncle Khi's ear.

'This morning, he said this would be the last funeral he ever played,' said Khi.

Hạnh held her daughter's hand and walked next to Nghĩa. Through the mournful sound of the trumpet, she heard Uncle Vạn's voice clearly, *Don't pity me. Go back to Nghĩa.*

The funeral procession crossed the Silver Stone Bridge and turned toward the pier. Hạnh gazed out at all the Đông villagers' faces. She understood that only she knew the true cause of Vạn's death.

A long line of villagers shuffled slowly to the village graveyard to say farewell to Nguyễn Vạn one last time, their white mourning headbands bobbing as if on waves in the bright spring light.

Acknowledgements

The translators are grateful to Dương Hướng for granting us permission to translate his incredible novel into English. During the course of translation, he kindly explained to us words and cultural references we did not understand or misunderstood. It took us three years to see this project finally come to life, and his patience with the long process has been much appreciated.

We are indebted to Nora Nazerene Abu Bakar, vice president of Penguin SEA, for seeing the value of this classic novel and for adding it to the Penguin Southeast Asian Modern Classics series. We thank Divya Gaur for designing the beautiful cover, Sneha Bhagwat and Surina Jain for their meticulous copyediting and suggestions for clarification, and the entire Penguin SEA team for their help making this novel available to international readers. Working with Penguin SEA has been a delight and honor for both of us.

Our appreciation also goes to Dr Đỗ Hải Ninh for writing the foreword and all the scholars/writers who have written blurbs for the book. The English edition of *No Man River* was made possible partly by the research grant the University of Montana Humanities Institute awarded to Quan Manh Ha, who sincerely values their generosity and support.

Additionally, we owe our families, friends, and colleagues a great debt of gratitude for their love, friendship, and encouragement: Noel Harold Kaylor, Ngô Văn Giá, Paul Christiansen, Quynh H. Vo, Jennifer Peeples, Owen Waugh, the Splinters crew, and so many more.

And last, but not least, thank you—our readers. Our translation of *No Man River* is for people like you who are curious about what the Vietnamese experienced before, during, and after the American War, how they remember that time, and most importantly what they sacrificed to bring to fruition their aspirations for peace and national liberty.

Printed in Dunstable, United Kingdom

82684142R00143